STAR TREK 61:
FROM THE DEPTHS

D0416103

STAR TREK NOVELS

1: CHAIN OF ATTACK

2: DEEP DOMAIN

3: DREAMS OF THE RAVEN

4: THE ROMULAN WAY

5: HOW MUCH FOR JUST THE PLANET?

6: BLOODTHIRST

7: THE I.D.I.C. EPIDEMIC

8: YESTERDAY'S SON

9: TIME FOR YESTERDAY

10: THE FINAL REFLECTION

11: TIMETRAP

12: THE VULCAN ACADEMY MURDERS

13: THE THREE-MINUTE UNIVERSE

14: *STAR TREK:* THE MOTION PICTURE

15: *STAR TREK:* THE WRATH OF KHAN

16: MEMORY PRIME

17: THE ENTROPY EFFECT

18: THE FINAL NEXUS

19: THE WOUNDED SKY

20: VULCAN'S GLORY

21: MY ENEMY, MY ALLY

22: DOUBLE, DOUBLE

23: THE COVENANT OF THE CROWN

24: CORONA

25: THE ABODE OF LIFE

26: ISHMAEL

27: WEB OF THE ROMULANS

28: THE CRY OF THE ONLIES

29: DREADNOUGHT

30: THE KOBAYASHI MARU

31: THE TRELLISANE CONFRONTATION

32: RULES OF ENGAGEMENT

33: THE KLINGON GAMBIT

34: THE PANDORA PRINCIPLE

35: THE PROMETHEUS DESIGN

36: DOCTOR'S ORDERS

37: BLACK FIRE

38: KILLING TIME

39: THE TEARS OF THE SINGERS

40: ENEMY UNSEEN

41: MINDSHADOW

42: HOME IS THE HUNTER

43: DEMONS

44: GHOST WALKER

45: MUTINY ON THE ENTERPRISE

46: A FLAG FULL OF STARS

47: CRISIS ON CENTAURUS

48: RENEGADE

49: TRIANGLE

50: LEGACY

51: BATTLESTATIONS

52: THE RIFT

53: FACES OF FIRE

54: THE DISINHERITED

55: ICE TRAP

56: SANCTUARY

57: DEATH COUNT

58: SHELL GAME

59: THE STARSHIP TRAP

60: WINDOWS ON A LOST WORLD

61: FROM THE DEPTHS

Coming soon:

62: THE GREAT STARSHIP RACE

STAR TREK GIANT NOVELS

STRANGERS FROM THE SKY

FINAL FRONTIER

UHURA'S SONG

DWELLERS IN THE CRUCIBLE

SHADOW LORD

PAWNS AND SYMBOLS

A *STAR TREK*® NOVEL

FROM THE DEPTHS

VICTOR MILAN

TITAN BOOKS

LONDON

***STAR TREK 61:* FROM THE DEPTHS**
ISBN 1 85286 467 2

Published by
Titan Books Ltd
19 Valentine Place
London SE1 8QH

First Titan Edition August 1993
10 9 8 7 6 5 4 3 2 1

British edition by arrangement with Pocket Books, a division of Simon
and Schuster, Inc., Under Exclusive Licence from Paramount Pictures
Corporation, The Trademark Owner.

British Library Cataloguing-in-Publication Data. A catalogue record
for this book is available from the British Library.

Printed and bound in Great Britain by Cox and Wyman Ltd, Reading,
Berkshire.

For Joan-Marie

Prologue

BLINKING INTO molten silver sunlight, Aileea dinAthos emerged from the ranch house to find her father sitting on the afterdeck, clad only in khaki shorts. A cup of black *chai* steamed in his hand. A white eyeshade shielded his face from the glare of tiny Eris, burning a hole in the blue-white sky to the east, not far above the ocean that was their world.

She stood on tiptoe, stretched arms high above her head, hand locked on wrist, back arching. She wore just a white thong swimsuit bottom and a sidearm belt. Eris light fell on her bare brown skin like a rain of needles. The sky was clear but for a bloated gray worm of smoke sprawled across the southern horizon and a bank of slate-colored clouds to the northeast. That would probably not last past noon, but like any true Vare she was prepared to enjoy the moment to the fullest.

She came up behind her father then, making no

1

more noise than she customarily did, which was none, despite the light fall of volcanic ash that dusted the deck. Before she reached the edge of his peripheral vision, he said, "You're up late. A body comes by slovenly habits in the city."

She laughed and sat down on the arm of his chair. A mild sea was washing over the white flotation cylinders that supported the deck. The float rocked gently. A soft breeze ruffled her shag-cut hair.

"If that's the worst habit I've picked up in the city," she said, "we're all luckier than I thought we were."

Aagard dinAthos saluted his daughter with his mug, which was white porcelain and chipped at the brim. Much as it exasperated her, he refused to throw it away. It had history, he claimed.

"It's never too late to come home. Ranch life is hard, but it's honest and clean."

"My work's honest, too," she said. She stood up quickly and instantly regretted her sharpness of tone. Her father just grinned at her through his short grizzled beard and nodded.

She sighed. She knew her father both loved and respected her. And she had been a full adult for years, since her fourth birthday, self-owning and self-reliant. She was seven and a quarter now, but he had never let go of testing her.

It was a major reason she could never come home to stay.

When Mom was alive, it was different. Aagard and Aileea dinAthos were made of the same stuff. Sanabar —gentle, resilient, and utterly unlike her husband or her daughter—had been the safety rod that prevented them achieving critical mass. One of the sudden terrible storms that wracked the planet had washed her from their lives, leaving a void that could not be filled.

There were many reasons they called the world Discord.

Aileea wandered near the rail, shaded her eyes to gaze away to the smoke bank in the south. Nearer to hand a pair of Hinds floated above a raft, each on six red wings, seeking the life-forms crawling in and on the matted seaweed.

"New volcano?" she asked. "We never wandered out this way when I was a kid."

"Just sticking her head above water," her father said, nodding. "That's why I'm keeping the float ever so slightly under power, so that we can steer clear of the plume. May even have to lay on more thrust, bear a hair north"—he brushed at the gray grit film that had accreted on the arm of his chair—"so we don't have to go around wearing respirators."

She nodded. "Maybe I'll scoot down that way and have a look at our new arrival."

"Best take a flyer. She's an active baby." As if to emphasize his words a rumble, almost subliminally low-pitched, rolled in from the south to vibrate in their bones and teeth.

Before her the surface of the Ocean of Discord bowed upward and then broke with a quiet, insistent rushing, not twenty meters from the ranch house. Water cascaded from the mottled dark blue back of a prawn. The Waverider crest had been laser-burned a centimeter deep and a meter wide in the beast's carapace, which was thick as battleship plate and nearly as hard. Like most of Discord's native life-forms, the giant crustaceans metabolized and made use of the metals superabundant in the planet's crust.

3

As always, Aileea was awed watching the beast's back, ten meters wide at its broadest, rolling like the top of a great wheel turning, to vanish again beneath the waters. The house rocked to the swell of its passing. The fifty-meter-long prawn was a sea grazer, utterly nonaggressive, relying on size and armor sufficient to deter even the rapacious predators of the world called Discord. A constant tone emitted by the household sonics, inaudible to the ears of Aileea and her father, kept the beast from approaching dangerously close.

The breeze blew the rank salty smell of sea life to her, and something else, at once sweet and pungent. "That's Old Lucy, isn't it?" she asked.

"The matriarch herself."

"She's ready to be scraped."

"True enough. But she's just done spawning. Didn't want to gripe her."

Out on the water the wavelets danced white-bright like broken porcelain shaken on a table. A scooter skimmed the surface, snaking a line of froth across the shards. A ranch hand, riding herd on the pod of giant crustaceans or inspecting the pod-shaped robot "wranglers" that contained and guided the huge sea beasts. The figure raised an arm and waved.

"Who is that?" Aileea asked, waving back. "I can't make out."

"It's Gita, of course," her father said gruffly. "You can tell by the reckless way she careens around."

He eyed his daughter critically. "Your childhood playmate, and you don't recognize the way she rides?"

Aileea felt her mouth tighten. She was all too aware of the gap that now yawned between her and the woman who had been a virtual sister to her. Not that

4

she didn't get along with Gita. It was just that they had . . . grown apart, and she felt an aching hollowness within.

"It's been a long time since I've seen her ride, Father."

"You're losing touch with where you came from, girl."

She glared at him. He regarded her with eyes sharp and black as obsidian. "Come home, Aileea," he said in a quiet voice. "You know the sea as well as any Vare—you're a very part of her. And you'll soon pick the ranching life back up, right enough."

He showed her a sardonic grin. "And I don't think you'd need worry about growing bored. We see action aplenty."

A grimace flickered across her face like a cloud transiting the sun. "I've seen all the action I ever want to, Father. And then some."

She paced the slow-rolling deck, hugging herself. "The Stilters come frequently?"

"Very much so, these days."

She turned. "But you're handling them?"

It was a foolish question, she realized at once. *Evidently. Or we wouldn't be here.*

"Well enough," her father said. "But it's starting to cut close—"

A shrill beeping sounded. He reached down, picked up a palmreader, and frowned at the screen.

Aileea felt a chill run down her spine. "The perimeter wranglers are picking up something on sonar." It was not a question.

Her father nodded, murmuring quick commands into the handheld unit. Cable of lightweight high-tensile-strength alloy played out of a housing atop the ranch house, allowing the radar eye slung beneath the captive polymerized aluminum balloon to ride higher, to see farther past the horizon.

"Speak of Leviathan," Aagard dinAthos muttered when he saw what it showed him. "Speak of the Devil in the Sea. . . ."

"Get below," Aileea said sharply. "You can control the wranglers from the command center."

"I can control them from here, too, daughter," he said, rising to his full height, which was impressive for a man of their Gens. He spoke without heat, but firmly.

Her eyes fell away from his. It was a measure of the strangeness of her chosen profession that for a moment she had been unaware of the incongruity of casually giving orders to not just her father, but any Vare.

She didn't have a lot of time to stand around being abashed; at once she was in motion, across the deck in a flash of long slender legs burned dark by the relentless sun, into the cockpit of her own scooter, moored at the stern of the float. It retracted its fragmentproof canopy to her word of command. Despite her state of undress she slid into the form-fitting black seat without hesitation and slipped on the lightweight headset. She had no need of an emergency flotation vest or a breather, but she might have reason to miss the environment suit she was accustomed to wear to work, if only for its armor.

She cast off, started the electric impellers cycling water through tubes that ran the length of the tiny craft. As it picked up speed she allowed herself the luxury of a glance back at the float where she had been born and raised. Her father still stood on the afterdeck, arms crossed over his wiry-muscled chest, staring off at the horizon over which the intruders would soon appear. She caught a glimpse of giant Mansur hulking in the doorway with his cleaver in his hand, and then she turned her eyes forward and gave the scooter full acceleration.

Head-up holos sprang into existence between dark jade eyes and the windscreen, feeding her simultaneous streams of information. Still several minutes until contact; she left the canopy back. She would feel the wind in her face and her hair as long as she could.

"Waveriders," she said to the communicator. "Who's out there this morning?"

"Sleep late enough, Aili?" Gita came back.

"Almost too late. Who else?"

The others sounded off crisply: Krysztof, Lev, Haidar, Jasmine. Not just employees, they were all stockholders in the ranch. It was their home and their property they would be defending.

She would give instructions and they would follow them, though they were Vares and fiercely protective of their liberties. Not simply because she was the senior stockholder's daughter, nor even because they were all friends and Krysztof and Haidar had, like Gita, been her childhood playmates. Hers was not the most respectable profession, perhaps, but her expertise at it was unquestioned.

"We have three bogies inbound on bearing two ninety, speed one hundred fifty klicks per hour," she said, reading the data relayed from the wranglers and the household sensors. "Look like hydrofoils, sixty-tonners. *Cossack* class."

The Stilters were getting smarter. In the past they had favored conventional surface craft, larger and full of firepower but slower. That made them potent foes—but also inviting targets for Vare missiles and torpedoes.

Their advisers from the stars were teaching them well, it seemed.

"Kofirlar," snarled Lev. None of them knew it had once meant "religious infidels"; to them it signified "intruders, interlopers." It was the name they gave their ancient enemies' new friends.

"They'll be there," Haidar agreed, "but just a few. The crews will be Stilters."

Holding her lower lip between her teeth, Aileea nodded. Haidar had the knack of looking at the brightest available side of things, but he was most likely right.

"Moment," Krysztof said in his slow, heavy way. "I'm getting a return from Seventeen. Vessel in the thousand-tonne range, same bearing, fifty kilometers farther out."

"That'll be the carrier, the mother ship," she said.

"Keeping out of our range," Lev said.

"Do you blame them?" Haidar asked with a laugh.

"There are still seventy and more of them to the six of us," Jasmine warned.

Gita's laugh pealed in Aileea's ears. "Unfair odds," she said. "Perhaps half of us should stay behind."

As they spoke the six were riding an intercept course, spread out in an arc covering three kilometers of ocean. The scooters were tiny craft, without armor to speak of, relying mainly on speed for defense. But like so many of Discord's smaller life-forms, each carried a deadly sting.

She called for the data from Wrangler 17, quickly skimmed it, brought up the feed from the robot's camera. "That's a tender, all right. Looks like a *Goebbels*."

She used the Vare codename for the craft. She knew the Stilter name for it, too—Vare electronic surveillance was good, much better than Stilter countermeasures, and after almost forty years of constant warfare Vare and Stilter could translate one another's language. But the Vare names were easier on the mouth —speaking Stilter was like trying to tie a half hitch with your lips.

She frowned. "The Goebbels is built to carry four Cossacks. Stay alert, everybody—there might be another one out there."

"Should some of us hang back and keep an eye out for him?" Krysztof asked.

"We're too few as it is," Jasmine said.

"She's right," Aileea said. "Now be careful. We'll be in range of their rockets soon."

Up ahead she saw them now, three notches of white cut from the blue horizon, the bow waves of the speeding hydrofoils. She brought up a magnified display. Cossacks, all right, stubby wedge-shaped hulls painted in jagged patterns of blue and black and white to break up their silhouettes, bristling with weaponry like a seaspine on a reef. And clumped much too close together, in approved Stilter fashion. She wondered if the Kofirlar were trying to break them of that.

She punched up a private sideband. "Dad, did you catch that? There may be a bogey unaccounted for."

"I'll be fine, child. I've been fighting Stilters longer than you've been alive."

"That's Stilters, not these new friends of theirs, with their alien technology and their energy weapons."

9

"Fah. They aren't superhuman."

"At least go below, please, Father? You'll be safer below the waterline, and you can read your displays as easily in the command center as on deck."

"I have no desire to be safe while my people fight. Including my own flesh and blood."

She bared her teeth in a grimace of defeat. It was an expression she'd had little use for in her life—except for her dealings with her father.

"It's a free planet," she said wearily.

"That it is," her father said. "That's why we fight." His image vanished.

There was a ripple of flashes as the starboard hydrofoil launched rockets. Surges of water foamed over Aileea's bare legs, left and right, as she zigzagged her craft. Up here in the forties of latitude the water was blood warm, but it felt chill after Eris's hot caress. Its coolness exhilarated her. The spray in her face and the moist salty air and the nearness of danger filled her with searing wild pleasure.

She looked across the sea, which was beginning to chop as the wind freshened. There was Gita, canopy back, her nebula of heavy dark hair flying free behind. She seemed to sense her old friend looking at her and raised a fist in joyous defiance.

Aileea grinned and waved back, but she was already forcing down the sense of exaltation. It didn't do to get too giddy. She wondered if Gita could control her own exuberance in action.

The rockets struck, creating a brief flurry of geysers far astern of Aileea's scooter. The outriders quickly called in. She already knew the volley had fallen wide.

"Uh-oh," Haidar said from her right. "Someone's locked onto me."

"Go deep!" Aileea yelled.

Her old friend was already sealing his canopy as he threw his craft into violent lurches Gita might envy. He extended his dive planes and began nosing under even before it closed. The scooter vanished.

A second later water fountained from the roil of water left by the submerging craft.

"Haidar!" No answer. She had come almost abeam of the starboard 'foil, swinging wide and then curving toward the craft at full throttle. The three bigger craft sped on toward the float. They were after bigger game than the scooters.

Aileea raked the 'foil with her twin machine guns. They were light weapons, too light for the work. The hydrofoil showed no sign of damage.

Haidar's scooter burst from the sea like a broaching *volk*, clearing the water in an upward avalanche of spray. Aileea watched with her heart in her throat, fearful that Haidar had pushed his luck too far and was about to smear himself all over the uneasy plane of the sea.

He struck down amid a splash like another missile going off. Aileea saw his scooter begin to drift counter-clockwise. Then it straightened and streaked away. A line of lesser spouts from a Stilter automatic canon stitched across its wake. Haidar's triumphant shout burst in Aileea's ears.

An indicator in Aileea's head-up display flashed, showing she had a lock-on. She quickly triggered a missile of her own toward the nearest 'foil. An orange box surrounded it in her display, allowing her to follow its flight. It guided true, curving slightly to intercept the craft.

At the last instant the hydrofoil banked hard into its

port foil, throwing up a crescent ridge of water. The missile blasted through the top of this bow wave, skipped twice on the surface of the sea, and exploded harmlessly half a kilometer beyond its target.

"Damn!" Aileea cried, frustrated. One thing the Stilters were good at was dodging. And, unlike their bigger ships, the hulls of their new hydrofoils were largely nonmetallic composites, giving Vare targeting radars little to bite on.

So far she had had to give few instructions—and now her comrades were doing something she wouldn't dream of asking them to do. They had begun darting back and forth in front of the 'foils, dangerously close to the dazzle-painted hulls. The 'foils were not notoriously stable beasts. Though they dwarfed the scooters, a collision with one at speed would tumble a 'foil if not tear it to pieces. The bigger craft were slowing down and beginning to swerve themselves to avoid their tormentors. Aileea turned her scooter and raced to join their dangerous game.

Stilter gunners blazed enthusiastically away at the scooters. Their targets were small, fast, and agile, and the Stilters were outstandingly bad shots. As they lost way, though, the 'foils' hulls settled back into the water. It slowed them down, but it also rendered them less vulnerable to impact.

The vessel she had shot at was headed away in a wide arc west, possibly running, possibly circling to come in again. For the moment it was out of the fight. Aileea overtook what had been the central craft, turned to cross its bow. Ahead of her she saw Gita, actually steering toward the 'foil, guns firing.

The hydrofoil lunged forward at full power, trying to catch the outrider before its foils bit and lifted it out of the water again. Aileea shouted wordlessly as she watched the big craft run her friend down.

She hurled herself at the 'foil, which was continuing to accelerate, hoping to surprise the outriders and break past them to the ranch float. Aileea streaked down the vessel's flank, raking it fore to aft with a shuddering burst of her guns, fighting to hold the scooter steady against the recoil. The water seemed to boil around her as the 'foil gunners opened up on her with everything they had.

Then she was past, circling the hydrofoil's stern, cursing that she was now too close for her remaining missile to arm itself. She prepared for another run along the central 'foil's other side. It would expose her to the point-blank fire of two enemy craft. She didn't care.

As she lined up for her pass something flashed through the corner of her peripheral vision. The hydrofoil's stern exploded into two pulses of yellow-orange flame.

Victory cries rang from her communicator. She sheered to port and let her scooter lose way as the hydrofoil began to settle by the stern. Long-legged figures darted the canting deck in panic, tumbled, thrashing, in the water. Later she would see to rescuing survivors—if a later happened.

Half a kilometer astern of the burning 'foil, dead between the spreading legs of its wake, a single scooter bobbed.

"Gita?" Aileea said.

"I dove under the seaslug," her old friend's voice came back. "I guess I fooled him. Fooled you, too, didn't I?"

Aileea opened her mouth, but her words clogged her

throat. "Some vacation, huh, Aili?" Gita said with a laugh like a silver bell.

Lev uttered a harsh cry of triumph as the third hydrofoil turned right about and fled. The vessel Aileea had launched at, meanwhile, was making good progress toward the horizon.

"Good job, people," Aileea said.

"Daughter," Aagard dinAthos's voice said, "well done—"

"It was Gita, Father."

"But I'm afraid it isn't over yet."

The image of another hydrofoil appeared in her display, transmitted from the float. Beside it was a map, showing a blinking red dot rapidly closing upon the steady white glow that represented the ranch house.

"Father!" Aileea exclaimed, blasting power to her impellers. "Why didn't you warn me?"

"You all were busy. I didn't want to distract you." As he spoke he worked controls outside her field of vision. At his back she saw blue-white sky. He still stood on deck. "Besides, I have the situation under control."

She felt her lips peel back from her teeth. The other riders were lining up in a V formation, trailing to port and starboard of her. They rode flat out, bouncing off the wavetops like skipped stones. It was a race to see who would reach the ranch house first, scooters or lone 'foil.

Aileea's eyes flicked desperately from windscreen to display. Seven hundred meters, six, five. The enemy vessel was only a little farther from the float.

"I think they're going to try to board, Father," Aileea said.

Aagard dinAthos uttered a caw of triumph. "No chance of that now! I've got—"

A lance of red light struck Aagard. For an instant he became a figure of light, pale in the sun's glare. Then the red beam vanished, as did Aagard dinAthos and a section of the rail.

"Father!"

Water spouted from beneath the Stilter craft's starboard foil as a wrangler, transformed by Aagard's signal into a homing mine, struck. The foil itself was torn away. For a moment inertia carried the vessel along, poised on one foil. Then, with apparent deliberation, it began to tilt toward the water. It veered right, went broadside, went over. And then it was bouncing up again, stern high, tumbling across the waves, disintegrating as it went. When Aileea flashed past the float, the foil was no more than a finger of burning wreckage pointing toward its intended victim.

"Aileea," Krysztof said. "The tender is preparing for missile launch."

"I am taking appropriate steps," came the basso rumble of Mansur. "Aileea, I am sorry about your father."

Aileea cried out in grief and frustration and rage. The Stilter over-the-horizon missiles weren't very accurate, but they were big enough that you didn't want to linger too near to where they might be landing.

"Scatter!" she yelled to her friends. She herself turned and lined out to the north at full power.

Behind her, the float on which she had begun her life began to sink beneath the waves.

The headquarters had been hewn from lava rock by raw gouts of power. Only the floor had been fused to a glassy smoothness. Walls and ceiling remained jagged, ready to claw at the unwary.

Klingons were not indifferent to comfort. But they liked to act as if they were.

The young ensign prostrated himself on the polished black stone where he had been thrown by two burly ratings. *"Qeyn HoD wa'DIch,"* he said to the polished boots of the man who stood before him. "We lost two craft—*Pajwl'* and *'urng* died with them."

He raised his head. His face was young and pale. A burn glowed on one cheek. His beard was still far from full and resembled seaweed trailed across rocks by the tide.

"The herd beasts ran again, First Captain," he said. "The fault is mine. We failed."

A rumble ran through the officers assembled at the captain's back. They had been on this accursed planet for nearly half a Klingon year, fighting with one arm tied against a foe far more resolute and resourceful than their allies. Frustration and the grinding discomfort of life on this hot, wet, foul world was beginning to eat away at morale like the surf that battered down islands almost as quickly as the planet's hyperactive mantle could cast them up.

Captain of the First Rank Kain gazed down on the youth with his one good eye. He stroked his long chin, which was shaven clean in a departure from the normal Klingon style. As if to compensate, his mustache swept dramatically to either side of his full-lipped mouth. Tall, broad in the chest and shoulders, narrow in the hips, he was a striking figure, by Klingon standards or by human.

For a moment the black-gauntleted tip of a thumb brushed the patch that covered his right eye.

"I know the taste of failure," he said in a resonant voice, far smoother than the usual guttural Klingon snarl. Those who didn't know him sometimes made fun of what they considered his prissy mode of speech.

Once.

"Likewise its price." He dropped his hand to the hilt of a curious circular, multiple-bladed weapon slung at his waist.

The ensign lowered his cranial ridge to the floor. "I request permission to die by my hand, to atone for my failure."

"Denied."

The youth looked up. Again the rumble from behind Kain's shoulder, louder this time.

"We are few," Kain said, "too few to waste. *luHoHta'.*" The last was spoken over his right shoulder to his aide, a handsome young woman who wore the insignia of a senior lieutenant on her gold rank sash. "The ensign is sentenced to ten minutes' confinement in the *QIghpej.*"

The face of the young ensign sagged in a parody of relieved disbelief. Ten minutes in the agonizer booth, which directly stimulated the pain center of the brain, was a virtual eternity. Yet it would mean he lived, and kept honor intact.

Such lenience was an act of grandmotherly kindness.

Behind First Captain Kain's left shoulder a heavy face twisted in a snarl and a heavy hand snatched for a phaser. "Your father's toadying to the *tera'ngan* turned you soft and spineless as they are!" the grizzled operations officer roared. "Die, worm!"

At least he meant to roar. The words got lost in the sudden gout of blood around the *kligat,* the curious throwing weapon that was suddenly lodged between his beard and the collar of his tunic.

For a moment Kain stood looking down at the would-be mutineer as his life gushed onto polished black stone. "That *kligat* slew my bond-brother, Juk," he murmured. "It's really more than you deserved."

He bent, pulled forth the weapon, wiped it carefully clean on Juk's tunic. He held it negligently in his hand as he turned to face the other officers.

"Is anyone else inclined to mistake judiciousness for weakness?" he asked. No one spoke.

"Let us not forget what we do here," Kain said, raising his voice so it rang off the snag-toothed walls. "We have not come to wrest this planet from the lost *tera'ngan* on behalf of our foolish allies. When the time comes we shall take it for ourselves."

He made a snatching gesture with his free hand. The others nodded and growled assent. This was how a Klingon talked. Juk must have been crazy.

"It matters little how the war goes. All that matters is that it goes. We are here to forge the weapon that will split the hated Federation asunder—here to serve the Devil in the Sea. And we are *bait*. Set to draw the Earther who has done our empire more harm than any other."

He slung the *kligat,* walked to the ensign, and hauled him to his feet by the back of his torn tunic. He sent him stumbling toward *luHoHta'* with a shove. She caught his arm and held him upright without deigning to show strain.

"Already the rock rolls downhill, gathering momentum. Our allies have summoned the Federation, thinking it is their own idea. When that rock strikes bottom"—he smiled—"it will crush the man who cost me my eye and my brother.

18

"And we are the stone upon which James Kirk and his Enterprise *shall be broken!"*

And his officers, one again with him, raised their hands to the air and roared in the happy fury of the hunt.

Chapter One

"MR. SCOTT," Captain James Kirk said in surprise. He was walking back toward a corner of Min and Bill's Pub in Starbase 23, to a table where Lieutenant Commander Montgomery Scott sat with his legs stretched out before him and a book in his hands. The pub had a very relaxed atmosphere, which made it a popular place for crews in from space to dissipate tension. At the moment, though, the captain and Scott were the only patrons visible. "I'd never expect to see you here, with the *Enterprise* undergoing such an extensive retrofit."

Scott started, and looked up guiltily. "Captain," he said, placing the book on the table and starting to his feet, "I'd be right there overseeing 'round the clock— you know that, sir—if only I could. But Commodore Snodgrass made me leave! She said I was working m'self to death." He shook his head. "Imagine! Tossing me out of my own engine room. If she wasn't a woman, I'd give her a piece of my mind."

"Then be glad she *is* a woman, Mr. Scott. People who try the commodore on for size usually wind up with more than their minds in pieces." The chief administrator of the Starbase's extensive drydock facilities had a reputation for being a poor choice to trifle with.

Kirk slapped Scott on the shoulder. "Sit down, sit down. If the commodore has actually gotten you to take a break, I don't want to cause such a heroic achievement to go to waste. Here, what're you reading?"

He glanced down at the book. Its screen showed a column of English phrases accompanied by transliterations of equivalent phrases in an alien tongue. It made Kirk's throat hurt just to read the rasping consonants, harsh gutturals, and glottal stops.

And then the sounds came together in his mind, and he raised an astonished gaze to his engineering officer. "Mr. Scott," he said, "a *Klingon* dictionary?"

Scott nodded. "Aye, Captain." He wouldn't meet Kirk's eye.

Trying to hide a grin, Kirk sat down. "Regardless of what Captain-Lieutenant Korax said back at Station K-7, half the sector is *not* learning Klingon. You'll remember we got the better of them pretty decisively on that occasion—not to mention a few times since."

"Oh, aye," Scott said, nodding and smiling at the reminiscence. Though he wasn't carrying too much extra flesh—all things considered—his chin tended to double when he nodded. "I guess we taught those Sassenach to speak ill of the *Enterprise.*"

"Ah—yes. I guess we did." Kirk sat down. "Why are you learning Klingon, then, Mr. Scott? I didn't know you had a passion for languages." *Almost five years with this crew,* he mused, *and I'm still finding*

22

things out about them. The fact did not disturb him; it was just another voyage of exploration, and that, after all, was what he lived for.

"Oh, I do not, sir," Scott said. Kirk raised an eyebrow at him, a gesture he'd unconsciously absorbed from his first officer. "It's just that, what with the Klingons giving technical assistance to the Romulans, and then this latest round of peace talks with the Federation, there's a great lot of Klingon engineering manuals floatin' around—"

Kirk gazed at his chief engineer and sighed a deep sigh. "Scotty, you truly believe you *are* relaxing, don't you?"

Scott looked at him. "Why, of course, Captain. What else would you call it?"

The chirp of his communicator spared Kirk having to respond. He took the unit from his belt and flipped it open. "Kirk here."

"Chekov, acting captain, *Enterprise*," a voice said. Though the starship was currently in the charge of Commodore Snodgrass and her merry elves, she was still Kirk's responsibility. Kirk could hear the young officer's pride at being in command of the mighty vessel—and therefore due the courtesy title of captain—warring with his impatience at having to stay aboard while the rest of the bridge crew got shore leave. "Admiral Satanta requests your presence in his office as soon as convenient, sir."

"Is Mr. Spock aboard?"

"No, sir. He's currently at Rosa's Cantina."

Kirk was taken aback again; hanging out in a bar was not a common form of recreation for his Vulcan first officer. "I'll collect him myself, then—it's on the way. Thanks." He started to close the communicator, then raised it again. "Carry on, *Captain.*"

23

"Aye-aye, sir!"

Scott looked up from his book, which he'd snagged the instant Kirk's attention was deflected. "Will you be needing me, sir?"

"No, no, Scotty. Stay here and—relax."

Beaming with relief, Scott stuck his nose back in his book. Kirk swung toward the door and almost bumped into Min, the stout, cheerful Terran proprietress, bustling up with her apron and her tray to take his order.

"I'm sorry, Min. Have to run."

"Hurry back, Captain. You're always welcome here." She smiled a great smile of welcome. Most of the Terran crew of the *Enterprise*—most of the humanoid crew, in fact—said Min reminded them of a favorite grandmother. It was one of the reasons the place was so popular. Of course, the crew didn't spend *all* their R and R time there.

Behind the bar loomed her husband, Bill, washing glasses. The Atarakian was over two meters high, with long, jointed antennae and huge, yellow, self-luminous eyes, which his species, incapable of speech, used as signal lamps for communication. He nodded his great green chitinous head to Kirk, flashing his eyes—literally—at the captain's wave of greeting and farewell.

The corridor of the Starbase's civilian reservation was beginning to fill with Starfleet personnel and the crews of ships from half a hundred planets, members and nonmembers of the UFP (United Federation of Planets) alike. Starbase 23 was not built on a planet, or in orbit about one; it had been carved out of a metallic asteroid floating in the debris belt of a blue giant whose enormous, rapidly rotating mass was too great to permit the formation of worlds. Instead of day or night, the lives of its occupants were ruled by shift change.

The arched ceiling of the passageway was high, and deliberately left rough, to provide a contrast to the rectilinear regularity of most starship interiors. The irregular metal surfaces caught and danced with blue and orange and red and yellow glints thrown out by the taverns and bars, the restaurants and cabarets and shops, and the meditation rooms of myriad faiths and philosophical disciplines.

Kirk sidestepped a snouted Tellarite, who was rolling down the passageway with a pugnacious swagger, paused to allow a pair of Vulcans in the yellow robes and filigreed golden ear clasps of savants from the lyceum to emerge from a coffeehouse, and nodded greeting to a blue Andorian standing before a shop that offered for sale the *Hii-dou-rai* ceremonial stones, bits of petrified wood laboriously hand-rubbed into glossy-smooth round shapes, for which his race was admired throughout the galaxy. The Andorian bobbed his antennae politely.

Kirk continued, but had to brake almost at once to avoid blundering into an altercation that came crashing out the front door of an Orion pub. Two pale pink-skinned male humanoids pummeled each other with their fists, fighting with more passion than skill. Whether either or both were Terran, Kirk couldn't tell, though to his annoyance one wore a red Starfleet General Services tunic.

Starfleet service was less onerous than virtually any military service in the history of any of the galaxy's known warrior races, among whom Earth's humans were prominent. Starships were spacious, clean, and well appointed. Most menial tasks of cleaning and maintenance were performed by machines. And

Starfleet personnel were all well-trained professionals, not grunts or swabbies and particularly not conscripts. They were where they wanted to be, and had worked hard to get there.

But Starfleet was a demanding master. While combat was only—thankfully—a minor component of Starfleet's job, its main missions of the policing of the Federation, internal and external diplomacy, and its overriding task of scientific exploration were extremely high-tension pursuits. Stress was as much a part of a starship's atmosphere as oxygen, especially here, near the Federation's outward fringe.

And despite everything twenty-third-century technology could do, space was still a harsh, hazardous environment. A moment's carelessness—or even blind chance—could kill not just a crewman or -woman, but an entire ship.

So for all the Federation's psychology and human engineering, space crews were not much less prone to the more extreme forms of blowing off steam than their surface-navy predecessors had been. The only consolation was that—with a few exceptions, like the ultra-self-disciplined Vulcans—the Federation's other races were little better behaved than humans.

Kirk felt conflicting impulses—the one to lay the hard arm on both combatants for the breach of discipline, the other to find out who was at fault and knock him on his fanny. What he did was wait a moment until the pair fell down on the walkway, then step gingerly over the writhing, punching tangle, through the cloud of profanity and the aroma of cheap Orion distillates they exuded, and go his purposeful way. Satanta was a friend of long standing, but when a flag officer invited a captain to wait upon him at earliest convenience, it meant "Shag butt down here at warp factor eight."

Rosa's Cantina wasn't exactly en route, but it wasn't far off, either—a jog down a dark and narrow side passage that at first glance didn't seem meant to carry traffic at all. Access way or afterthought, a few steps along it curved left and led Kirk into the sound-and-light spill of Rosa's.

The cantina was darker than Min and Bill's, and the atmosphere less wholesome—it was the sort of place the crew went when they grew tired of Grandma. The music floating out the open door surprised Kirk—not the usual jarring Saurian jazz or Orion Chrome-5, but the unmistakable, near discordant wail of a Vulcan lyre. Accompanying it was an equally unmistakable contralto voice.

"Lieutenant Uhura!" Kirk said, stepping into the cantina. It was dark, scarcely lit by dim swirls of red and violet light. It was packed with bodies, standing or perched on high, narrow stools. Kirk recognized scattered *Enterprise* crew. In a clear corner stood Uhura in a fall of yellow light, her voice filling the bar without necessity of a microphone. Sitting behind her playing a swan-necked instrument was none other than the *Enterprise's* first officer.

The communications officer was just finishing her song. Kirk made his way to her side through the applauding crowd. She met him with a radiant smile.

"My set's over, Captain," she said. "Sorry you didn't get here sooner."

"So am I. I have to admit I'm a bit surprised to see you here, though." The *Enterprise's* communications and electronic-warfare suite was undergoing an even more extensive upgrade than her engines, and the newly promoted communications officer was, if anything, more obsessive about overseeing work done on her system than Scott was.

She laughed. "If I had my way, I'd still be aboard making sure everything was done just right," she said. "But I didn't have any choice in the matter."

"Oh? Did Commodore Snodgrass run you off, too?"

"No," a gravelly voice said from behind Kirk, "*I* did."

"Bones?" Kirk said, turning.

Dr. Leonard McCoy nodded. "I swear, I've got a crew of compulsives to try to keep inside their skins. You, Uhura, Scott—each of you is worse than the next. You just don't know when to quit. At least Sulu has his hobbies to keep him sane."

Ignoring the obvious implication, Kirk said, "What about you, Doctor? Between you and the commodore, Uhura and Scotty are taking time out. Even Mr. Spock is letting his hair down."

Placing his instrument carefully on a stand, Spock shot him a scandalized look.

"You, on the other hand, are still on duty, aren't you?" said Kirk. "Looking after your charges like a mother hen."

"Confound it, Jim, that's different," said McCoy.

Kirk nodded. "Uh-*huh.*"

Spock straightened. "You were coming to ask me to accompany you on some business, I believe, Captain."

Kirk looked at him. "How'd you know that?"

"You strode in here in a highly purposeful manner. You showed surprise at seeing Dr. McCoy and Uhura, but none on seeing me. Therefore, it was I whom you were seeking. And the tendency which you are visibly struggling, not entirely with success, to control—to bob upon the balls of your feet—indicates impatience to be somewhere."

"'Brilliant deduction, Holmes.'" He held out a hand. "Shall we?"

Spock turned to Uhura. "It was, as always, an honor to accompany your singing, Lieutenant. The mathematical subtleties displayed—"

"Spock!" McCoy exclaimed in disgust. "You'd explain away a sunset, too, wouldn't you?"

The Vulcan cocked a brow. "What is so esoteric about that, Doctor? It is merely the occultation of the primary—"

Kirk took him by the arm. "If you'll excuse us—" He towed Spock out the door.

Five meters down the alley, an eight-foot-tall Gorn was hoisting Sulu into the air by the head.

Chapter Two

"SULU!" Kirk whipped his hand phaser from his belt and pointed it at the monster's scaled back.

The reptilian creature lowered Sulu until his boot soles touched the stone floor. It removed its taloned hands from his head.

The helmsman rolled his head on his neck. "That's much better," he said. "I don't know if it'll ever replace *shiatsu,* but it works."

Kirk glanced over his shoulder at Spock. The Vulcan stood a step behind him, erect and unruffled. "Gorn massage techniques are renowned for their therapeutic qualities," Spock said. "Their rather rough-and-ready nature has, however, made their acceptance slow within the Federation."

"Captain—Mr. Spock," said Sulu, nodding past the enormous masseur. The creature started to turn. Kirk hastily stuck his phaser back in his belt, thanking fate that the Gorn had a predator's forward-looking eyes. "I'd like to introduce my friend, Mr. Horatio Hornblower."

"Horatio . . . Hornblower?"

"Your people cannot pronounce my name," said the Gorn via the translator medallion hanging over his steel-hard pectoral scutes. The unit was set to produce a high, almost adolescent voice. "Among you I have chosen to go by the name of a great hero of your history." He held out a scaly claw.

Kirk hesitated just an eyeblink, then took the creature's hand and shook it firmly. "Our—history. Ah, good choice. You pay great honor to our traditions."

The being swelled visibly, which Kirk took for a good sign. His sole personal experience with the Gorn race had not been a particularly happy one. Since that time the warlike reptilian beings' relationship with the Federation had regularized somewhat, and was for the most part peaceful.

"To brave the fearful great expanses of your planet's seas must have required an extraordinary man," the Gorn said. "Such bravery—to risk one's life to an environment so powerful and chaotic."

"Not much open water on the Gorn homeworld, Captain," Sulu explained. "Horatio, here, is science officer on a Gorn exploratory vessel undergoing repairs in drydock."

"Captain," Spock said.

"Right, Spock. Mr. Sulu, I'll let you get back to your discussion of comparative therapeutic techniques. Next time you're thinking of trying any radical experimentation, though, you might first check with Dr. McCoy."

Sulu laughed. "I'll do that, Captain."

* * *

As a student at Starfleet Academy, Kirk had gotten the impression of then-Captain Douglas Satanta as an individual who seldom sat. As a lecturer in Principles of Exploration he had not been a nervous man by any means; when he stood he stood still, except when he talked. Then he accompanied his baritone voice with deliberate, powerful sweeps of his hands.

The admiral was standing with his back to the door when it hissed aside to admit Kirk and Spock. He seemed to be studying the image of a world on a wall-sized viewscreen. At least Kirk guessed it was a world; all he could see around the admiral's looming figure was featureless blue disk, as if the Starbase's computer were tardy at drawing in the planet's terrain.

The admiral turned. Black hair hung in glossy braids to the epaulets of his Starfleet uniform, framing a heavy dark face, massive through cheek and jaw. The face was scarred and pitted as an asteroid. Satanta had been a planetary scout and first-contact specialist before he became a fighting starship captain. He was a man who seldom spoke of his exploits. Plenty of others were more than willing to do that for him.

He nodded deliberately. "Kirk. Mr. Spock." His formality told Kirk that something was up; otherwise that ominous-looking face would have split in a starling grin, and it would have been "Jim," an engulfing handshake, and a clap on the shoulder.

"Admiral. I came as quickly as I could round up my first officer." He gave Spock a sidelong glance and grinned. "I found him in a nightclub on Third Level."

Satanta raised his eyebrows. "Mr. Spock, carousing in a pub?"

"Lieutenant Uhura requested that I provide instrumental accompaniment for her singing," Spock said imperturbably. "I have observed that her voice has a salubrious effect upon the morale of the crew—therefore, it was only logical to comply. Besides, she was most insistent." He cocked his own eyebrow. "With all due respect I believe that hardly comprises 'carousing,' Admiral."

"If you gentlemen have finished your male bonding rituals," a cool voice said, "I believe we have business to attend to."

Kirk turned his head. A woman in civilian clothes of conservative and expensive cut sat in a chair swiveled away from the conference table. Dark red hair was pulled back from a stern face. Her eyes were green. He had the impression that she was tall, but that might have come from the stiffly erect way she held herself.

"Commissioner Wayne is correct," Satanta rumbled, his normally deep voice dropping an octave. "Commissioner, may I present Captain James T. Kirk of the starship *Enterprise* and his first officer, Mr. Spock. Captain, Mr. Spock—Moriah Wayne, the Federation deputy commissioner for interspecies affairs. She monitors compliance with the Prime Directive."

"It's a pleasure to meet you, Commissioner," Kirk said.

"I've heard a great deal about you, Captain Kirk. In fact, certain of your accounts of first contact with nonhuman races are required reading for our department."

"Ah," Kirk said, trying not to make himself look furtive by sneaking a glance at the admiral.

"Your approach is direct, not to say abrupt, and frequently lacks sensitivity. Your handling of the Gamma Trianguli VI situation, for instance. On that occasion you definitely violated the letter of the Prime Directive, if perhaps not its spirit."

Kirk's expression hardened.

"A Starfleet review board found the captain's actions were entirely justified," Spock said. "After all, the computer named Vaal was in the process of attempting to destroy the *Enterprise* when Captain Kirk destroyed it."

"Your defense of your captain does you credit, Mr. Spock, but it is unnecessary," Wayne said. She rose, only slightly less briskly than if she were standing to attention, and gave Kirk a look of frank appraisal. She *was* tall, he noted. "The qualities he displayed on Gamma Trianguli VI may be precisely what we require for our mission."

Now Kirk did look at Satanta. The admiral nodded.

"We're pretty much on the fringe of the galaxy here, as well as Federation Space," the admiral said. "There isn't much beyond us for a couple of hundred million light years, till you get to the next galaxy. But there are a few systems out past the boundaries of the Federation. One of them contains a planet called Okeanos."

He stepped aside to clear their view of the great blue disk. It appeared as featureless as before.

"It was found by a ship of the First General Survey, UES *Hernán de Soto,* back in 2092. The primary is called Joan-Marie's Star, after the navigator. It was her turn to name something. The chief steward, of all people, named the planet itself. Its classification is M. Computer, rotate."

At first the disk didn't change. Then dots appeared halfway down its curve—chains of islands, twining back and forth across the equator like tawny snakes. A few of the islands were respectably large, but none approached continental size.

34

"As the name suggests, it's a water world. Land masses represent less than three percent of the surface. Beyond that not much is known. The *de Soto* gave it a once-over with scanners and went its way."

"Why was not more attention paid to the planet?" Spock asked. "In the early days of Terran space exploration, human-habitable planets were at a distinct premium."

"The classification is a generous one, Mr. Spock," Commissioner Wayne said. She had a good voice, a rich, well-modulated alto. "The planet is nearly as hot as Vulcan, and equally bombarded with ultraviolet radiation. In addition, it has a dense crust, containing a high proportion of heavy metals."

"Which means high levels of background radiation," Kirk said.

"Earth humans cannot survive long on the surface without drugs or shielded environments," the admiral said.

"Not exactly a tourist paradise," Kirk said.

"But a beautiful world, if one is prepared to meet it on its own terms," the commissioner said, looking at the image with half-closed eyes.

"You have a great love for the sea, Commissioner?" Kirk asked.

"I have a great love for any world where the elemental forces of nature still hold sway, unconquered by our so-called civilization. I'm an ecologist by training, Captain."

"I see."

"The survey crew was surprised to find the planet in the first place," Satanta said. "Outside the spiral arm, all you generally see are ancient Population Two stars, which almost never have planets—and when they do, they're gas giants. The ship was actually making a side

35

trip to do a close-range study of a pulsar twenty-five light-years distant from Okeanos. Spectroscopic observation revealed the nearby presence of a Population One star, and a closer look showed it had solid planets, including several in the biozone."

"So the *de Soto* decided not to waste much time on a marginally habitable world and moved on to look at the pulsar," Kirk said. "I'm a little unclear as to what this all has to do with the *Enterprise,* Admiral."

"You're going there," Satanta said. "More precisely, you are transporting Commissioner Wayne there."

In surprise Kirk looked first at the admiral and then at the commissioner. At close range she was as tall as he was. She also might conceivably have been called attractive, if she hadn't gone to such lengths to make herself look like a stern schoolteacher.

"Your commission concerns itself with the affairs of newly discovered alien races, does it not?"

"We prefer the term 'sentients.'" Wayne gave a slight smile. "They're not alien to themselves, Captain. But yes."

"Then what official interest do you have in an uninhabited, radioactive swimming pool at the tail end of the Milky Way? However beautiful it may be."

"In their haste to return to more congenial reaches of space, Captain, the crew of the *de Soto* overlooked a few important details," Wayne said. "Such as the fact that the world they called Okeanos was inhabited by an intelligent species."

"They call themselves the Susuru," Satanta said. "We know nothing about them beyond the fact that they contacted us by subspace radio sixty-two stardates ago."

"I'm sure the commissioner is eager to meet this new race and make certain that the Prime Directive is honored. But the *Enterprise* is still undergoing upgrade. She's scheduled for twelve more days in drydock."

"You'll be cutting that short," the admiral said. "Starfleet orders."

Kirk frowned at him. Frowning at a flag officer was not usually considered healthy for one's career, but Kirk had never been one for letting his career get in the way of doing his duty as he saw it.

Fortunately, Satanta was no man to hold it against him. "Jim," he said, "you haven't heard the whole story yet. According to the Susuru, they are not alone on Okeanos. There are also Earth humans."

"Oh?" Kirk turned to Wayne. "So you're going to Okeanos to open relations with both groups."

She shook her head firmly. "According to the Susuru, the humans are unwelcome intruders," she said. "They're doing what Earth humans always do—oppressing the native peoples and ravaging the environment.

"I am going to Okeanos to convince them to leave—with the *Enterprise* to back me up."

Chapter Three

"HAVE YOU NOTICED, CAPTAIN"—Mr. Scott's voice came echoing back past the seat of his uniform trousers—"how these Jeffries tubes have the nasty habit of getting narrower and narrower as years go by?"

Kirk let the hand that held the palmtop screen displaying the blueprints for this sector of the ship rest on a rung of the vertical access tube and sighed. Scott was his senior by a respectable margin. It was only natural that he should feel a certain discomfort at the constant widening of the gap between him and his youth.

Telling yourself that is a great way to avoid admitting that you've been noticing the same thing, said Kirk's internal voice. A side of his mouth quirked up in a grin; strange how much that voice had come to sound like Bones's. When it didn't sound like Spock's.

"Marked and recorded, Mr. Scott," he said. "Carry on."

"Well, one thing's for certain, Captain. No matter how often they lift her face, she's always the same, and always a lady."

Kirk grinned at Scott's boot soles. The romantic side of his own nature was stirred by Scotty's undying devotion to his first and only true love. But the sad fact was, a man far gone in the grip of his passions could get to be a dead bore. Even to someone who, like Kirk, shared that passion to a large extent.

"And speakin' of the ladies, Captain," the engineer said, turning a grin down past his paunch at Kirk, "you'll no doubt be aware our distinguished passenger is by way of a bonny lass herself."

Kirk met his eye. "Really, Mr. Scott? I hadn't noticed."

The engineer turned a grin down to him. "Oh, aye, Captain, I understand. I do indeed." And he winked.

Kirk scowled, but held back the angry words that rose in his throat. *What am I getting so testy about?* he chided himself. The chief engineer was just making conversation as they worked.

They were in the process of refamiliarizing themselves with the starship. Though the *Enterprise*'s overhaul had been interrupted by the mission to Okeanos, much had been completed, and the journey was serving as a shakedown cruise. In fact, the ship carried several dozen technicians from Starbase 23 who were still hard at work installing and fine-tuning.

Naturally, Mr. Scott had to eyeball each and every "improvement"—quotation marks his—himself. And now he had no gimlet-eyed commodore to send him packing.

Kirk felt bound to accompany him as much as he could. Generally Kirk didn't have a great deal of patience with detail. His tendency to improvise had early been marked by his instructors at Starfleet Academy, and not with unqualified approval. That tendency—and ability—had kept him and most of his crew alive through nearly five years of galactic exploration. Even if it did tend to make his superiors tear their hair.

But one area where Kirk had a positive hunger for detail was the *Enterprise* herself. He believed in knowing his ship to the finest resolution possible, making her every capability and weakness as much a part of him as his DNA code.

"Bridge to captain." Spock's voice echoed down the Jeffries tube. There were intercom panels in the access passageway, of course, but none happened to be convenient.

Kirk unclipped his communicator from his belt and snapped it open. "Kirk here."

"Commissioner Wayne requests your presence on the bridge at your earliest convenience, sir."

Kirk frowned. Was Spock's voice even crisper than usual? The deputy commissioner had permission to be on the bridge, as a matter of courtesy—it was neither Starfleet's policy nor Kirk's to be too stiff-necked about that kind of thing. But what she might be up to requesting the captain's presence there he couldn't imagine.

"I'm on my way, Mr. Spock." He snapped the communicator shut. "Well, Mr. Scott, it looks as if I'm going to have to leave you to your own devices for a while. Have to keep our distinguished passenger happy. At least, if there were anything seriously wrong, like a Romulan attack, I'm sure Mr. Spock would have mentioned it."

"Our fair commissioner can't seem to get enough of your manly presence, Captain," Scott said. "The lass'll scarce give me the time of day herself. I reckon there's no accounting for taste."

"That will be more than sufficient, Mr. Scott," Kirk said briskly, and scrambled down the handholds to the passageway below.

"What seems to be the trouble?" Kirk asked as he strode onto the bridge.

Commissioner Wayne stood beside Spock, who occupied the captain's chair. She held her head high, as if in defiance. Her hair was wound into a tight bun that glistened like spun copper. With her body language it made her look haughty, almost aristocratic, rather than severe. Her skin looked smooth and shiny and hard, as if it were covered in glaze, or a coat of ice. She wore a tight tunic and trousers in black and gray in a style currently fashionable among the UFP bureaucracy.

Kirk sensed tension, and it didn't take him long to localize it. Spock was unreadable as always. Sulu— Sulu customarily sat at his helmsman's station in a posture of relaxed alertness, flexible but ready to respond instantly. Now he held himself rigidly erect, his spare frame drawn so tight he practically vibrated.

"Captain Kirk," Wayne said, turning to face him as the elevator doors hissed shut behind him. "I regret to inform you that your Mr. Sulu is in serious violation of Federation law."

Kirk stopped, and looked from the civilian to Sulu. Sulu looked straight ahead, at the field of stars seemingly rushing into the main viewing screen. The stars were beginning to thin out as the starship drove into the outer reaches of the galaxy at multiples of the speed of light.

"What's the charge? Reckless driving?"

41

"This is hardly a joking matter, Captain."

"Very well." Kirk's expression hardened. "We will discuss this in the briefing room. Mr. Kyle, you have the con. Mr. Spock. Mr. Sulu. If you'll accompany me."

"Aye, Captain," Sulu said. He rose, still not looking at either Wayne or the captain. Kyle slid into his seat.

"Commissioner," Kirk said.

"Surely we can discuss the matter here as easily—"

"Now."

"Computer," Mr. Spock said as they entered the briefing room.

"Recording," said the computer in a feminine voice.

"That won't be necessary, Mr. Spock," Kirk said, seating himself near the three-faced screen at the table's head. No one else made a move to sit. "This is not yet a formal proceeding. Computer, don't record these proceedings."

"Acknowledged, dear," the computer said.

Kirk felt his face get hot. The commissioner's eyes were darting green laser beams at him.

"I thought we had that little problem fixed," he said apologetically.

"This isn't a court martial?" the commissioner asked with a poisonous smile.

"No. It's a simple discussion at this point."

"I thought the military mind loved its little formalities."

"This military mind loves having a firm grasp of the facts before taking action. Excuse me, Mr. Spock?"

"Just clearing my throat, Captain."

Kirk gave him a few heartbeats of hard eye. The first

officer remained unruffled. Kirk turned back to Wayne.

"Now, just what is it that Lieutenant Sulu is accused of, Commissioner?"

"I overheard him talking on the bridge. He spoke quite candidly of transporting possibly dangerous life-forms in his quarters."

Kirk cocked his head. "Really, Mr. Sulu? What exactly are you keeping in there now? Denebian slime devils? A mugatu? Tribbles?"

"No, Captain. It's a mycellium."

"A what?"

"A walking slime mold, from the Gorn homeworld. Mr. Hornblower gave it to me. It's really a fantastic organism, Captain. It's a kind of carnivorous yellow and purple carpet. It can travel up to half a kilometer a day." Sulu was a man of many enthusiasms, and he was warming up to one of them. "That's something of a record, sir."

Kirk looked at him a moment longer. "A slime mold." He gave his head a little shake.

"It is truly an unusual organism, Captain, possessing many unique attributes," added Spock.

"Thank you, Mr. Spock. Is that what you heard the lieutenant talking about, Commissioner?"

"Yes, Captain."

He took a deep breath. "I fail to see how a walking slime mold constitutes a threat to the security of the Federation. No matter how fast it walks."

"Certainly, Captain, the potential for ecological devastation is enormous should such an organism be released on a world other than its planet of origin," Spock said.

Wayne shook her head. "I find it unsettling that a

man in your position could be unaware of such a basic fact."

"Commissioner, I'm not unaware of the danger. Neither is Lieutenant Sulu. And I'm sure he has no intention at all of letting his . . . specimen . . . go, on anybody's planet."

"But the danger of accidental release always exists," Wayne said. "That's why Federation law explicitly forbids the transportation of such organisms."

Kirk sat back in his chair and drummed fingers on its padded arm. "Commissioner Wayne, we are transporting you to your destination in what I'm sure you'll admit is a fair degree of comfort. But that does not mean we're a cruise liner. Nor is Mr. Sulu an irresponsible tourist trying to smuggle an exotic alien animal home with him for a pet.

"The *Enterprise* is a ship of exploration. Her crew are picked and trained specialists in exploration. Collecting—yes, and transporting—alien organisms is an important part of our mission."

"The law—" Wayne began.

"Does not apply in the present case, Commissioner," Spock said. "Section Five-oh-Four A, paragraph three, of the Federation Environmental Statutes clearly provides an exemption to exploratory and scientific vessels and their crews."

Kirk stood up. "Really, Commissioner, Mr. Sulu's slime mold will not be ravaging any ecosystems. We know how to handle these things."

Commissioner Wayne exhaled and lowered her head, seeming to lose a centimeter of stature. "Very well. I won't pursue the matter. Mr. Sulu, I hope you understand there's nothing personal involved. I'm just trying to do my duty, to nature and the Federation. Sometimes"—the ice cracked, ever so slightly—"sometimes I can be a bit overzealous."

Sulu glanced at the captain. "Sure, Commissioner. I understand."

"That will be all, gentlemen," Kirk said.

The two men left. Wayne started to follow.

"Commissioner," Kirk said. "A word with you?"

"Certainly." She let the door slide to behind her and leaned back against it. It seemed mildly out of character for the unyielding Federation commissioner.

"I understand that you have to do your job as you see fit, just like the rest of us aboard," Kirk said. "But I would appreciate it if in the future, should you have any accusations to make against any of my crew, you come to me directly. Public humiliation is not exactly good for morale."

The commissioner frowned. Kirk met her furious gaze head on.

Her expression softened particle by particle. "Fair enough." She paused, studying him as if she had never really looked at him before. "You're very solicitous of your men, aren't you?"

The question took Kirk aback. Almost in spite of himself he smiled. "That's my job."

"And you're very good at it."

"Starfleet seems to think so. They let me keep it. Now, Commissioner, if you'll please excuse me, I have a starship to run."

Chapter Four

WITH A SHRILL YIP Lieutenant Sulu sprang forward and struck Captain James Kirk on the side of the head with a stick.

The helmsman stepped back. "You need to keep your left-hand stick higher, Captain," he said, his voice muffled by the duraplast faceplate of his protective helmet. "You make it too easy to sneak one in, otherwise."

Kirk resisted the urge to try to rub the side of his head. His helmet was thoroughly padded, as were his hands, knees, and elbows, not to mention his protective cup. The sticks, half-meter lengths of hard polymer, were likewise padded. Still, the blow had stung. Sulu possessed a wiry strength that was surprising in view of his size. "Shall we try again?"

"Sure, Captain. Remember—in a lot of ways *escrima* is a lot like boxing. Martial arts all pretty much work according to the same principles." They had the aerobics room to themselves. Sulu's words echoed slightly. "You're a pretty fair boxer, so you should pick it up fairly quickly."

Kirk raised an eyebrow. Pretty *fair?* he thought. He had been the consistent runner-up in the middle-weight division at Starfleet Academy, losing year after year to the detested Finnegan. His tormentor graduated at the end of Kirk's junior year. It still rankled Kirk that only as a senior, without Finnegan to face, had he finally been able to take the championship.

He had not kept up with boxing. It was hard enough to find time to stay in shape, even with Dr. McCoy harping at him constantly. But Sulu's words pricked his vanity.

He raised his sticks. "Look to your own guard, Mr. Sulu," he said, and launched a quick swing at the helmsman's head.

Sulu danced back, and Kirk took great satisfaction in the fact that his parry seemed rushed. He aimed a whack at Sulu's advanced left knee. A beat later he fired an overhand stroke at Sulu's head. There were advantages to a combat art that used two weapons, he thought.

To both sides. Sulu countered both strikes with solid blocks and leapt to the offensive. He became a whirlwind. Kirk found himself staggering back, batting ineffectually at the sticks that whistled and flashed inches before his face.

Sulu's left stick darted around and down, delivering a resounding whack to Kirk's unprotected ribs. As Kirk tried to block, Sulu's right came down in an overhand blow that landed directly between the captain's eyes. Kirk reeled back three steps and sat down hard on the resilient mat that covered the gym floor.

Sulu was instantly at his side. "Captain, are you all right?" He tried to help his superior up.

Kirk waved him off. "I can stand on my own, Mr. Sulu. Nothing's hurt except my pride."

He caught the helmsman trying to swallow a grin. "I think you're enjoying this altogether too much, Mr. Sulu."

"Oh, no, Captain," Sulu said a little too quickly. "But maybe we should take it a little slower, until you get the hang of it?"

Kirk shook his head. "I won't be coddled, Mr. Sulu. You can instruct me on the niceties of form later. If I'm going to spar, I'll spar all out."

A trickle of sweat ran tickling down his nose. He removed the helmet. "I think I will take a bit of a breather."

Sulu nodded, took off his own helmet, and tucked his sticks under his arm. Kirk turned away to mask his hand feeling gingerly at his ribs. He'd been lying when he said the blows hadn't hurt. He felt as if he'd been kicked by a horse.

"I thought you were devoted to fencing, Mr. Sulu," he said, a trifle plaintively.

"That's still my first love, Captain. But I don't spend all my time with it. I don't want to go stale."

Reflecting that there wasn't much risk of that happening to his mercurial helmsman, Kirk went and got a drink from the water fountain. Sulu followed.

"I'm working my way through the martial arts, actually," Sulu said. "I've been studying Orion dance-fighting, which is a lot like Brazilian *capoeira.* Before that I did Tellarite *dag-jumag,* except to really get that right a human-sized person has to practice it on his knees, which gets wearing. *Escrima*'s a lot of fun. And it's very practical. Did you know Ferdinand Magellan was killed by an *escrimador* with rattan sticks?"

"I can't tell you how reassuring that is," Kirk said as the other bent to drink, "since I'm in the same line of work Magellan was."

"From what I've heard, you're a lot nicer to work for," Sulu said with a grin.

Into the exercise room came Commissioner Wayne, wearing a pink leotard over white tights. A cloth circlet consisting of a pink roll braided together with a white one kept the sweat that sheened her forehead from dripping into her eyes. Apparently she had been working out on the machines in the neighboring compartment.

"Oh, Captain," she said. "I heard voices—I hope I'm not disturbing anything."

"Not at all," Kirk said, wiping his face with a towel. "Mr. Sulu was just instructing me in the fine points of Filipino stick-fighting."

"Uh, Captain—if you don't mind, I'd better go. I'm on duty soon."

"Certainly, Sulu. And thanks for the workout."

"Sure," the helmsman muttered. He nodded to the commissioner without looking at her and sidled out of the room.

She looked after him with a puzzled expression. "He seemed uncomfortable. I wonder why he hurried out."

"You don't know?" Kirk said, surprised. She shook her head. "You did accuse him of a serious crime, Commissioner. One that carries a very stiff sentence."

It was her turn to look surprised. "But I was only doing my job!"

Kirk shrugged. For an obviously intelligent woman,

who had risen high in the ranks of Federation official-
dom, she showed some startling gaps in her knowledge of people.

Wayne looked at the helmet, sticks, and gauntlets
Kirk had left sitting by the wall. "Are you a martial
artist, Captain?"

"No. Not really. I try to stay limber enough to stay
alive on strange new worlds."

She laughed. "Ah, yes. Landing Party Kirk. Never
content to stay behind on the bridge while others
beam down into danger."

"You seem to know a lot about me," Kirk said,
starting to feel nettled.

"Is that so surprising, Captain? You've become
quite a legend in the Federation service in the last five
years."

She gave him a sidelong glance, half sly, half shy.
"Would you care to spar with me? Or don't you fight
with women?"

He rubbed his aching ribs. "I have an unfair advantage in mass," he said. "I'm a good deal heavier than
you."

"But I'm not exactly small. And I'm pretty good
at taking care of myself. My father insisted that I
learn."

Kirk looked her over appraisingly—something he
had not really done before. His status inhibited him
from dealing with her entirely as he might another
woman, he had to admit to himself.

He knew she was tall, and not overweight. The
utilitarian clothes she affected did not conceal those
facts, but also failed to call attention to any particulars. Now he saw that she had a lithe, long-legged
ranginess to her—a figure carrying little excess pad-

ding, but still entirely feminine. She moved with a dancer's grace and held herself well balanced.

He gestured at the *escrima* props. "Are you a stick-fighter too?"

She shook her head. "Bare-handed."

He shrugged. They stepped out on the mat and faced each other. "Any rules?" she asked.

"Don't do any damage my ship's doctor can't fix."

"Fair enough."

She began to circle counterclockwise. Crouching, hands up, he turned to keep facing her. After half a minute it became clear she was waiting for him to initiate an attack. Obligingly he came forward in a half-speed lunge.

She grabbed his hand, turned away from him, and jackknifed forward. He went flying over her shoulder to land flat on his back with a resounding whump. All the air exploded out of his body.

"I'm sorry," she said, standing over him. "I thought you knew how to land."

"I . . . do," he said. He felt as if he were lying there in several pieces. It took some time to pick himself up. "You just took me by surprise."

She grinned at him. "Try again. As if you mean it this time."

If that's what you want. He swung a right-handed blow for the side of her head, palm open. The fact was he didn't want to hit her with his bare fist. Also, he knew he'd likely bust his knuckles.

She whipped her left arm up in a forearm block. At the same time she stepped into him, thrust her right leg and hip past his, and drove the heel of her right hand into his sternum with a snap of her hips.

Kirk cartwheeled. This time he got a shoulder

tucked and rolled properly, taking much of the force out of the impact.

"Very good landing," she said, as he climbed to his feet.

"You're not so bad yourself," he said dryly.

She laughed. "Aikido and judo are the styles I learned. I don't believe in causing unnecessary harm. Even to an attacker."

"You're a pacifist, then," he said, massaging his breastbone.

"Not entirely," she said, "but close."

He lunged for her, trying to grapple and power her down. She grabbed his right wrist and he found himself spinning through the air again. This time he had no time to tuck; he landed flat and hard.

Instead of lying there stunned he rolled onto his side and swept the commissioner's legs out from under her with a scissors kick. It was her turn to go down hard and get the breath knocked out of her. Before she could recover he was lying half on top of her, pinning her wrists to the mat.

"So," she gasped when she could breathe again, "you're not just another military jock, loaded down with male chauvinism masquerading as chivalry, after all."

He had to admire her for getting the speech out. "Maybe I am," he said, lifting himself off her. "But I also hate to lose."

He held out a hand to help her up. Her eyes narrowed, and the strength of her glare rocked him back on his heels. Then she took his hand and let him pull her upright.

For a moment they stood nose to nose, their bodies touching. Wayne looked into his eyes with an expression he couldn't read. It seemed almost like wonder.

A heartbeat before he reached for her she pirouetted away. "I'd best not keep you from the bridge any longer, Captain."

He let go a ragged breath. "You're right, Commissioner. Duty calls."

They showered and dressed out in their respective locker rooms. In the foyer to the gym complex they met. "Will you walk with me to the bridge, Captain?" she asked.

It was on the tip of Kirk's tongue to ask why she felt she needed to *be* on the bridge. Master of unarmed combat though she might be, she was still a high-ranking civilian official, and he knew all too well that such officials had their foibles. Even if they did happen to be decidedly handsome women.

"My pleasure," he said, and gestured for her to go ahead.

Dr. McCoy was just walking toward them, down the corridor from the turbolift. "I just ran into Sulu," the doctor said, his round face crinkled with concern. "Shall I have Nurse Chapel bring a gurney for you?"

"Very funny, Bones."

"I'm just an old country doctor," McCoy said, "so you don't have to pay me any more mind than you usually do. But if you won't stop gadding about the surface of every hostile planet we make orbit around, at least you can refrain from getting yourself knocked to pieces in the safety of your own ship."

"Healthy exercise does him a lot less harm than sitting in his captain's chair getting fat," Wayne said. "I should think you'd know that, Doctor—unless your medical ideas are as antiquated as the speech patterns you affect."

The doctor stiffened. "Among my *antiquated* ideas are certain notions about the proper manner for a gentleman to address a lady," he said. "On the other hand—"

Kirk held his hands up. "Bones. Commissioner Wayne. Peace. Dr. McCoy and I are old friends, Commissioner; we've been going on like this for years, and we're both too old to stop."

"Speak for yourself, Captain," McCoy said.

"Do you think it's appropriate for a subordinate to address you that way?" Wayne asked. She seemed sincerely puzzled.

"Yes."

McCoy's blue eyes bored into her. "Do you think it would be better for morale if we had a uniform shirt stuffed full of Starfleet regulations for a captain? Our people aren't Romulans."

"Perhaps the Federation would be better off if they were," Wayne said. "Our citizens are undisciplined and self-indulgent."

"I thought you were the grand antimilitarist, Commissioner," McCoy said. "Why are you suddenly hipped on discipline?"

"Discipline and a military mind-set are not synonymous, Doctor. For all the efforts of the Federation government to mandate an environmentally sustainable lifestyle, the fact remains that—"

"I find this debate endlessly fascinating," Kirk said. "But unfortunately I have to go to work. If you'll excuse me?"

"I'll be in sickbay," the doctor said, eyeing Wayne with distaste, "puttering with my horse needles and patent medicines."

He stalked away. "A strange man," Wayne said. "And an angry one."

"He just likes to act irascible. It's part of his self-image."

The commissioner gave him a skeptical look. He thought of pointing out that she didn't strike him as being all that different from McCoy. Then he thought better of it.

They walked down to the turbolift. The crewfolk that they passed smiled and nodded to the captain. Kirk returned the greetings.

In the lift, Wayne said, "Your crew seem to like you, Captain."

Kirk shrugged. "I just believe in treating people decently."

"They're not required to salute you?"

Kirk laughed. "Excuse me, Commissioner. I don't mean to be rude. But I have to say that, while you seem to know a lot about me personally, you have some gaps in your knowledge about Starfleet."

"You're right. Your contacts with xenoforms fall under the Commission's purview. Starfleet protocol does not."

She studied him under lowered brows. "Captain, we're going to be working together very closely under circumstances that will no doubt prove extremely trying. I know your dossier well, but I don't really know *you*. It would be appropriate for us to become better acquainted. Perhaps we should have dinner together."

"An excellent idea." Without thinking, he added, "My quarters, twenty hundred hours?"

Commissioner Wayne looked at him with eyes like chips of sunstruck glass. He froze, belatedly considering the consequences should the prickly commissioner misconstrue his invitation. He was no careerist, but he did like his job.

She smiled. It made her seem a different person.

"I'd be honored, Captain. I'd like to show you that I'm not the total ogre I sometimes seem to be."

Chapter Five

"I HOPE OUR CUISINE is up to the standards you're accustomed to, Commissioner," Kirk said.

"My main concern with food is that it should be nutritious and wholesome, Captain."

"I . . . see. Will you take some more wine?"

A pause, a hesitant smile. "Yes, please."

Kirk poured, hoping the gesture would distract attention from his expression. He was seasoned in the ways of Federation bureaucrats, not to mention women. But he was having a hell of a time reading her signals.

Moriah Wayne sipped her wine. To his surprise she had turned up in a simple gown of a dark lustrous gray, one that left her arms bare and emphasized the color and clarity of her eyes. She wore her hair tied up at the crown of her head—a less severe bun than usual, at least.

"I see you surround yourself with relics of the sea,"

she said. Kirk's quarters, while spacious, were a long way from luxurious. The main decorations were the artifacts she referred to—the wooden wheel of an ancient sail ship, a ship's bell, a model of a three-master under full sail. "You asked me back at Starbase Twenty-three if I have a great love for the sea. I might ask you the same question."

Kirk *did* care about food. Tonight's fare—tournedos of beef with asparagus tips and steamed Andorian *taqq*—was special even by the *Enterprise's* usually excellent standards. He ate with his usual appetite and savored his meal well.

Between bites he said, "I do love the sea. But my first love is exploration. Look around, and you'll also see a model of the original Lunar Excursion Module and the first manned starship."

"Men and their toys," she said, smiling and shaking her head. She sat slowly back in her chair. "I thought your first love was the *Enterprise.*"

A shrug and a laugh. "Perhaps I'm fickle."

He leaned forward, holding up his hands—and trying not to think about McCoy's frequent observation that if you chained his hands behind his back, Kirk would be mute.

"I'm an Iowa farmboy who grew up loving the stars. I *wanted* them. There was so much to see in the universe, so much to learn, to do." He sat back and grinned. "The *Enterprise* gives me the stars. So maybe I'm not faithless, after all."

"So do you love the end, then—or the means?"

Kirk stared into his own wineglass. Then he laughed. "I don't think I'm prepared to be that profound, just now. And I'm doing all the talking."

"Well. . . ." She had eased her plate to the side and

held the wineglass on the table before her, rotating the stem slowly in her fingers. "I'm a city girl myself. I was born on Jotunheim."

"The industrial world?"

She nodded. "A huge ball of metal circling a dim red sun."

That explained why she had given him so much trouble in their sparring match. Jotunheim had a gravity a bit over 10 percent greater than Earth's. She had grown up working her muscles proportionally harder than a woman on Terra would.

"Growing up in the domes . . . I hated it. It was like living in a terrarium. You grew up longing for the stars. I grew up longing for the warmth of unfiltered sunlight on my face, the wind in my hair, the feel of grass beneath my feet. For air that didn't smell of the millions of other people who breathed it and moved in it and sweated in it. The recyclers and the hydroponic trays never could make the air smell fresh. . . ."

Her words dwindled away. A strand of her hair had fallen free and hung beside her face, gleaming like burnished metal. It made her look vulnerable—and entirely beautiful.

Her reminiscence reacted in Kirk's mind with something McCoy had said. "Jotunheim—are you related to Councillor Wayne?"

A sad smile. "He was my father."

"I see." Cornelius Wayne had spent twenty years as Federation Council member for Jotunheim. He had been a notable foe of Starfleet, insisting that it posed a threat of military dictatorship. A lot of older Starfleet officers spoke of him with the fondness they usually reserved for Orion pirates, Klingons, and the catastrophic decay of dilithium crystals. Kirk himself had no particular feelings about him; he had died of a brain aneurysm shortly before Kirk entered Starfleet Academy.

"My father died when I was an adolescent," Moriah said. "I—I guess I was angry at him for a while, for abandoning me. He was a harsh man in a lot of ways—not very easy to get along with. He wasn't abusive, don't get me wrong—nothing like that, ever. Really. He was just . . . demanding.

"Soon after he died I went away to college on Earth. He wanted me to go to Harvard, as he had, become a lawyer, and go into government right away—as he had."

She seemed to be gazing at the point of Kirk's chin. But her eyes were focused beyond, years ago and light-years away. "I went to the University of Oceania instead, for their environmental sciences program. I knew what had been missing in my life when I was a child—closeness with nature. We evolved outdoors, Captain—"

"Jim," he said, sipping. "Please."

A beat. "Jim. We humans spent millions of years on the savannas of Africa. Only for the past six thousand years or so have we had cities. That's not long enough for us to adapt to a total artificial environment—to life indoors, to life under glass."

Spock would probably quibble with that, point out that on world after world—Earth included—life tended to adapt very rapidly to changes in surroundings, if it adapted at all. If it didn't, it died.

But Spock wasn't here. "I agree," Kirk said.

"I thought if I became an ecologist, that would get me outdoors. And I really was concerned about the environment. All I had to do to see what was at stake was look at my homeworld."

She held forth her glass. "May I?"

"My pleasure." Kirk poured.

"I know the Federation had reasons for allowing unrestricted exploitation of Jotunheim—no atmosphere, no life, no environment to protect. But the industrial 'plexes, the mines gaping like open wounds . . . they were *ugly.*"

"But the Federation is very concerned about the environmental welfare of *living* planets," Kirk said.

"To an extent." She shrugged. "I wanted to do *more.* That's why I chose that school and that major."

Kirk had finished his own meal. He sat at ease, looking at her. It was an easy thing to do.

"Was that the only reason?" he asked after a time.

She dropped her eyes. *Is she actually blushing, or am I seeing things?*

"All right." She brought her face up sharply. Spots of color glowed on the prominent cheekbones, and her eyes were hot. "You're right. I was rebelling against my dead father—the rebellion I never had the guts to make when he was alive. Does it make you feel more manly to score a few cheap points off me?"

He held up his hands. "A truce. Please."

He felt a touch of guilt. That crack about men and toys had stung; he wanted to see if he could shake Wayne's forbidding composure. He was beginning to realize that the game, as Bones would quaintly put it, was not worth the candle.

"I was teasing, I admit it. Please accept my apology. It was inappropriate."

"No, no. Please." She reached across the table, took his hand, squeezed it. Then pulled her hand back as if it were in danger of being bitten. "I don't always react well. It's my fault. I've never been that good with people, I know. I didn't have much social life when I was young. I was always—you know—studying and training."

A wan smile. "My father had high expectations of me. I was his only child. And after all, it was a sign of high regard that he never settled for anything but the best from me."

"I—uh—I suppose so." Kirk rose, went to the wall near his model of the Old Ironsides, and pressed a button. A panel slid open, revealing a wide-bottomed bottle of brown glass. The neck was long, and curiously angled.

"Would you care for a taste of Saurian brandy? I've been saving the bottle for a special occasion. If the presence on board of such an illustrious personage doesn't qualify, I don't know what does."

"I'd be delighted."

She stood. At a spoken command from Kirk table and dirty dishes retracted into the wall. Kirk opened the bottle and poured a minuscule portion of the amber liquid into two brandy snifters.

"I'm not being stingy," he said, bringing a snifter to her. "This stuff is as potent as mercury fulminate and should be treated the same way—gingerly."

"Oh, I know. I've had it before."

"I guess you probably have."

Kirk sat in a chair facing the commissioner. He held up his goblet, admiring the way the faint light made golden play in the depths. "To what shall we drink?"

She leaned forward. "To success."

"I'll always drink to that," Kirk said. They drank, and savored, and settled back into their thoughts.

In time Wayne raised her eyes to his. They met with something like a shock, locked, and held for half a dozen heartbeats that seemed to ring very loudly in the ears of James T. Kirk.

She rose and came to him. She stood above him and held out her hands.

He took them and stood. "I must be going," she said. "I'd like to thank you for a truly wonderful evening."

He felt the warmth of her body washing over the front of him like surf. "It was my pleasure," he said.

She swayed forward against him. By reflex he slipped an arm around the small of her back. She let her head fall back, eyes almost shut, lips parted.

He kissed her.

Her body seemed to flow against his, like water joining water. Her mouth opened under his. Her tongue flicked against his, tentatively, then surged against it.

And her eyes snapped opened, and rolled, like the eyes of a trapped animal. The muscles of her back turned to wound wire beneath his hands. She backed out of his grip as if breaking bonds, stared at him with wild eyes, and was gone.

Two days later they reached the system of Joan-Marie's Star.

Chapter Six

"JOAN-MARIE'S STAR," said Spock, bending over so that the displays of the science console licked at his face with light. "General Survey number one dash one-one-two-three dash five-three-seven. Spectral classification F0, yellow-white, diameter one point seven-two times ten to the sixth kilometers, mass one point nine-two Sol, luminosity nine point eight-oh Sol. Surface temperature, seventy-five hundred degrees Celsius."

He straightened and looked at the star's image blazing on the main viewing screen. "It is rather unusual for such a hot sun to possess habitable planets, Captain."

"I have the impression, Mr. Spock, that we're going to encounter very little at all that is usual on this mission. Mr. Sulu, go to half impulse power."

The door to the turbolift hissed open. Moriah Wayne stepped onto the bridge. She was wearing a somber navy and black today.

She nodded politely to Kirk's greeting. He looked hard to see more than politeness in the glass-green eyes, but if it was there it eluded him. As she had been eluding him the last couple of days.

He shrugged. He'd been more than busy enough, surveying the alterations to the *Enterprise* with Scott, helping oversee the technicians who continued to work on his ship. He'd been running himself to the edge of exhaustion, in fact. He had more important matters on his mind right now than an ambiguous encounter with Wayne.

"The star possesses an Oort cloud of comets and seven planets," the science officer continued. "The outermost two are gas giants. Our objective is the fifth planet from the primary."

"Mr. Sulu," Kirk said, "can you give us a look at Okeanos?"

"Aye, sir." He manipulated controls on his console. A cloud-marbled blue disk expanded to fill the screen.

At the navigator station, Chekov let out a whistle. "Look at that storm system in the northern hemisphere!"

"In truth, Mr. Chekov, it would seem to differ little from the storm system visible in the southern hemisphere," Spock said.

He resumed his recital. "Okeanos orbits at a distance of three point one-three astronomical units, with a period of three point nine-nine-six Standard years—"

The turbolift door opened again, this time to admit Dr. McCoy. "So that's our destination," he said, peering at the viewscreen. "I hope I'm in time for Spock's lecture. He's as close to a textbook case of numerolalia as I'm ever likely to see."

"The compulsive uttering of numbers, to which I

presume your unwieldy neologism refers, is not a syndrome recognized by the Federation Psychiatric Union, Doctor."

"It will be, Spock, once I publish my paper on you." He gestured at the screen. "Say on, say on. Science is waiting."

"The planet has a diameter of twelve thousand seven hundred seventy-five kilometers, and a gravity of one point two. Its rotational period is fifty-five thousand nine hundred five seconds. Does that satisfy you, Doctor?"

Sulu whistled. "Fifteen and a half hours."

"Fifteen hours, thirty-one minutes, and forty-five seconds," Spock said.

"Isn't he beautiful?" McCoy said.

"You'd barely have time to go to bed before it's time to get up again," Sulu said.

"I think they make up in quality of daylight what they lack in quantity," Kirk said dryly.

"Indeed, Captain," Spock said. "While Okeanos receives almost precisely the same amount of irradiation as Earth does, a much higher percentage of it is in the form of ultraviolet light."

"We'll have to remember to wear our sunscreen," Kirk said.

"The atmosphere consists of seventy-eight percent nitrogen, twenty percent oxygen, and two percent argon, with traces of carbon dioxide and water. Concentrations of sulfur compounds range from annoying to hazardous, depending on proximity to volcanic activity."

"Twenty percent oxygen's pretty thin for a man to breathe," McCoy said dubiously.

"A greater atmospheric density than Earth's brings

66

the oxygen content well within the range of human comfort."

"I don't get the idea *comfort* is a word it's going to occur to me to use much in connection with this planet, Spock."

"Unfortunately not, Doctor. However, I anticipate that I shall find the climate eminently salubrious. The average daytime temperature at thirty degrees latitude is three hundred eleven degrees."

Wayne had been gazing raptly at the screen. The statement jolted her from her reverie. "Three hundred degrees? My God, that's almost as hot as Venus. How can there be liquid water?"

"Mr. Spock is using the Absolute scale," Kirk said, eyeing his science officer. "He means thirty-eight degrees Celsius."

"Which is still almighty hot," McCoy said. "Reminds me of a story from back home. A Southern gentleman once remarked that if he happened to own both hell and Texas, he'd rent out Texas and live in hell." He gestured toward the screen. "Obviously, he never heard of this place."

"Obviously, Doctor, since that quote predates even the crudest spaceflight by almost a century."

Wayne made an irritable gesture. "Your numbers are just that—numbers. This is a beautiful planet, Mr. Spock."

"But potentially a very deadly one."

"All planets are potentially deadly, Spock," Kirk said. "If there's one thing our travels have taught us, it's that."

Commissioner Wayne crossed her arms. "How very *masculine,* to see the unknown as a threat."

"I beg your pardon, Commissioner," Lieutenant

Uhura said, "but on the *Enterprise* we've found that very often the unknown *is* a threat."

The commissioner turned a glare on her. Uhura didn't flinch.

"Captain—"

"What is it, Mr. Sulu?"

The helmsman frowned. "I'm not sure, sir. The planet's magnetic field is extremely powerful, and the flux is incredible. It's causing my sensors to give back anomalous readings, but I'm getting something— *there.*"

His finger stabbed a button like an entomologist pinning a rare insect. A little designator box appeared at the lower left corner of the disk. "There's a vessel in orbit around Okeanos, Captain. Just coming around the edge of the world."

"Shields up, Mr. Sulu. Go to full impulse power." Kirk leaned forward unconsciously. "Can you bring it up on the screen?"

"Aye, Captain. Going to full magnification . . . now."

The ship resembled a sinister bird, with down-turned wings and a long, slender neck. Commissioner Wayne caught her breath.

"Klingon battlecruiser," Ensign Chekov said in wonder.

"It's magnificent," Commissioner Wayne said. She held the fingertips of her right hand pressed against the notch of her clavicle, as if she were touching an invisible amulet.

"It's just what we needed," Kirk said. He was almost amused by the situation. Fate never threw him a fastball down the middle, that much was certain.

"Captain, the vessel is broadcasting a standard

Klingon recognition sequence," said Uhura. Kirk made a sound low in his throat.

"What are they doing here?" Wayne asked.

"No good, no doubt," Kirk said. "Open hailing frequencies, if you please, Lieutenant."

"Aye-aye, sir. Hailing frequency open, sir."

"This is Captain James Kirk of the USS *Enterprise,* calling the Klingon ship in orbit around the fifth planet of this system. Identify yourself, please."

A snarl of syllables that sounded like a lion gargling came from the bridge speakers. "—*taj may'Duj tlhIngan wo'—*"

The translator kicked in. "—Imperial Klingon Battlecruiser *Dagger.* Leave the system at once or you will be destroyed!"

"It's nice to be made to feel welcome," Kirk said.

"They're not transmitting any visuals, Captain," Uhura said. "No, wait—I'm getting something now."

Wayne had stepped forward. "I am Federation Commissioner Moriah Wayne," she said. "I demand to know—"

A face appeared on the screen. It was darkly handsome, notwithstanding the bony ridge that thrust up from the crown of the skull to part heavy black hair that hung to broad shoulders. A long face, gaunt almost, with black mustaches sweeping down to either side of a full-lipped mouth and a jutting narrow chin. A pale scar slashed down from the high forehead and across the right eye to gouge deeply into the cheek. The eye itself was covered with a black patch.

His good eye more than made up for its lack of a partner. It was as hot and black as the core stuff of a sun. Energy and dangerous charisma seemed to shine from him like hard radiation.

"To know"—Moriah Wayne stood openmouthed, making a vague spreading gesture of the hands— "what you're doing here."

"We tender fraternal assistance to the natives of this world, who are being unjustly oppressed by members of your race."

"This from the galactic experts on the subject," McCoy muttered under his breath.

Apparently failing to hear him, the face turned. "Ah, Captain Kirk! Welcome! You honor us with your presence." The speaker settled back in his command chair, which had the shaggy black and purple pelt of some animal thrown over it. The motion permitted the watchers on the *Enterprise* bridge to see more of him. He wore the customary Klingon jerkin of silver mesh, and over it the gold sash of his rank. "I see, Captain, that the years have been kinder to you than they generally are to members of your species."

Kirk was trying not to stare. It was not the Klingon way to so much as offer greetings. Here was a Klingon being effusive. "You have the advantage of me, I'm afraid."

A black-gauntleted hand dropped to the hilt of a curious multiple-bladed knife slung at the Klingon's waist. "Much time has passed since last we met in the flesh, Kirk. I am Kain, now Captain of the First Rank and officer commanding the Klingon Imperial advisory detachment to this unhappy world."

Kirk sat back in his chair as if the other had reached through the screen and punched him in the sternum. *Kain!* The years, the savage scar—if he looked beyond them, Kirk thought, he could just recognize the youthful junior lieutenant, fresh-faced for a Klingon and painfully eager to prove himself, who had stared

70

warily out from behind his father's shoulder in the receiving line.

"The Axanar peace conference," Kirk said. "It has been a long time, Captain."

"Our paths have crossed since then," the Klingon said.

"They have?"

"Indeed. I was a senior lieutenant on the *Fist of Retribution* at Endikon, Captain. I commanded a certain landing party."

Kirk goggled. "That was you?" *I can't laugh. Now, of all times, I have to keep a straight face.*

Kain nodded. "We Klingons believe that third meetings are fateful, Captain."

"Is that your ship in orbit?" Wayne asked.

"It is, Commissioner. I am not aboard her, however. I speak to you now from our mission on Homesward, the chief island of the Susuru archipelago."

He smoothed a wing of his mustache with a thumb. "Now perhaps you would be so kind as to tell me what you are doing here."

"We're here in response to a call from the Susuru," Wayne said. "They are being victimized by human interlopers."

"So they say," Kirk said.

"You have summed the situation admirably, Commissioner. Yet I admit I'm puzzled. Klingon generosity is widely known."

"That's true," Kirk said. It was known in precisely the same way Klingon mercy was—for the purity of its absence.

"We have come to help them, with strong hands and strong hearts. Why then would they summon"—he was able to keep most of the contempt from his voice—*"Earthers?"*

Kirk sucked briefly on his lips. "Their message to the Federation said, 'They are your people—come and get them.'"

Kain laughed. It was a hearty, rich laugh. It put Kirk in mind of flaying knives and white-hot pokers.

"So they do not slight us. It is good." The Klingon smiled. His teeth were very white. "I must say, Captain, your arrival greatly eases my mind."

"It does?"

Kain nodded earnestly. "The situation here is highly volatile—skirmishes and worse occur daily." He leaned forward. "Surely with your powerful assistance we will find a peaceable solution to the problems of this world."

"No doubt we shall," Kirk said, "one way or another. Captain-First, it's an honor to speak with you, but I have to cut this short. I have other people to talk to."

Kain nodded. "I await your call, Captain. And that of your very capable commissioner."

The screen went blank. "Now, how did *he* know she was capable?" Dr. McCoy asked.

Wayne was staring at the now blank screen as if she still saw something there. "What an extraordinary man," she breathed.

"He is that," Kirk said.

The commissioner beamed. "With him working together with us, surely we'll have the situation here cleared up in just a few days."

Kirk took a deep breath. "Commissioner," he said, "I certainly hope so. Lieutenant Uhura, see if you can find me a channel to the Susuru."

Chapter Seven

A MOMENT'S DISLOCATION, and then Kirk was standing shin deep in grass. He looked down, surprised, then glanced left and right at Spock and Commissioner Wayne, who had beamed with him to the surface of Okeanos.

"Greetings, Captain Kirk, Commissioner Wayne," a familiar voice said. Kirk looked up to see Kain striding across the sere grass at him. "And you, of course, are the remarkable Mr. Spock."

"I am."

Kain walked up to the commissioner, took her hand, and raised it to his lips. Her hand looked fragile and white against his black gauntlet.

Kirk restrained the impulse to either goggle or roll his eyes. Instead he blinked past Kain's shoulder. Despite the grass, the coordinates to which they had beamed were indoors. The ceiling seemed to be a low, flattish dome with a broad circular skylight to admit the light of the brief Okeanos afternoon. The glare of

Joan-Marie's Star was muted heavily by red filters, so that the chamber was filled with a murky dimness.

"I hardly expected to find you here, Captain-First," Kirk said. "Where are our hosts?"

"We are here, Captain," said a voice like water over smooth stones. A figure resolved itself out of the gloom, with a number of others trailing behind.

The creature was small, perhaps a meter and a half tall. It walked tentatively on the toes of long slender forelegs—which looked horribly uncomfortable to Kirk, who was feeling the pressure of 20 percent-greater-than-usual gravity in his knees and ankles and lower back. Its hind legs were held together at the rear of its short and narrow but long torso. Slim hands were folded across each other on the body's centerline.

The head was narrow and long, with huge forward-looking liquid amber eyes above a muzzle covered in soft, honey-colored fur. The nostrils were wide and sensitive-looking. The ears rode high up on the crested skull, long and pointed and mounted to track in all directions, like a Terran horse's. At the moment their focus was twitching nervously from Kirk, to Wayne, to Spock, and back to Kirk again.

The being stopped three meters in front of Kirk, performed a complicated gesture that was part prancing, part genuflection. The captain saw that the fur of his muzzle was hoary. His hands were almost human, bony knuckled and sparsely furred. They gave the impression of substantial strength despite their slenderness.

"I am Swift," the creature said. His front teeth were broad chisel-shaped incisors, yellow and worn. "The Susuru follow where I walk."

74

"I am Captain James Kirk, USS *Enterprise*. This is Mr. Spock, my first officer, and this is Deputy Commissioner Wayne, of the Federation."

The Susuru was backing slowly away as Kirk spoke. The other twenty Susuru backed with him, scrupulously maintaining position so that he stayed in front. When he had retreated to about seven meters he stopped and raised his head. His body was golden, with white on the belly and a ruff like a collie's around his neck of darker fur shot through with gray. The tips of his ears were black.

"And these four Fives are They Who Walk in the Vanguard," Swift said, indicating his companions. "You would call them our council of elders. The fifth Five, who brings the number to perfection, is, of course, myself. We bid you welcome."

The other Susuru spoke what Kirk took for a ritual greeting in chorus, and performed an abbreviated version of Swift's earlier gesture.

"Our browse and water are yours," said Swift.

Commissioner Wayne walked forward. The Susuru leader went rigid. The others backed away, whining softly.

"Commissioner," Spock said, "I believe you are invading Swift's personal territory."

She turned a furious look over her shoulder. "Mr. Spock, I'll thank you to let me do my job! I *am* Deputy Commissioner for Interspecies Affairs."

Spock raised an eyebrow. Wayne turned back to Swift, who cringed visibly.

"You communicated your need to the Federation," she said. She dropped to one knee. "I have come to help you."

The Susuru had pulled up one foreleg. The toes

were long and tipped with thick pads. The creature leaned so far back it seemed impossible that it didn't topple backward.

"You are not planning to leap for my throat?" Swift asked, tucking his chin deep in his ruff.

Wayne gave him a wondering look. "But I'm from the Federation. I'm here to *help* you."

"Besides," Kain boomed in his rich baritone, "I am here to keep you safe."

"If you'll forgive my curiosity, Captain," Kirk said, "just why *are* you here? Are you seriously expecting the commissioner to leap for his throat?"

Kain chuckled. "Not at all. I'm here to advise the Lead Walker. Their experiences of your fellow Earthers has been anything but reassuring."

"They are your people." Swift's sibilance turned to a jagged shrill keening, with a piercing fingernails-on-blackboard edge that made Kirk weak at the knees. "Come and take them! They despoil our world. They enslave our wild sea beasts, they rape our ocean bottoms and befoul our water with their mining! All to serve their insatiable greed."

The Vanguard Walkers set up a wail, rising higher and higher in pitch even as Swift's voice dropped.

"And they kill us. Our youths who venture upon the sea, our mothers and young in our bomb-shattered habitations. *Your* people. Yours!"

The wailing rose until Kirk's eardrums bulged inward.

"Oh, you who run in the vanguard of your human herd," the Susuru leader cried above the intolerable sound. "The blood of innocence cries out for justice. Hear now my words: should you not act, in two fives of days, with the aid of our friends from far stars, we

76

shall mount a mighty offensive and scour your folk from the face of the planet!"

Dr. McCoy was waiting as they stepped off the transporter platform back aboard *Enterprise*. "Well? How'd it go?"

Moriah Wayne held her fingertips over her ears and shook her head. "That wailing! Such grief—I can't get that awful sound of loss out of my ears."

"That well?" McCoy said. Kirk shrugged.

"It is illogical to give such free rein to the natural response of grief," Spock said.

"How can you speak of *logic* at a time like this?" Wayne flared at him. "We are talking about *pain,* Mr. Spock. The pain of the loss of loved ones. Or does your green Vulcan blood run too ice cold for loss to have any meaning to you at all?"

"I never thought I'd say this," McCoy said, "but you took the words right out of my mouth, Commissioner."

Spock looked at her. "I, too, have known loss, Commissioner," he said. "Even Vulcans mourn. But there is a danger in abdicating control so completely. It is frequently difficult to regain."

"Lieutenant Uhura," Kirk said as he strode onto the bridge, "see if you can raise one of the human cities."

"They're very impressive structures, Captain," Sulu remarked. "The Okeanians aren't going to be happy to leave them behind."

The *Enterprise*'s sensors had revealed seven of them, sprawling metallic clusters apparently floating free on the endless ocean. Four occupied the northern

77

hemisphere, three the south. None approached the equator nearer than twenty degrees latitude. There was a great deal of broadcast traffic between the cities, as well as with a multitude of smaller settlements. Few of these encroached far into the equatorial zone.

"They don't have any choice in the matter," Wayne said crisply, stationing herself next to Kirk's command chair even as he settled into it. "The only question is how many transports we'll need to take them off-planet."

"That's not necessarily the *only* question, Commissioner," Kirk said. "We haven't even spoken to these people yet."

She stared at him in disbelief. "But didn't you hear those beings down there? Didn't you feel their loss reverberating in your bones?"

"Believe me, Commissioner, I heard them. But we have not yet heard what the humans on Okeanos have to say."

She tossed her head. "What difference does that make? They're intruders. They have to go."

"Situations are seldom as clear-cut as they seem upon cursory examination, Commissioner," Spock said. "Surely we cannot take action on the basis of such incomplete data as we now possess."

"Captain," Uhura said, "I can't seem to get anybody to respond to me."

"What do you mean, Lieutenant? Are you trying to tell me that no one's the least bit interested in being contacted by visitors from outer space?"

"No, sir, that's not the problem. Everyone I reach is willing to talk. They're bubbling over with questions, in fact—and they all seem to be able to speak English."

"Well, at least we won't have to rely on our translators." The "Universal Translator" AI technology was relatively new. While Starfleet made extensive use of it, it was known to display some highly embarrassing glitches from time to time. "What seems to be the problem, then?"

She swiveled her seat to face him. "I can't find anybody in a position of authority, sir. Everybody I speak to just laughs when I ask to be put in touch with their planetary or local government."

"Maybe they don't have one," McCoy said.

"Ridiculous," Wayne said. "They possess cities and technology. They can't be complete anarchists."

"If they have had extensive dealings with the Klingons," Spock said, "perhaps they have grown wary of spacefaring cultures in general."

"That sounds dangerously close to bigotry, Commander," Wayne said. "Captain Kain is obviously a man of great integrity and sensitivity."

"Those aren't traits the Klingon culture values highly," Kirk said. "It's hardly bigotry for Mr. Spock to base his observation on facts that are, after all, pretty widely known."

"What is widely known, Captain," Wayne said, "isn't always true."

"She's got you there, Jim," Dr. McCoy said.

Kirk rubbed his jaw. "I know," he said.

"Captain," Uhura said, "I have somebody who's agreed to speak to you."

Kirk raised his eyebrow at her and sighed. "Are they transmitting a visual?"

"Yes, sir."

"Put them on the screen, if you please."

The screen showed three people seated in a room. It was dark except for three lights shining down on them from the ceiling. What he could see of the room was devoid of decoration. The three occupied a low dais. At their backs a window opened on night and a gray sea whipped to thrashing frenzy by a storm.

He took all that in in a flash. Then his attention snapped to the people themselves.

"What?" whispered Moriah Wayne. She didn't seem aware that she had spoken.

Kirk tried hard not to stare himself. *These are supposed to be humans. What's going on?*

The three individuals onscreen appeared to belong to three entirely different species.

"I am Captain James T. Kirk of the United Space Ship *Enterprise*. We have come in the name of the United Federation of Planets—"

"We offer you and your people an enthusiastic welcome, Captain," said the man who sat in the middle. He looked entirely normal—a light-skinned black, theatrically handsome, with pronounced epicanthic folds to his eyes. He was dressed in a russet jacket and trousers over a collarless black shirt, with black thong sandals. "But you might as well save your breath. It doesn't matter to us whom you claim to represent."

"Oh, really?" Kirk said. In the corner of his vision he noticed Uhura paying perhaps stricter than regulation attention to the spokesman.

The man nodded. "Really. But I forget my manners. This is Aileea dinAthos of Securitech, and this is Mona Arkazha, representative of the Deep-ranger Syndicate. I am Jason Strick. I'm an arbiter by trade."

Kirk frowned. "Are you speaking for the duly constituted government of your planet?"

That elicited polite laughter from Strick and the woman named Aileea, who sat at his right. "There isn't any such thing," she said in a singsong accent much like the man's. "Unless you talk to the Susuru." Her face hardened. "They seem to have a lot of fancy ideas along those lines."

Lightning cut a brief purple wound across the sky at their backs. Kirk studied dinAthos briefly. She looked to be in her early thirties, and wore a dusty-green vest over a white top that left her midriff bare, and dark green slacks. She looked human, too—beautiful, in fact.

But the hair she wore in a shag to her shoulders was a deep green, and down the sides of her slim neck ran slits that reminded him of gills.

"Just whom *do* you represent?" he asked.

"Ourselves," said the third person. She—Kirk saw —was a squat being, hairless, with rubbery-looking black skin. A clear respirator mask covered the lower half of her broad face. A dark metal yoke enclosed her short neck and flowed down over the tops of her shoulders. It surrounded her with a constant iridescent shimmer of mist. She had webbed hands and feet, two vertical slits for a nose, no external ears—holes in the sides of her head. Where the skin was close to bone, on knuckles and feet and under her square jaw, it showed yellow highlights. She wore no clothes except for the mask and yoke, and a harness holding small implements whose function Kirk didn't recognize. She looked like some kind of amphibian, only vaguely humanoid.

"Jason says I speak for my syndicate, and in some matters I do. In this matter I have no authority beyond my own skin." Her accent was harsher than the others', and sounded somehow familiar. "But understand something, Captain—you are unlikely to get a different answer from anyone else on Discord."

"Discord?"

81

The man held his hands out. "Our world. This world."

"It isn't your world," said Commissioner Wayne.

"And who are you to say so?" demanded Arkazha.

"I am Moriah Wayne, Federation Deputy Commissioner for Interspecies Affairs."

"The what?"

Wayne drew herself up. "I have been sent to prepare you to evacuate this world in order that it be returned to its rightful owners."

Lightning blazed again, powerful enough to tumble the image momentarily into a flurry of horizontal lines.

When reception cleared the green-haired woman was standing, legs braced, fists clenched. Kirk saw that she wore a heavy-looking handgun on a belt at her hip.

"This is our world!" she exclaimed. "Our ancestors came here when Earth rejected them. They mixed their blood with sea and crust to make it theirs."

"The Susuru—" Wayne began.

"The Susuru are the interlopers! They weren't here when our mothers landed. And they are murderers, Captain. We're willing to let them have the land, and the freedom of the seas. But they want it all—and they want our lives as well."

"Aileea, please—" Strick said.

"If the Stilters want to take one they'll have to take the other," dinAthos declared. "They'll have to kill us all."

She thrust a finger at Wayne. "You can have Discord on the same terms, *Commissioner*. And that's the only way you'll get it."

She sat down again, cheeks flushed, jade eyes glaring.

"Not so fast," Kirk said. "We're not going to rush

into anything here. Ms. dinAthos, I'd like to come down to the surface and meet with you in person, set up talks between you and the Susuru—"

"And what of the Susuru's new friends?" asked Arkazha.

Kirk shrugged. "We'll deal with them, too."

"What a merry party *that's* going to be," McCoy muttered.

Strick held up his hands. To Kirk's surprise they were callused hands, workman's hands. "You have the freedom to land where you will, Captain. In fact, I invite you and all your crew to come down freely as our guests. In this I do speak for most Discordians. We're a hospitable folk, and it's been a long time since we've had news from Earth.

"But if you're looking for someone with the authority to speak for all Discordians—that person doesn't exist. And please understand that, so far as we're concerned, you are here as private citizens. We do not recognize your Federation, nor any power you derive from it."

"You have no authority here," said Arkazha. "You are tourists—no more."

The screen returned to the image of Okeanos— Discord, the settlers called it. Wayne slowly unclenched her fists. "I don't think there's any more room for doubt," she said quietly.

"Doubt of what, Commissioner?" Dr. McCoy asked.

"That what those beautiful Susuru said was true? These so-called Discordians are no more than bandits."

Kirk sighed. "I'm calling a command conference in the briefing room to discuss the situation. Fifteen minutes." He rose.

"I thought the Susuru said the colonists were all human," Sulu said.

"Perhaps we all look alike to these Susuru," Chekov suggested. Wayne scowled.

"I have to admit I was somewhat startled myself," Kirk said. "I wonder what races were represented. I couldn't place the two of them, the dinAthos woman and Arkazha."

"Arkazha speaks with a good Russian accent, Captain," Chekov announced. "It has undercurrents of St. Petersburg."

"Thank you, Mr. Chekov. That's an interesting datum."

"Sensor readings"—Spock bent to the science console—"indicate that all three persons belong to the same species—*Homo sapiens.*"

He turned and straightened. "They are all every bit as human as you yourself are, Captain."

Chapter Eight

"THE PROBLEM we've got to deal with now," Kirk said, "is how to proceed from here."

"Surely that's self-evident, Captain," Wayne said. She alone declined a seat at the table. "The humans— if they can be called that—are invaders. Our instructions from the Federation require us to persuade them to leave. Duty and justice alike require that we carry out those orders."

"I dinnae like it, Captain," Scott said. "To uproot a whole people from their homes, move 'em clean across space to God knows where . . . it goes against the grain."

"Do you examine all your orders to make sure they're in accord with your sentiments before you obey them, Lieutenant Commander Scott?"

Scotty worked his mouth and glared, but could find nothing to say. "Mr. Scott," Wayne said, smoothing her tone. "It's not just a question of orders. It's a

85

question of right. If a burglar breaks into your house, does he have a right to be there?"

Scott eyed her suspiciously. "No, ma'am," he said. Since she was neither part of the ship's complement or the Starfleet chain of command, she didn't rate the honorific *sir*. Or at least he didn't feel compelled to apply it to her.

"But if he should somehow manage to stay a week—does that give him a right then?"

"No."

"What's the statute of limitations, then, Mr. Scott? When does theft turn into ownership?"

Scott moistened his lips. "I cannae answer that," he said. "But clever words and fair countenance do not make wrong into right, Commissioner."

"As distasteful as the fact may be," Mr. Spock said, "it is common knowledge throughout the galaxy that time does, in fact, confer such legitimacy. There are few cultures today who do not occupy at least some land that their forebears wrested from another culture."

"Because it's accepted, does that make it right, Mr. Spock? Is the Federation about righting injustice, or papering it over with rationalizations and legalisms and so perpetuating it?"

"Your arguments are at base emotional," Spock said. "Logic tells us that any attempt to systematize justice will entail a degree of compromise."

"Then set logic aside. What does your heart say?"

"My heart is incapable of speech, Commissioner."

Wayne stared at him. "Is he making a joke, Captain?"

"He's Vulcan," Kirk said. "He can't make jokes."

He saw the sideways flicker of McCoy's eyes, the ghost of a grin, hastily hidden.

Wayne walked around the table to stand near Spock. "Mr. Spock, tell me, as a Vulcan, how does it make you feel that your people are dominated by Earth humans." She held up her hands. "No, wait. I know Vulcans don't like to admit they have feelings. So—what is your response to the fact of your domination?"

"The Vulcans are not dominated, Commissioner," Spock said matter-of-factly.

"But look around you. What do you see? Vulcan faces? Hardly. Any nonhuman faces? None. Mr. Scott, the doctor, Lieutenant Uhura, Chekov, Sulu, the captain—all human. Doesn't that suggest an imbalance."

"Vulcan has its own space service. Most Vulcans inclined to venture into space choose to join it." He paused. "They find the Federation service somewhat beneath them."

"Aren't Vulcans superior to humans? Are you not stronger than a man? Are you not quicker, more resistant to heat and radiation . . . more intelligent?"

"I am."

"Commissioner," Dr. McCoy said, "do you really think the ends of this mission are served by inciting our first officer to rebellion?"

Kirk held up a hand. "Bones. Let her have her say."

"Then why is a Vulcan not head of the Federation? Why isn't one captain of this ship?"

"Because that would not be logical."

She blinked. "Not logical? How is it not logical?"

"Leadership requires a certain ambition, a drive, a desire to lead—or to conquer. We Vulcans lack that ambition. When we forswore emotion, Commissioner, it was in fact primarily to expunge precisely those drives, which had caused such great devastation to our people and our planet. Our Romulan cousins, on the other hand, indulge their ambition, to the detriment of their culture and galactic peace."

Wayne raised spread fingers near her temple and dropped them again in a gesture of defeat. "Doesn't anyone see what the Federation is like?"

"I see a century of peace and harmony," Scott said.

"Haven't there been wars, with the Klingons and Romulans and Gorn? Haven't you buried your own dead?"

"Relative to the bulk of human history, Commissioner," Kirk said, "I think one would have to say the Federation era has been one of unprecedented peace."

"How exactly does it come to pass that a high official of the Federation is arguing so vehemently against the Federation?" McCoy asked.

"Don't misunderstand me, Doctor. I'm not saying the Federation is evil. I'm saying it could be better. Don't you feel that the UFP has the obligation to be as ethical as possible?"

"Yes," he said reluctantly. "I do."

"The fact is that Earth humans dominate the Federation. That is wrong. The fact is also that that 'human history' you spoke of, Captain, is nothing but a litany of rape, degradation, murder, and exploitation. And that is what the Susuru are facing on Okeanos today."

"Commissioner," Kirk said, and then had to pause with his hands on the table before him to order his thoughts. "I—I can't agree that human history is as black a picture as you paint it. No, wait, please—that doesn't have any bearing on our discussion here—"

Wayne would not be restrained. "It has every bearing!"

"The key point is that we do not have all the facts

88

about what's going on down there. And as Starfleet officers, I submit, we have a responsibility to withhold action until we know more."

"Hear, hear," McCoy said. A ripple of concurrence ran around the table.

"You all saw the meeting with the Susuru leader on the viewing screen," Wayne said, almost pleading. "You heard his words, his passion. How can you doubt what he said?"

"His passion was no doubt authentic, Commissioner," Spock said. "Yet that does not mean that he told the whole story. I do not mean to imply that he lied. He may have told the truth as he knew it—and saw it. All we have to go on are unsupported allegations made by mutually hostile parties. It would be the height of recklessness to proceed on no better grounds."

Wayne looked around, her lovely haughty face with scorn. "How like Earth *men,*" she said. "What other Earth-derived men say is all that's important—the outcries of native beings count for nothing."

"Two of the spokespeople for the Discordians were women, Commissioner," Uhura said quietly.

Wayne dismissed the objection with a flip of her hand. "The leader was a man. They're a male-dominated, exploitative society. The women were figureheads—nothing more. They'll recite the lies they're told to."

"This ship is commanded by a man, Commissioner," Uhura said. "Does that mean I and all the other women aboard are nothing but puppets and empty-headed liars?"

"Lieutenant, I don't think I like your tone."

"Commissioner, I don't think I like yours."

"Crew," Kirk said, "Commissioner. Let's not descend to personalities. Commissioner Wayne, my bridge crew and I seem to agree that we need to learn more before we act."

"Do you run your starship as a democracy, then, Captain?" Wayne asked with a sneer.

"What's wrong with democracy?" McCoy demanded.

"The answer, Commissioner, is no," Kirk said softly. "The *Enterprise* is not a democracy. No starship is or can be. The decision is mine, and mine alone.

"But my officers are professionals, the best Starfleet has to offer. We have served together for nearly five years. They know my decisions may affect whether they live or die. When the situation permits, I respect them enough to hear what they have to say before I decide."

"Even if that brings you into conflict with your orders?"

"Even then."

She stared at him a long moment, nostrils flared. "Sometimes," she said quietly, "I feel as if I'm talking to myself." She marched from the briefing compartment.

Into the heavy silence, Kirk said, "Tomorrow we will beam down to the surface and see if we can't find out what's really going on here. Now, dismissed."

Kirk had just collapsed on his settee and pulled his boots off when the door annunciator chimed. "Damn," he said. He stood up and clumped to the door, dangling his boots from one hand.

The door opened to his command. Moriah Wayne stood there.

"I knew it was you," he said. "No one else would have timing that perfect."

Her face was serious. "Could I come in? I—I don't want to intrude."

He looked at her a moment, then shook his head. "You aren't intruding." He waved her in with the boots. "Come in. Make yourself at home."

She entered. He tossed the boots down by the door, walked wearily back to the settee, and dropped bonelessly onto it. "Would you like something to drink, Commissioner?"

She shook her head. She had walked over to stand staring at his model of the USS *Constitution* in its illuminated niche. The lights in his quarters were turned down to a mellow glow. The ship seemed to float in a pool of yellow glow. He noticed that two strands of her hair had come loose. They hung framing her face, softening, mellowing.

"If you're here to continue our policy debate, I'm afraid I have to disappoint you. I'm just not up to it."

"No." She reached out a finger as if to touch the model, with its bellying white sails and intricate rigging. He tensed. Irrationally, he didn't want her touching his ship.

Instead she withdrew her finger and turned toward him. "Why does the crew dislike me so? Everyone— they all seem to be against me."

He inhaled deeply and let it out through his nose with a sound like a snore. "Commissioner—"

"Moriah." Her eyes glowed.

He stood. She flowed forward to stand before him.

"Moriah, you have a positive talent for alienating my bridge crew. You accuse Sulu of a major felony, you patronize Uhura, you accuse Bones of being a male-chauvinist quack, not to mention impugning his standing as a Southern gentleman. You make Spock out as a puppet and a bad imitation human. All you need to do is call Scotty a whiskey-addled old soak who doesn't know his spanner from a hole in the ground, and you'll have made a pretty clean sweep."

"Am I so undiplomatic, Jim?"

"'Undiplomatic?' Moriah, you—" He held his hands up, almost cupping her face. "You make Kahless the Unforgettable look like Talleyrand."

She turned her face aside, took his right hand in hers, brought it to her mouth, and kissed the palm. He felt as if someone had touched a cattle prod to his coccyx. He straightened, fatigue forgotten.

"You're a strong man, Jim," she said, pressing his palm against her cheek. The skin was cool and smooth. "You stood up to me today."

"I hardly thought it was going to have this effect on you."

"I know you stand up for what you believe. That's important." She looked into his eyes. "We need a man like you."

"We?" He drew back, dropping his hands. "I'm not sure I understand."

"We. The Commissioner, me. The nonhuman races of the Federation. We need your strength."

"Moriah." He shook his head. "I don't know what to tell you. I—I care about the status of nonhumans. I don't think many Starfleet officers have introduced more new species to the Federation. I fully understand—I fully *feel*—the ramifications of what I've done. Even with the Prime Directive, and all the procedures the Federation has in place to ease the shock, contact with a galaxy-spanning civilization can be terrifically dislocating for a culture."

He turned away. "But I still feel that the Federation gives more to its members than it takes away. If I weren't convinced of that I could never do what I do."

He felt a hand on his arm. "James."

He turned. Her arms went around him.

"*I* need a strong man, too. It wears me down, always being so self-sufficient, so steadfast, me against the world. Sometimes I need a strong chest just to . . . lean against."

She laid her head against Kirk's chest. He held her to him and stroked her hair.

In time she raised her face to his. He kissed her.

This time she did not pull away.

Chapter Nine

LIGHT SPILLED DOWNWARD like a shower of gold dust from a point two meters above the deck. A shimmer, and Kirk, Spock, and Moriah Wayne stood on a mat of some woven sea-green fiber.

Kirk looked around. He and Wayne wore wraparound sunglasses with a chip inside that kept the fierce tiny dot of Joan-Marie's Star blacked out in a constant eclipse. Even at that his first impression was of ferocious glare.

His second impression was of body-blow humid heat, and a gravity that seemed much greater than one-fifth more than he was used to. His knees started to buckle. The world whirled around him.

Get a grip on yourself, he commanded sternly. *You're the intrepid explorer. It wouldn't do to set foot on a new world only to collapse in a helpless puddle of protoplasm.*

Grinning at the image, he grasped the rail—which thankfully was sheathed in some fibrous material that shed heat—and forced himself upright. They stood on an observation deck three stories above a city of glass and metal and open water, all dazzling in the sun's white glare. The city obviously lacked a powerful planning commission; it was a jumble, towers and turrets and domes and horizontal cylinders thrusting every which way, split by waterways of varying widths and linked by catwalks and skyways in a weird thronged web.

"Chaos," said Wayne, sniffing. "Total confusion."

"Commissioner," Spock said, "as of local sunrise this morning, our sensors revealed the presence of some one million, one hundred thirty-five thousand, two hundred sixty-two human occupants. Whatever system of living the inhabitants have evolved, it is certainly not altogether dysfunctional."

"It's a blight," she said. "A silver scab on the sea."

"Freefolk," a voice said from behind them. They turned into a wind tanged with astringent metal smell to see the trio they had spoken to last night emerging from a low domed metal structure. The light of the primary made it resemble the hemisphere fireball of a nuclear explosion at ground level, frozen in time. Behind it was sky like a gray blanket that had been slashed with a knife. Painful blue shone through the rents.

The speaker was Jason Strick. He wore a brightly colored dashiki over white duck trousers today. "Welcome to Discord."

"The city as well as the planet," added Aileea dinAthos. She wore a loose cream-colored blouse over khaki shorts, and soft knee-length moccasins. She was still wearing her gun belt. "They both have the same name."

"*Your* name," Wayne said, her words so frosty even

the sun couldn't melt them. "The natives no doubt call it something else."

"The Susuru call the planet by a name that means Island," Aileea said levelly, "if that's who you're referring to. The Susuru aren't native to this world, any more than we are."

"Thank you very much for your welcome," Kirk said loudly. "We're here to uncover the facts of the situation on this world, whatever it's called."

Strick offered his hand to Wayne, who accepted it after a moment's hesitation. DinAthos shook hands with Kirk. Her grip was surprisingly strong—strong enough that he had the impression she might have been able to crush his hand if she chose, despite the fact that she was shorter than Wayne and lightly built.

"That is very impressive technology," said Arkazha, shaking Spock's hand. "The means by which you arrived here."

"Transporter beams," Kirk said, shaking hands with Strick. He was armed, too, Kirk saw. The butt of a handgun projected from under the tail of his dashiki, behind his left hip. "A lot has happened on Earth since your ancestors left."

"No doubt," Strick said. "And we're eager to hear all of it."

"Those—transporters?—cause a lot of interference without communications," dinAthos said. "When you beamed in just now it made all our electronics go crazy."

"That can occur when transporter beams function near unshielded electronic components of a certain rudimentary stage of development," Spock said.

The three looked at him, more curious than miffed, it seemed. "I suppose we do seem primitive to you."

Wayne opened her mouth to say something. "Actu-

96

ally," Kirk said, "I don't think we're all that far ahead of you."

He glanced up at the sky, which was clear overhead, though cumulus balls rolled along the western horizon like white tumbleweeds. "I just hope we're not due for one of your colossal electrical storms. Big lightning discharges interfere with our transporters something fierce."

"Our meteorological observations indicate no major storm cells are likely to form in or move through this area for at least the next eight hours, Captain," said Spock. "And Mr. Sulu will, of course, alert us should conditions change."

"Excellent, Mr. Spock."

"Would you care to see something of our city?" Jason Strick asked. "We can walk a little ways, if our heat and gravity aren't too much . . ."

"We'll survive," said Kirk, who privately doubted it. As appalling as heat, humidity, gravity, and glare were, they were nothing compared to the invisible stuff—high UV output from the primary, background radiation from heavy metals in the crust. Dr. McCoy had fussed over the party before they beamed down, slathering them with sunblock and hypospraying them full of antiradiation drugs.

"This'll keep you alive," he said, "but nothing on Earth or Okeanos is going to make you comfortable."

"We call our sun *Eris,*" dinAthos said.

"For the Goddess of Discord, who disrupted the banquet of the gods by rolling the golden apple inscribed 'For the Fairest' into their hall on Mount Olympus, I presume?" Spock said.

"That's the one," the green-haired woman said with a grin. "An arbitrary bitch, but she keeps us all alive."

They walked to a broad stairway and down to ocean

97

level. The motion of the sea made itself felt as a gentle rocking, barely perceptible. The walking surfaces were all covered in the resilient fiber mats, which seemed a very efficient insulator. Not even colonists well adapted to this hellhole to go abroad in daylight lightly clad and bareheaded could endure contact with bare metal heated by the tiny sun.

"Captain," Spock said quietly from Kirk's left elbow. Their hosts were descending the stairs behind them, while Wayne preceded them, turning her head left and right with a pinched expression. "I find it remarkable that these people can have adapted so completely to the extremely rigorous local conditions in the two hundred years or less for which they can have occupied the planet."

"Two hundred years, Mr. Spock? You seem awfully definite."

"Zefram Cochrane demonstrated a practical warp drive some two hundred and seven years ago," Spock said. "Inasmuch as this planet is rather more than three hundred light-years from Earth, and human spaceflight of any kind is a mere three centuries old, it is highly unlikely that these colonists' ancestors departed Earth before the advent of warp drive."

"An excellent point, Mr. Spock," Kirk said. "The rapid adaptation of these Discordians is another mystery. As if we didn't have enough."

The spaces between buildings were full of people, walking, haggling, debating, splashing in the sea, batting a handball against a wall. The first thing Kirk noticed about them was that both Strick and dinAthos were fairly conservative in their style of dress. The norm seemed to be bold, almost gaudy colors in clothing of flamboyant cut in which coverage from the sun seemed a minor consideration and modesty none at all. People dressed like Arkazha were more in evidence than ones dressed like her companions, and not only the amphibians.

The people themselves presented a variety as astonishing as their garb. There were hulking humanoids covered in pliable gray armor plates like rhinoceroses, stocky men and women no larger than Tellarites, others the same height—waist high—but so slight Kirk at first took them for children. A creature like Arkazha leapt from a canal onto the walkway before them in a great surge of blue-green water, straightened, turned toward the approaching party, nodded politely, and walked past them. Wayne's eyes widened; the being was nude, and emphatically male.

A moment later a much more humanoid woman, equally naked, plummeted past Kirk's elbow in a dive from a third-story window. Kirk had an impression of aquamarine hair streaming back over a pale slim body with a delicate fringe of fin running down each arm from wrists to short-ribs. Then she was gone, leaving barely a ripple.

Wayne stopped and scowled back at Kirk, her arms tightly crossed over her sternum. "Are we going someplace, or just wandering at random through this warren?"

Aileea's jade eyes got narrow and dangerous. Strick smiled easily.

"At your pleasure, Commissioner," he said. "You are our honored guest. We'd like you to see something of the way we live."

"I've seen more than enough urban blight in my time."

The party caught her up and passed her by. After an angry moment, she followed.

"One thing puzzles me," Kirk said emphatically.

"Mr. Strick—ahh, is there any particular title I should call you by?"

"Mr. Strick is fine," Strick said with a smile. "Or Freeman Strick, or Jason. Or you can simply point—it's all the same to me."

"Just when did your ancestors leave Earth?"

"In two thousand seventy-two," dinAthos said. Wayne gave her a look that glittered like glass. She was white-faced and taut, and seemed to be building toward an explosion.

He felt disoriented. Last night they had been so close. Today they were walking a ragged edge. He had a long way to go to understand the commissioner.

"At the height of Earth's Third World War," Spock said.

DinAthos nodded. "You might say we sneaked out when no one was looking."

"And what had you done that made it necessary for you to sneak off?" Wayne asked.

"We were born," the Discordian woman said with a defiant head flip that shook green bangs from her eyes.

"We left to escape extermination," Mona Arkazha said. Her bulging eyes studied Wayne with evident disdain. "It seems our mothers chose wisely."

"Now, Mona," Strick said soothingly, "look at Mr. Spock, here. They allow Vares on old Terra, evidently."

Spock arched a brow. "'Vares,' Mr. Strick? I am unfamiliar with the term."

"Our own name for ourselves," Strick said. "It's from 'Variants.'"

"From the human somatotype," dinAthos added.

Spock blinked. "I beg your pardon, sir, but my own departure from the human norm arises from the fact that I am half Vulcan."

Strick stared at his face. Spock bore the scrutiny with his customary dignity.

"You mean you're half *alien?*" the Discordian asked.

"Xenoform," corrected Wayne.

"I am," said Spock.

Strick's face split in a huge grin. "Marvelous! So old Terra was able to overcome her fear of difference after all."

"Quite evidently," Spock said, "since the Federation now comprises several score of humanoid races."

Strick looked at his companions. "Maybe it's good our isolation's ended. Perhaps Earth is ready to accept us."

"Do not rush into happy conclusions, Jason," Arkazha said warningly.

DinAthos grinned. "He's a professional optimist. It serves him well in his line of work."

They had come into a sort of plaza around a broad artificial lagoon in which a dozen children—actually children, as a second look verified—of various types frolicked, without apparent consciousness of difference. People took late breakfast or early lunch under brightly colored awnings. Others browsed through stores selling underwater breathing rigs, entertainment electronics, and lightweight weapons systems for nautical vessels. Kirk noted that even those people who showed no obvious physical departures from the norm often showed flamboyant cosmetic differences, such as bright blue hair or orange skin.

He felt a prickling at the back of his neck and turned. A person who appeared to be half woman, half calico cat sat on a low wall covered in a fiber mat colored like a Persian rug next to a café whose name was written in what looked like Chinese ideograms.

She noted his attention and gave him a slow smile with a long, curved fang at either edge. Her eyes were yellow, with vertical slit pupils.

"Fascinating," he heard Spock murmur.

"Mr. Strick," he said, "there's no tactful way to ask this, but how in heaven's name do you come to be—that is, why—"

He held his hands up in a helpless gesture. Aileea dinAthos laughed.

"Why are we such an odd assortment of freaks, Captain? Genetic engineering."

"We are as we have chosen to be," said Arkazha.

Kirk and Wayne stared at them, thunderstruck. "You—gene engineer—*yourselves?*" the commissioner asked.

"The gene sculptors among us shape us to our request," dinAthos said, looking curiously and a bit warily at the commissioner. She got a queer tight smile. "That bothers you, doesn't it?"

"Of course it does!" Wayne flared. Her face was drained of color. "You people tamper with the natural order!"

"So does Dr. McCoy, Commissioner," Spock said, "when he cures someone of a disease that, if untreated, would otherwise prove fatal."

"But they're . . . perverting themselves. Their *children.* Twisting themselves into monsters on a whim!"

"Moriah, get hold of yourself!" Kirk snapped.

She glared at him. "Do you need further evidence? These people aren't just alien to this world. They're alien to the *cosmos!* They're *unnatural!*"

Jason Strick's cheeks looked as if they had been dusted with a fresh fall of volcanic ash. Aileea dinAthos was looking at Wayne as if she were a poisonous sea creature that had flopped up onto the walkway. Only Arkazha was showing no sign of response, though with her heavily modified physiognomy she probably had a limited range of facial expression.

Kirk took Wayne by the arm and steered her a few steps away. "Commissioner," he said, pitching his voice low, "you are comporting yourself in an entirely inappropriate manner."

"Inappropriate?" Her laugh was like glass shattering. "The very *existence* of these people is a crime!"

"We're not within the Federation now. Our laws don't apply."

"We have come to bring this planet under the rule of Federation law. Remember?" Color was coming back into her face now, starting with the points of her cheekbones. Her eyes were fever bright. "That's going to be a positive pleasure!"

Kirk moistened his lips, which were beginning to prickle a little from the incoming ultraviolet. He tasted the medicinal tang of sunblock. *Better not lick this stuff off,* he thought irrelevantly. It was supposed to be impervious to that, but experience had taught him better.

"I don't *know* what these people's status is under Federation law," he admitted. "But I won't have you abusing them. Your tone suggests mobs with torches and ropes, Commissioner."

"Are you speaking of lynch mobs, Captain? Or of those old horror movies, where peasants with torches storm the castle to destroy the mad scientist and his monsters?"

Kirk turned away in disgust. Strick and dinAthos stood with heads together, speaking in low tones. Spock looked up from conversing with Arkazha.

"Dr. Arkazha has been explaining something of the

Discordian culture to me. She and others of her Gens, for example, have been optimized to survive in the ocean depths without the need of life support or the need to decompress after returning to the surface." He tipped his head to the side. "It is, indeed, a highly efficient system."

Kirk felt a pulse of queasiness in his stomach and hated himself for it. Much as he found to admire about Moriah Wayne, he did not want to resemble her in any particular just now.

He put a hand on his science officer's biceps and steered him out of earshot of the others. Wayne continued to stand by herself, looking off into the sky.

"Spock, you know gene engineering of sentient species is forbidden under Federation law."

"But, Jim, these people don't belong to the Federation."

Kirk sighed. "That's true. But you have to understand. On Earth we had some very unfortunate experiences with genetic engineering of humans."

Spock nodded. "The Eugenics Wars of the last decade of the twentieth century."

"And you've seen firsthand some of the results of that conflict, not to mention one of the prime movers behind it. Like everybody on the *Enterprise*."

"The passengers of the *Botany Bay*."

"Exactly. We distrust gene-engineered humans. I know it's irrational—but you might say it's in *our* genes."

"Captain."

He turned, a little too quickly. "Mr. Strick."

"I understand why we might . . . unsettle you."

The Discordian spokesfolk had approached to a discreet range. "We left Earth to escape bigotry," Aileea said bitterly. "It's nothing new to us."

104

Strick held up his hand, "Aileea." She scowled but said no more.

"We make no apologies for the way we are," said Mona Arkazha. "In fact, it was in part to preserve the right to choose our forms for ourselves that we left Earth. But we did not, initially, become this way by choice."

"In fact, we owe our existence to an individual of whom you may never have heard," Strick said, "since his heyday ended almost three centuries ago. A twentieth-century tyrant named Khan Noonian Singh."

Chapter Ten

"Khan," Kirk echoed.

"You've heard of him?" Strick asked.

"There were so many dictators on Earth back around then," Aileea said. "Hard to believe you can even tell them apart after all this time."

"Mm." Kirk glanced at Spock and envied him his Vulcan poker face. "We have a very comprehensive political history program at Starfleet Academy."

"In fact," Spock said, "I believe I am familiar with a few of the particulars of your case. As I recall, your forebears were subject of UN Resolution Fifty-one, of two thousand thirty-eight. You will remember, no doubt, that was the resolution that determined that no Earth citizens could be held liable for the acts of their ancestors. A rider to the resolution confirmed the human status of certain human-variant strains who had been created in the gene research laboratories that created Khan and his fellow tyrants. This was the so-called 'Khan's Stepchildren' resolution."

"You're very diplomatic, Mr. Spock," Aileea said. "What they really called us was Khan's bastards."

Spock raised his brows. "Perhaps my sources elected to be circumspect."

"Captain Kirk," Aileea said with a flip of her head, "I apologize for speaking sharply to you a little while ago. I made the mistake of reacting to something someone said. Speech is free."

"That's why we fight," Strick added.

"No apology necessary, Ms. dinAthos," Kirk said.

"Why not let your people walk among us?" Arkazha asked. "They can decide for themselves whether we're monsters or not. Otherwise"—she hooked a thumb at Wayne, still standing off in splendid isolation—"all they'll have to go by is what *she* tells them."

Kirk rubbed his jaw. He looked at Wayne, looked around at the denizens of Discord City, and looked at Spock.

"Captain," his first officer said. "During our sojourn at Starbase Twenty-three, leaves were of necessity cut short. Indeed, a quarter of the crew got no leave at all. And leave within the sealed environment of an orbiting Starbase produces far less favorable effects upon morale than leave upon a planetary surface."

"You're the only person in our crew who'd find this an ideal port of call, Spock," Kirk said. As a Vulcan Spock needed neither sunglasses, shots, nor sunscreen.

Kirk thought for a moment, watching the children splash in the lagoon. These people seemed open and friendly enough. Still, there was the fact that they seemed fond of carrying weapons. And there were the Susuru allegations to consider. Wayne was certainly correct that they could not be dismissed out of hand.

I'm the one who talks about getting the facts before I

make a decision, he thought. A trickle of sweat ran down his neck into the collar of his shirt. *Maybe I should put that into practice.*

"I appreciate your offer of hospitality," he began guardedly. "But I'm responsible for the welfare of my crew. So far I've seen no more than a couple of blocks of your charming city. I'm not yet really in a position to evaluate the risks involved."

"Sonic fields keep the sea beasts at bay," Arkazha said. "The storms are savage, but if you stay inside a dwelling, you're safe enough, if not always comfortable."

"It's an unknown environment," Aileea said, somewhat to Kirk's surprise. "He's right to be cautious."

"He could let the crew decide for themselves what risks they're willing to take," Arkazha stated.

"Come, Mona, that's not their way," Strick said. "And it's hardly up to us to reform them, is it?"

"If we want to be left alone, we must know how to leave alone," Arkazha agreed. "You are correct."

"We cannot compel our people, you understand, but in fact you'll be welcomed almost anywhere you choose to go," Strick said. "We Discordians are mostly friendly folk, and I think most you run into will be as eager to hear about what's been happening on Earth and in the galaxy the last two hundred Terran years. I'd warn you to stay away from the equator, though."

"Why's that?" Wayne asked. "What've you got to hide?"

"Fools from harm—though that's not our usual way," Aileea dinAthos said. "Here at fifty degrees north you're fairly safe from Stilter attack. Close to the equator, you're fair game for them and their friends."

"Is there anything in particular you'd care to see?" Strick asked. "I should start calling soon, to make arrangements."

"The Susuru say you're destroying the environment," Wayne said abruptly. "How about showing us your mining and sea-ranching operations?"

"Destroying the environment?" Strick drew his handsome head back. "Why in Eris's name would we do that? We *live* on this planet! Why would we do it harm?"

"And what business is it of yours?" dinAthos demanded. "We don't live by your laws!"

Wayne gave her a look of ineffable smugness.

"That might be a place to start," Kirk said. "It would help us understand how you live." He looked at Wayne. "And it might lay certain ecological misgivings to rest."

"Apparently environmental self-righteousness still persists on Earth," Arkazha said, "as well as fear of Variants. Perhaps not that much has changed, Jason."

Strick ran his hands backward through his short, crisp hair. "In fact, I think the welfare of our planet means more to us than it *can* to you. Most of us live on intimate terms with the sea."

Wayne gestured around her. "All I see is that you surround yourselves with steel and glass. Artifice, not nature."

"This is a *city*," dinAthos said. "Don't you have cities in your Federation?"

"Far too many."

"If we were to commence our tour," Spock said, "it might save us all a great deal of profitless debate."

Arkazha showed her teeth in a startling grin. They were wholly human, which made her appearance all

109

the more jarring. "I like you," she said. "You are a man after my own heart. Practical."

"Logical," Spock amended.

Strick nodded and reached for his waist. Wayne stiffened, eyes going wild, but he merely came up with a hand communicator of his own.

"I should call and arrange a flyer first."

"That's hardly necessary," Kirk said. He grinned. "How would you like to experience our 'impressive technology' firsthand?"

The Discordians looked at him like kids at Christmas. "Could we really?" Strick asked, forgetting for the moment to be cool and dignified.

"You can do more than that." Kirk flipped out his communicator. "Kirk to *Enterprise*. Mr. Sulu, lock onto my coordinates." Kirk turned to Strick. "Care to show us the scenic sights of Discord?"

It was night at the mine at eighty degrees south. A low black cone thrust up from the ocean, its outline vaguely saw-toothed, like a fractal design. Waves driven by a fifty-kph wind hurled themselves against it, as if trying to batter it down for its presumptions in challenging the supremacy of the sea.

Spotlights poured light out in actinic pools on the seamount. In their glow, forms moved, human and mechanical. The wind and waves did not seem to hamper their activity.

"I don't envy them out there," James Kirk said, face almost pressed to the armored glass port of the submersible.

The small craft lurched as a wave too big for impellers and gyros to compensate for rolled past. Kirk clenched his jaw and thought about the men who had ventured forth on the sea in the wooden sailing ships whose models he displayed in his quarters. Then he tried *not* to think about them.

"If the motion of the sea troubles you," Arkazha said with a slight smile, "be thankful for your wonderful transport beams that placed us here directly without the need to traverse many uneasy kilometers of sea."

"The workers don't envy us," said Aileea. She turned a frankly malicious glance at Wayne, who sat next to the port across the cabin from Kirk and Spock. Her pale redhead's skin had taken on a greenish tinge that made her almost look as though she had Vulcan blood. "They're Grunts. They were bred for heavy labor—strength, endurance, low volition and intelligence. When we were freed, they chose to reclaim their wills and intellects."

"Now they can perform physical tasks virtually on autopilot, leaving their higher minds free," Strick said. "They give us some of our greatest philosophers and theoreticians."

"The wind and the spray don't bother them?" Kirk asked. The thick hull muted the fury of the wind, but he could feel its howl in his bones, a lonely soul-devastating sound.

"These chose further modification for this environment," Strick said. "You see, we Discordians prefer to shape ourselves to our environment as much as possible, instead of vice versa."

This last was directed to Wayne. Unlike their other two guides, Strick was still making every effort to win the commissioner over. She ignored him, though whether she rejected what he said or was merely too seasick to respond, Kirk couldn't tell.

"There would seem to be a risk entailed in adapting yourselves too closely to a given environment," Spock said. "Throughout the known universe, overspecialization is a consistent road to extinction."

"As individuals, our human intellect always gives us further scope to adapt," Arkazha said. "Our minds help us adjust to changing situations, as humans have through history. If you consider us as a whole population, I think you would agree that we maintain an adequate degree of diversity."

"Indisputably, Doctor Arkazha."

Kirk glanced at his first officer and friend. Spock was showing the Discordian more deference than he generally offered humans. The keen intellect she displayed, notably unblunted by sentiment, obviously commanded his respect.

"Ready to dive?" The voice of the pilot came back over the intercom. She was a beautiful woman of early middle years with orange hair, cropped close and shot through with gray. She was also one meter tall. She belonged to a strain known as Micros, or sometimes Pixies, who had been developed by the Eugenicists as pilots and operators of craft where mass or volume were at a premium—fighter aircraft, space vehicles, deep-sea probes. They had faster-than-normal reflexes, greater tolerance for G-loading and pressure, and keener eyesight. "I'm getting tired of fighting the seas with this bitch."

"We're ready, Mattie," Strick said, and the craft submerged.

Bubbles seethed upward past the ports as ballast blew. The pitching instantly eased as the drive planes bit and carried the submersible below the action of the waves. The moaning of the storm went away.

The craft canted to port and swung around. Even Wayne could not restrain a muted exclamation of wonder as the seamount came into view. The seamount was a hive of activity in the blaze of spotlights. The lava upthrust was honeycombed with tunnels. Deep-rangers—Vares similar to Arkazha—moved in and out, wrestling cutting lasers and guiding ore pods.

"They work the most recent flows," Strick said. "The metals just lie there in layers, from beryllium, cobalt, and copper, down through iron and iridium and on to uranium. There for the taking."

Spock stirred himself. "He has a tendency to over-simplify."

Mona Arkazha said. "But not by much, in this case."

"Do you restore the habitat when you've finished with your plunder?"

"Not much of a habitat to begin with," Strick said. "We catch the seamounts as soon as they seem to have grown dormant."

"What if you guess wrong?"

"Accidents happen," Arkazha said. "Life goes on."

"Life is cheap, to the exploiters," Wayne said.

"Exploiters?" Arkazha's rubbery lips proved more than adequate to sneer. "We need the metal. We pay to get it. Where is exploitation?"

"What about the workers?" Wayne asked, gesturing out the port.

"I was one such worker, for this very corporation, when I was young. I was born in Exile, which floats not far from here. As a deep-miner I earned money for school."

Her tone got distant. "I saw friends die, when a plug blew. Life is risk."

113

A trio of Swimmers, as Aileea's Gens was called, swam slowly past the submersible with lazy sweeps of the fins strapped to their feet. They wore goggles and wetsuits, but their necks were bare, to allow their gills to work oxygen from the water.

"Why do they wear suits?" Kirk asked.

"We don't have polar caps, the way Earth does," dinAthos said. "But the water does get a bit chilly way down here."

"You know a lot about Earth," Kirk said.

"We remember where we came from."

"Would you like to visit Earth?"

Aileea gazed out the port. "I'm happy here."

Outside the city Storm, where it was afternoon, they looked at a surface plant where minerals were extracted from seawater. In the city itself they saw an artistic competition, where looming metal sculptures were revealed to the discordant electronic music and the cheers—or catcalls—of crowds packed into stands.

It was morning at Qara-Qitay. An Asian-looking Micro flew them over the city, a loose and sprawling collection of metal structures anodized in shades of gold and yellow, then landed them on a float next to an electronics plant on the fringe. They spoke to a foreman, a rhino-skinned Grunt with a hardhat perched atop his disproportionately small head. He assured them that by-products were preserved and sold to other fabricators who could make use of them.

"Discord is rich, but harsh," he said in a high-pitched whisper. "When we first came here, it was a struggle just to live. We learned to throw away as little

114

as possible." A mountainous shrug. "Besides, there's money to be made selling what we can't use."

Wayne sneered.

In Harmony, where insulative matting was made from seaweed, the people displayed few weapons of any kind. In the baking heat of their central square they besieged Spock with questions about Vulcan philosophy, and even listened sympathetically to Wayne when she criticized their fellow Discordians as self-centered individualists. They in turn pressed upon her their theories of nonauthoritarian communal living. Their efforts were hampered by the tendency of the proselytizing to dissolve into shouting matches, until the whole plaza was packed with learned discourse carried out at the tops of lungs and the party gratefully escaped via transporter beam.

Rakatau drifted through the Sea of Smokes. Despite a brisk rain even Spock had to don a respirator against the stinging sulfur fumes issuing from seamounts and bubbling up from subsurface vents. Neither stench nor downpour bothered either their hosts or the locals, whose faces showed strong Malay traits—even the heavily gene-modified ones. They wore colorful sarongs and carried wavy-bladed *kris* daggers in preference to firearms. They mined the vents and seamounts, and built ships and habitations. They didn't seem to draw much distinction between the two.

Wayne asked a passing Swimmer with long black hair and a profusion of gold jewelry bright against her mahogany skin if the city discharged its wastes into the sea.

"Of course not!" the Swimmer replied, gills flaring

in indignation. "It's broken down by gene-engineered bacteria and sold as fish food. Eris, what a question. We *swim* in this water!"

There was excitement in Serendip. At twenty degrees north it was the closest of the Discordian cities to the equator, and suffered accordingly. A Susuru surface force had attacked a fishing fleet thirty kilometers to the southwest of the city, sinking two boats and killing eight. Casualties among the Susuru were reported to be high. Kirk knew full well that reports of damage inflicted on an enemy tended to be floridly optimistic. Still, the distant black column of smoke rising into mauve dusk indicated that someone or something had been damaged severely.

Since the Klingons' arrival, the Susuru had become aggressive about launching over-the-horizon missile attacks to test the Discordian antimissile defenses. So far these had proven excellent. When the party arrived the city was just coming off an alert.

When Aileea dinAthos learned of the attack, she walked to a rail and stood staring off at the setting sun for a few moments before rejoining the others.

Serendip by sunset had a pronounced Indian flavor, with skirling music and exotic cooking smells riding the breeze off the sea. The dusk light was an alkaline white, which seemed to cut age deep into the faces it touched.

The sunset itself was beautiful and somehow ghastly. Distant Eris had an apparent size less than a sixth that of Sol as seen from Earth. The tiny ball had fallen into a puffy pile of cumulus way beyond the horizon, with dense slate bands of cloud in front of it, and lit it into a yellow fireball. The surfaces of the cloud slabs above and below the sun glowed yellow like heated metal; the sky between them was lemon yellow as well. Above and below the sky shaded orange, then red. With a start Kirk realized it looked like nothing so much as pictures he had seen of thermonuclear explosions.

It seemed ominous, given the fact of the earlier raid. Would the Klingons give their clients nuclear weapons? He shook his head. Kain was a rogue, but no account had ever made Kain out to be a fool. Not even the fact that Kirk had bested him on Endikon—Kirk had been quicker then, that was all. Introducing nukes to a planetary conflict like this would bring a Federation battlefleet at warp factor eight, with the full weight of the Organian Peace Treaty to back them up.

He found his mind adrift, as the cities themselves drifted on the endless face of the sea. He was feeling sunburned, footsore, and utterly spent. Discord's gravity and heat had been squeezing him for hours like a giant hand; the rapid shuttling back and forth between the surface and the climate-controlled comfort of the *Enterprise*'s transporter room had reached the point of overstressing his system rather than refreshing him. The arc welders of the great Indra shipyards spouted eerie spumes of blue light on the horizon, but he couldn't take any more.

"Let's call it a day," he said. Nobody argued.

Chapter Eleven

STEPPING GRATEFULLY OFF the transporter stage for what he hoped was the last time today, Kirk turned to his three hosts. "I thank you all for a most educational day," he said. "Now, in a small way, perhaps I can repay the favor. If you'll just follow me—"

On the bridge Kirk was pleased by the effect his starship had on his erstwhile guides—they reacted like kids at the zoo. At the sight of Discord spread out in all her blue-and-white-whorled glory on the main screen, Aileea cried out in wonder, momentarily a little girl again. Jason Strick stared about him with wide amber eyes.

Even Mona Arkazha seemed impressed. "The engineering that has gone into this creation," she said. "Magnificent!"

Kirk smiled indulgently. "You'll have to meet my chief engineer. If he hears you talking like that, you'll have a friend for life."

DinAthos turned toward him. "Captain, this is wonderful. But I'm afraid we're going to have to cut this visit short."

"Why is that, Ms. dinAthos?"

She was vigorously massaging her upper arms. "Because we're *freezing* to death."

Commissioner Wayne did not accompany them back to the transporter room. No one complained at her absence. Spock took over the bridge.

"What do you think of my earlier invitation, Captain?" Strick asked, trying to stop his teeth chattering.

"I think," Kirk said, "that I'll just take you up on it." He stepped to the wall communicator. "Kirk to bridge."

"Spock here."

"Mr. Spock, kindly see to having a schedule of leaves drawn up. I'd like to give the crew a chance to stretch their legs."

"Certainly, sir."

"Kirk out."

He turned away to find dinAthos standing behind him, well within his personal space, looking at him challengingly. "Well?" she demanded. "What have you decided?"

"To permit my crew to beam down for leave."

"No, Captain. What are you going to do about *us?* Are you ready to start driving us aboard the cattle cars, the way *she* wants you to?"

She really is most breathtakingly lovely, Kirk thought, and then: *Whoa, son. You've already let your romantic nature complicate the situation once this mission.*

"No. Speaking frankly, I hope it never comes to

119

that. But keep in mind, Ms. dinAthos, the Susuru are threatening to launch a final offensive to wipe you out."

Her eyes blazed dark green fire. "Let them try! We're ready."

"What I most want," Kirk said levelly, "is to institute peace talks between you and the Susuru. Maybe it's time your peoples tried to learn to coexist."

Aileea's face seemed to snap shut. She whirled away and walked to stand by the transporter platform, looking away from him.

"I take it that plan doesn't meet with her approval," Kirk said to the others.

"She's had a loss, Captain," Arkazha said. "The Stilters raided her family's ranch two weeks before you came. They killed her father and sank the house. Or maybe these Klingons of yours did it; they used one of their off-world energy beams that makes a man vanish if it so much as brushes him."

"She's still on compassionate leave, Captain," Strick said. "That's why she has the leisure to help serve as liaison. The thought took her by surprise, that's all. Like most of us, I'm sure she'd like to see the war ended."

"Keep in mind that it will be a complicated process to get us Discordians to agree on the terms of a peace. Most will not honor an agreement they were not personally party to," Arkazha said. "Still, we do not attack—much as some of our hotheads would like us to. We defend only. If the Susuru quit molesting us, there will be peace in fact."

Kirk nodded. "That's my first goal, then. To tell you the truth, peace negotiations are never anything but a complicated process, and in my experience 'brief peace talks' is an oxymoron as great as 'military intelligence.' Getting the parties to talk is usually the most important step."

Arkazha and Aileea made brief farewells. DinAthos wouldn't meet Kirk's eye.

"Captain," Strick said, sounding almost diffident. "A word with you before we beam back down?"

"Certainly."

They walked a few steps aside. "That communications officer of yours, the one with the lovely eyes—"

"Lieutenant Uhura."

"That's the one. I'd like to extend my personal invitation to introduce her to our world."

Kirk looked at him oddly. "Let me see if I get this right—you're asking me for permission to ask my communications officer on a date?"

Strick laughed. "I don't want to violate your customs, Captain. So far you've been scrupulous about honoring ours."

"The lieutenant is one of my most valued officers. She's one of the most intelligent people I know. She possesses excellent taste and judgment. That being the case, all I can say is"—he shrugged—"go for it."

Bone-weary though he was, Kirk called a command meeting in the briefing compartment to relay what had been learned that day. "The customs of the human colonists of Discord—and never forget, please, that they are all just as human as we are—are so different from ours that they might as well be aliens. Still they seem reasonable enough, and by no means belligerent, in spite of the sidearms. Therefore, it is my judgment that tomorrow we shall get in touch with the Susuru and try to get peace talks going between the warring species. Any comments?"

"I'm a doctor, not a diplomat," Dr. McCoy said, "but it seems to me it's always better to have folks talking than fighting."

"For once your sentiment is in accord with logic, Doctor," Spock said.

The other bridge crew murmured agreement. Kirk was just nodding, pleased at the easy consensus, when Commissioner Wayne spoke from the far end of the compartment, where she stood with arms tightly folded.

"Your plan is unacceptable, Captain."

"In . . . what . . . particular," Kirk asked deliberately. He was trying to hold his temper in check.

"Our mission is not to serve as peacekeepers. Our purpose is to remove alien organisms that have illegally been introduced into the planetary environment."

"You're talking about people as if they were vermin again, aren't you?" McCoy asked.

"Doctor, from an ecological standpoint, people are the most destructive vermin of all."

"Might I remind the commissioner," Spock said, "that Starfleet's primary mission is *always* keeping the peace."

"Not when orders signed off on by Captain Kirk and stored in your computer memory countermand it," Wayne said. "Starfleet instructed you to help me remove the colonists."

She looked around. "And frankly, all this talk of peace strikes me as unutterably naïve. Despite your captain's remarkably ingenuous assessment, these people spring from an armed and neurotic society, poised always on the edge of violence. There is no doubt in my mind that they will resist our carrying out our mission with the fury of cornered rats."

"People's being willing to resist being taken from their homes by force doesn't make them psychotic, Commissioner," Uhura said.

"You're forgetting that these people are outlaws," Wayne said. "They reject the concept of authority within their own culture. They practice a technology that has been banned, on Earth and later by the Federation, for almost three centuries. And they conduct wanton attacks against the rightful inhabitants of the planet."

"They defend themselves," Sulu said.

"So they say. Are you so prejudiced that you reflexively take the word of a human over the word of a nonhumanoid?" She tossed her head. "Or do I even need to ask?"

Sulu's handsome face darkened, and he looked quickly down at the table.

"She makes a good point, Jim," McCoy said ruefully. "We can't just take what these people say at face value simply because they're human."

"You are, of course, correct, Commissioner," Kirk said. "I have every intention of examining the story more thoroughly from the Susuru's side. Tomorrow."

"I think you'll find the charges substantiated," Wayne said. "After all, their allegations of ecological devastation have been amply borne out."

"What?" exclaimed Kirk. "Commissioner, that's ridiculous. We've just spent an entire day in that pressure cooker down there looking at recycling measures and hearing sermons on ecological consciousness that would do credit to a twenty-first-century city council! What in the hell are you talking about?"

"Commissioner," Spock said, "a single moderately active volcanic vent of the Sea of Storms discharges more waste into the ecosystem in one hour than all human habitations upon Discord do in one day. Simple mathematics suggest this to be true, and sensor readings confirm it."

"What about waste heat?"

"As we observed today, the human settlers make extensive use of solar, wind, and wave power," Spock said. "None of these energy sources introduces extra heat into the system."

"They also have fusion generators in those cankerous cities of theirs."

"Computer," Kirk said.

"Yes, darling." Wayne flashed her eyes at him. He ignored her. "Show us the planet listed in your memory as Okeanos."

"Yes, dear." The cloud-swirled blue disk appeared in the three-faceted viewer at the table's head.

"Now display all hot spots of, oh, one hundred degrees Celsius over ambient temperature. On second thought, make it fifty."

The image glowed with red spots as if it had developed a bad case of acne. "Now subtract all those sources that are of artificial nature. Flash each one white as you delete it."

"Yes, dear."

"Stop that."

"Affirmative . . . dear."

Kirk sighed. Dots flickered out, one by one. He noted that about twenty percent of them were on islands in the Susuru archipelago.

"That leaves," he said, "almost all of them. That's *lava*, Commissioner, being discharged by the tonne in some places. The level of human activity we're observing isn't making much dent in that."

"The humans still commit ecological rape on an enormous scale, Captain," Wayne said primly. "You saw the way they ravaged the seamount. You saw the factories by which they plundered the sea of its very substance."

"If such standards were applied across the Federation," Spock said, "they would seem to forbid any level of technological activity at all, or indeed any form of interaction with the environment. Surely you're not proposing the end of all of technic civilization, Commissioner?"

"I'm not too sure that's a bad idea," she said.

"What about beavers?" Sulu asked.

"Or mud daubers?" asked Uhura.

"They're part of nature," Wayne said.

"Unless you subscribe to certain fringe theories to the effect that sapience was taught to the ancestors of all present sentient races by some undiscovered agency," Spock said, "intelligence evolved quite naturally."

"The Susuru had their hot spots, too, Commissioner," Kirk said, "from power plants and foundries."

"Incorrect," the computer said.

Wayne turned him a look of triumph.

"Explain," Kirk said.

"Five heat sources are identified as foundries, six as assorted manufacturing operations, and four as fission-fired nuclear power plants. The remaining three sources are imperfectly shielded mobile matter-antimatter generators of standard Klingon issue."

"'Imperfectly-shielded?'" Mr. Scott echoed. The

computer's words had jolted him loose from the polite fugue in which he always spent conferences not directly connected with nuts and bolts or matters of immediate survival. "But any decent m/am unit converts output into usable energy with a hundred percent efficiency."

He shuddered at the shoddiness of Klingon design. Kirk grinned at a vision of him chucking his Klingon dictionary and technical manuals down a disintegrator chute at the first opportunity.

"All this is entirely off the subject," Wayne said stiffly. "You have your orders, Captain, and frankly it is unacceptable for you to waste further time in implementing them."

Kirk lowered his chin to his clavicle and stared at her. "Then orders be damned, Commissioner. To herd those people into transports at gunpoint and whisk them away from the planet on which every last one of them was born would be an act worthy of a Hitler—or a Khan."

He raised his head. "You will recall that, in both of those cases, 'only following orders' failed miserably as a defense."

"Captain, I warn you—"

He held up a hand. "Save your warnings, Commissioner. If on the conclusion of my investigation I ascertain that the presence of Earth human settlers upon Okeanos places an intolerable burden on the planet or on any of its indigenous species, I will see to their removal. By whatever means necessary."

McCoy started to his feet in outrage. "Jim—"

"Sit down, Bones. I'm a Starfleet officer. I've sworn to follow my orders—we all have. *If* those orders are lawful. If in my judgment they are not, *Enterprise* will return to Starbase Twenty-three with those orders unfulfilled. In no case will I take action until I'm certain it is the right action to take."

Wayne dropped her voice. "This could cost you your ship, Captain," she said, almost sadly.

"I'm aware of that," he said. "But it won't cost me my soul."

Chapter Twelve

"Lieutenant. May I speak with you a moment?"

"Why, certainly, Captain."

The briefing was breaking up, the bridge crew returning to their duty stations or, in the case of Uhura, heading for their quarters. As Kirk himself hoped to be soon.

"Do you remember the spokesman for the Discordians—the man who came up to the bridge with the two women?"

"The tall one with the gorgeous eyes—is that the one you mean, sir?"

"Um. Yes. I believe he's going to offer you an invitation soon."

"Oh, *really.*"

"Yes. And while it wouldn't be wise to get too tangled up with a participant in a dispute we're going to try to settle—whether the Commissioner wants it settled or not—there's no reason you can't"—he made a rotary gesture with his hands—"enjoy yourself."

"I certainly will, Captain," the lieutenant said with a gleam in her eye.

"Of course, you know a degree of discretion is called for—" *How is it that so often I wind up sounding like a father lecturing his adolescent daughter?* he wondered.

"I'll uphold the finest traditions of Starfleet, Captain," Uhura said, "and I'll be sure not to do anything *you* wouldn't do. Good night, sir."

"I was afraid you'd say that," he said to her retreating back.

"Captain."

Kirk stopped. Seeing the expression on his face, the crewfolk walking the other direction along the passageway gave him plenty of sea room. Or remembered errands they'd forgotten back the way they had come.

"Commissioner," he said, as the purposeful footsteps caught up to him.

Moriah Wayne's face was white with fury. "Why wasn't I consulted on allowing the crew leave among the settlers?"

"I'm the captain. This is my ship and my crew. How I schedule my leave rotations is my concern. It's no more my job to check with you on the subject than it is for Bones to ask your permission to order more supplies for sickbay."

Her eyes took on a dangerous glint. "I believe you are deliberately trying to sabotage this mission, Captain," she said. "My report will so state."

He stared at her. "Because I'm allowing shore leave?"

"Precisely. You're playing on the crew's natural sympathy for humans over what they think of as aliens—even though those, those ersatz humans below, are at least as alien as the Susuru. You want to create a situation in which it will be impossible to compel the settlers to evacuate without risking mutiny."

"Mutiny?" His first impulse was to roar at her. That died quickly, to be supplanted by the urge to laugh in her face. He gave in to that one.

"Commissioner, really. You have the most amazing view of how Starfleet operates."

He held up a finger. "First of all, let me remind you—*Enterprise* is not a democracy." Another finger. "Second, let me point out to you that everyone on board, except a few civilians and yourself, has sworn an oath to uphold the laws and ideals of the Federation, and to obey all lawful orders of their superior officers, regardless of their personal preferences. These are people who have already obeyed my orders many times when they might have preferred not to, even at the risk of their lives."

"What about the example you gave them earlier in the evening by defying my orders?"

"You're a civilian, Commissioner. You're outside the Starfleet chain of command. And every man and woman in the crew knows that, should you profess charges on my return, I will face a board of inquiry— or a court-martial. There's a price to disobedience, one even I am prepared to pay."

He held up his hands before him. "Don't you see how you're insulting them, Commissioner, when you suggest they'll mutiny if I give them an unpopular order?"

She sagged so abruptly that he was afraid she would collapse to the deck. Instead she leaned her back against the bulkhead.

"Jim," she said, "I'm sorry. I . . . I guess I'm getting too close to the situation."

He turned away from her, raised a forearm, and braced it against the bulkhead. He could not honestly have said what he was feeling at that moment.

A touch on his arm. He spun angrily away from it.

"What are you trying to do to me?" he demanded.

The planes of her face shifted, as if she were trying on various emotions and finding none of them fit. She settled on something that seemed halfway between hurt and haughtiness. "I might ask you the same thing."

"Moriah, I'm trying to keep separate my dealings with you as a person and my dealings with you as a Federation commissioner. You're not making it particularly easy."

"You're angry with me because of our policy disagreements."

"Policy disagreements? You keep telling me how you're going to have my job the moment we set foot back on Federation soil, over just those 'policy disagreements.'"

"You really can't separate the business from the personal, then?" she asked in a hollow voice.

"That's not it," he said, facing her once more. "Or that's not *all* of it. It's just—" A chopping motion of one hand. "I remember what you had to say about the Discordians this morning, Commissioner, and the tone of voice in which you said it." He shook his head. "That showed me a person I don't find it very easy to like."

131

She came to him and clutched at his arm. "But, Jim, you don't mean that old movie remark? That was a joke! That's all it was."

"It wasn't easy to tell, under the circumstances."

She laughed weakly and shook her head. "I guess that's another area where I've got a lot to learn about dealing with people."

He sagged at the knees. *Is this conversation for real?* "Maybe it is. But, Moriah, you had plenty to say about the colonists, and I don't think it was all supposed to be funny."

"No. It wasn't. Maybe I reacted a little strongly— but it was an honest reaction."

She drifted a few steps down the corridor. "I remember reading about the Eugenics Wars when I was a little girl. I saw the pictures of the devastation Khan and the others wrought. And I saw the pictures of the *things* they'd created in their labs."

He came up behind her and put a hand on her shoulder. "Don't you see that these people were Khan's victims? They didn't ask him to experiment on them."

"Khan and his cadre and the other tyrants were products of gene engineering, too, don't forget."

Kirk winced. He couldn't very well forget, since two years before the *Enterprise* had come across the *Botany Bay* adrift in space—the sublight "sleeper" colony ship in which Khan and a handful of his comrades had fled Earth in 1996. Khan had taken the *Enterprise* by treachery, and several crewfolk died before the ship was recovered. Kirk had marooned Khan and his followers, including the *Enterprise*'s historian, who had become infatuated with him, on Ceti Alpha V.

"They were the rulers," he said. "A self-proclaimed

master race. These people were bred to be their *slaves,* Moriah."

She pivoted toward him. "But you're missing something vital. They *perpetuate* it. I've been reading about their ancestors in the computer's historical archives. After Khan fell, the tyrants' altered humans were declared wards of the United Nations. They were sent to live in a series of camps in isolated areas. Normal humans had suffered enormously in the wars. Some blamed Khan's creations for their hardships—made them scapegoats, I'm aware of that. Others simply feared them. So they had to be kept carefully segregated and under guard."

"That's a terrible tragedy, Moriah. It seems to me someone of your pronounced compassion might find some to spare for people whose forebears went through a thing like that."

"But don't you see? The United Nations banned gene engineering of humans. As I said at the briefing, it's still illegal. I was raised to regard the very concept with horror. So were you, Jim. So was every other human child in the Federation."

"Well . . . yes. That's true."

"They kept it alive *themselves.* Defied the UN ban, kept passing the forbidden knowledge along, kept the equipment carefully hidden away in the camps. They not only passed their own artificial traits onto their children, they created new ones. They made that decision for their children—imposed it on them, for all their atomistic raving about the sanctity of individual choice. Can you honestly say that isn't monstrous?"

"I don't know. You met those people. You talked to them. Do they really seem like monsters to you?"

She turned away. "Yes. And the testimony of the Susuru bears that out."

He threw up his hands. "Commissioner, I suppose we will have to agree to disagree. *Until* our fact-finding mission bears fruit. Now—good night."

A hand on his forearm. "Jim." Her eyes glowed as if they had incandescent arcs behind them. "Let's go to your quarters and talk about—other things. About your plans and aspirations. About the future. About *us.*"

He filled so full of things to say that none of them made it out of his mouth.

"Not tonight," he finally managed to say. And he turned and left her standing alone.

Chapter Thirteen

"BEHOLD," said Captain of the First Rank Kain with a grand sweep of his gauntleted hand. "The majesty of Island."

Standing next to Spock, Dr. McCoy, and Commissioner Wayne on a weathered granite knee looming high above the ocean, Kirk beheld. It was morning and the sky was miraculously clear. He had to admit the sight was majestic indeed, despite the awful heat.

At eleven hundred meters the promontory was the highest point in the Susuru archipelago. A few active seamounts were higher, but there was no current volcanic activity along the equator. Across a strait so blue it was painful to look at lay the western end of Madagascar-sized Homesward, colored more shades of green than Kirk ever knew existed, from the dark green of the interior jungles and terraced mountainsides to the pale yellow-green of the cultivated coastal areas and cleared plateaus. To left and right other islands shouldered up from the sea, some large enough for habitation, others little more than the nubs of long-dead seamounts, all so thickly furred with the vegetation that sprang up whenever and wherever it was given a chance that they appeared to be wearing green wigs above the black margin where wave action kept the lava scoured clean of growth.

Kain pointed out the most prominent of them: "There lie the Sea Dragon's Teeth, there Fever Tree, Tribulation, Sulfur Island. That bare spit of black stone, the nearest point on Homesward, is known as Cape Sorrow."

"Gloomy damned set of names," remarked Dr. McCoy.

"Okeanos—Island—is a harsh world," said Wayne in a distant voice. She stood atop a small boulder, apart from her Federation companions and rather nearer the Klingon. She had her arms crossed and a dreamy expression on her face. The brisk breeze whipped loose hair like whisks of copper wire against her forehead. "She lays a heavy burden on her children."

"You are very perceptive," Kain said. "It is a world not unlike my own."

"Leaving aside the fact that Klingon is cold and dry," McCoy said, "whereas this place is the Devil's own sauna."

"Its similarity lies in the fact that both worlds are exacting environments, Dr. McCoy," Kain said. "But the very ferocity of the world adds savor, do you not think? Beauty without danger is insipid, like a rose without a thorn."

He walked forward to stand next to Wayne and point out a particularly interesting feature to her. McCoy put his head near Kirk's.

136

"Now, tell me if the sun's getting to me," he said, "but I thought the Klingon appreciation for natural beauty ran along the lines of, 'Up on that crag a few well-armed warriors could stand off an army.'"

"Maybe our Captain Kain has the soul of a poet."

"Maybe pigs have wings."

"Gentlemen," Kain called in his molten-amber baritone, "shall we head back down to the flyer? We are due to meet with the Lead Walker soon. Permit me, Commissioner." He held a hand up for Wayne. After a heartbeat's hesitation she took it and jumped down.

"Beware of Romulans bearing gifts," McCoy said under his breath, "and polite Klingons."

Kain and the commissioner led the way down the long, slow slope that fell away inland from the promontory. The trail vanished almost instantly into a tunnel hacked through unbelievably dense vegetation. Humidity and the smell of green decay seemed to enfold their heads like wet blankets.

"Confounded steep mountains they have on this planet," McCoy said, batting at a gigantic fleshy triangle of leaf that Kain had happened to allow to swing back into his face.

"Notice that the extremely durable stone of the outcrop on which we stood was polished quite smooth by erosion," Spock said. "The archipelago is quite ancient."

"Given how jagged these islands still are after millions of years of being exposed to the tender mercies of the elements," Kirk said, "I think I'm just as glad I wasn't around when they were formed."

"There just isn't much peace to this planet, Jim, and that's a fact," McCoy said.

The ground leveled off into a broad extended hip. The flat expanse was occupied by a clearing, natural or otherwise. The flyer that had brought them here was parked at the far side.

"I feel like, if I were wearing snowshoes, I could skim right across the tops of this stuff," McCoy said as they trudged through the grass, dew heavy and knee high.

"Hardly practicable, Doctor," Spock said.

"But I know what you mean, Bones," Kirk said. "This is unbelievable growing land—soil to gladden a farm boy's heart."

"It is fortunate for the Susuru that the soil is so fertile," Spock said, "since such a small percentage of their land is arable."

"I wonder why this plot isn't under cultivation?" Kirk asked.

"Because it's a park, Captain," said Wayne, who had paused to let the others catch up. "Look."

To the side of the clearing a Susuru family frolicked, two children racing in circles about what might have been a mated pair of adults. As Kirk watched, the larger adult, possibly the male, darted toward one of the young ones with an exaggerated spraddle-foot walk. The young Susuru promptly fell down in a tangle of gawky forelimbs. Its sibling hopped from foot to foot, hooting at it. The elder Susuru extended a foreleg to help it up. Then the three skipped through a complicated trefoil dance while the smaller adult sang in a sweet soprano voice.

"Look at them," the commissioner said. "Peaceful, playful. *They're* not carrying guns." She headed off toward the Klingon aircraft.

"Y'know, Jim," McCoy said. "When I look at these

138

critters the main word that comes to mind is *cute.*" He shook his head. "Hard to see them as the demons the colonists make them out to be."

"But the colonists do not demonize the Susuru, Doctor," Spock said. "They speak of them mainly in terms suggesting amused contempt."

Except Aileea, Kirk thought, vaguely troubled. *And she's not without a reason to dislike them.*

He wondered then why he cared how dinAthos felt about the Susuru—and why he made excuses for her.

The larger of the two young Susuru froze, legs apart, the fur of its ruff extended, staring across the grass at the little group of humanoids. It uttered a whinny of fear, stamped its forelegs. The other Susuru looked around, saw the party for the first time, and bolted into the undergrowth.

"Most curious," Spock said.

The flyer grounded in a field on the outskirts of the largest city of Homesward. A trio of field workers fled at their approach, running with startling leaps across orderly rows of bushes with thick-lobed, succulent-looking leaves. Ignoring the fact that the field was cultivated, the Klingon craft settled down, crushing several rows of bushes into the friable black soil.

Showing no concern, Kain leapt down from the craft and assisted Wayne out after him. The Klingon pilot followed, and all three tramped off across the cultivated rows.

Kirk, Spock, and McCoy climbed out more ginger-ly. "These Klingons sure have quite a way about them," McCoy said, eyeing the Susuru farmers who watched from several hundred meters away, twitching from forefoot to forefoot in agitation.

"For a fact, they seem a bit abrupt for 'fraternal advisers,'" Spock said.

"Klingons have a different concept of brotherly love than the rest of us," Kirk said. "It's an example of what the commissioner would call cultural diversity."

They set off after Kain and the commissioner. The city was laid out in concentric rings, with progressively decreasing distances between them. As the rings grew closer together, the character of their surroundings changed from rural to urban. The structures tended to be low and sturdy, to stand up against the violent weather—pentagonal structures of cement and stone that had been melted and poured into forms. The doorways and windows were all five-sided polygons, with vertical sides parallel and two shorter sides angling together in an arch at the top.

"Observe, Captain," Spock said, "how the number of structures in a ring is always a multiple of five."

"Play us some slack, Spock," McCoy growled. "We don't all have a surveyor's transit for eyes."

Spock raised a brow. "Doctor, surely you're aware a transit is used to measure angles, not as an adjunct to enumeration."

"You should learn to listen to what I *mean*, man, not what I say."

"Your request is illogical, Doctor. I can hear only that which you actually deign to vocalize."

Kirk listened to their banter with half an ear. Usually he took an active interest in their fencing matches, even after five years of listening to them; they were inventive, if nothing else, each one always finding something new to tweak the other with. More to his surprise, he was paying little attention to their surroundings, although the thrill of encountering an alien civilization close up for the first time was usually his intoxicant of choice.

Instead he kept watching Wayne and the Klingon captain walking side by side, close together, and speaking very earnestly.

Except for Spock the Federation representatives were all staggering visibly when they reached the innermost circle, a broad green lawn around the sprawling pentagonal building that housed the seat of Susuru government. There was no pavement. The Susuru Lead Walker and his entourage emerged from the grand five-sided portal and went down a short flight of steps directly onto the grass.

"Delay is unacceptable!" shrilled Swift as the off-worlders approached. "The humans must leave our planet or face extermination!"

"I have tried to impress the urgency of that fact upon the captain," Wayne said. "So far I have failed."

"Lead Walker," Kirk said, "just how well do you know your enemies, the Discordians?"

Swift snapped his fingers, an apparent sound of annoyance. "Well enough. They are intruders and ravagers." He glanced at Kain, who stood with Wayne by his side. "What more do we need to know?"

"Perhaps if both sides understood each other better, you'd feel less like booting them off your world," McCoy said.

The Lead Walker eyed him narrowly, with his ears angled down and out. Then he looked at Kirk. "You permit voices to speak from the herd? Anarchy, anarchy."

"The doctor is one of our own ruling Five," Kirk said. "And I can only echo his sentiment. Why don't you sit down with the Discordians and talk? You might not find them that unpleasant a set of neighbors."

Swift stamped his right foot. His Vanguard Walkers set up an ear-piercing ululation.

"No! They are not our neighbors! They plunder, they kill—"

"Perhaps if you were to show us some of the damage they have done to your dwellings," Spock said, "it might help us to frame a more perfect understanding of the situation."

Swift went up on his toes, leaned back as if to flee, and looked at Kain in something like panic. The captain only smiled back encouragingly—if a Klingon's smile could be said to be encouraging.

"It cannot be," Swift said slowly, lowering his weight again. "Security concerns forbid."

He dropped his muzzle to give Kirk a glance of sly appraisal. "They are your fellow humans, after all. How do we know you won't report to them what we show you."

Kirk felt his cheeks get hotter than the sun was already making them. "I am not human," Mr. Spock said. "I can assure you of my complete impartiality."

"You all look alike to me," Swift said suspiciously.

"As Commissioner Wayne said at our first meeting, we have come to help you," Kirk said, back in control of his temper. "But surely it will be easier for us to help you if you'll meet us halfway."

"No! No halfway!" Swift's grizzled ruff bristled. "This planet—ours! You are humans. The intruders are human. We called you to take your people off. Take them off, or we destroy them!"

"It is our impression that you have been waging warfare with the humans for almost forty of your years," Spock said. "In all that time, neither side has achieved a decisive result. How do you propose to defeat them now?"

Swift thrust his muzzle at Kain. "Our friends from the stars. They give us much—show us much."

"Introducing advanced weaponry to a planetary conflict constitutes a violation of the Organian Peace Accords, Captain," Kirk said. "The Discordians describe new weapons being used against them since your arrival, which sound suspiciously like phasers."

"They lie," Wayne said.

Spock arched a brow. "Indeed? How then could they describe them so accurately?"

"My people are warriors, Captain, as you're well aware," Kain said. "They are under strict orders not to violate the Peace Accords. Nonetheless, in the heat of battle, their blood might overwhelm even their sense of duty." A shrug. "I shall make inquiries."

"I trust the usual Draconian standards of Klingon discipline will be applied," Kirk said.

"Of course." Kain fingered the hilt of the bladed weapon at his belt.

"Then what is the answer to Mr. Spock's question?"

"Really, Captain Kirk, do you think it's appropriate to badger him?" Wayne demanded.

"The Susuru are apt pupils," Kain said. "In fact, properly stimulated, they have a marked talent for tactical innovation. The Earther colonists can expect no end of surprises in the not-too-distant future."

"But those who walk before you have ordered you to help us, Captain," Swift said. "We will not need those surprises—will we?"

"Lead Walker," Kirk said deliberately, "the uprooting of an entire people is something that the Federation views very gravely. Under most circumstances" —he looked at Wayne—"it is considered a heinous crime. I appreciate the depth of your feelings. But I am not willing to undertake an act of this magnitude without exhausting every possible alternative."

"No alternative!" cried Swift. He calmed himself, looked at Wayne. "You speak for those who walk before all, whom all follow. Do they not command him to our help?"

"They do."

"Do you then disobey your leaders, Captain?"

"In the Federation we have a rule of laws, not of beings. I am faithful to those laws. I intend to go on being so. Accordingly, I'm not going to take any action until I get you and the settlers together to talk. Do you understand?"

The twenty elders started screeching again.

"And that damned racket isn't going to make me change my mind!"

Swift stamped his foot. The wailing ceased.

"There's something I must ask you, Lead Walker, something that might work to your benefit. My crew need recreation, need to feel the wind and sun on their faces . . . even this sun. Will you let leave parties beam down among your islands so that my people may walk among yours and learn of them? It would help us to better appreciate your plight."

"No." Swift was too angry even to shriek. The guard hairs of Swift's ruff quivered to the intensity of his emotion. "This world is ours. Ours alone. We will have no humans upon it. Not the ones who invaded from the sky forty years ago. Not the ones you bring with you on your ship, with your flat faces and your thick, ungainly, ill-placed legs."

He drew himself up to his full height. "Island belongs to us. We want it back. There can be no negotiation. Remember, Captain—nine days. And then . . . annihilation."

Chapter Fourteen

THE DOOR ANNUNCIATOR to Kirk's cabin chimed. Sitting at his desk reading a digest of reports on Okeanos —or Island, or Discord—James Kirk lifted his head, thought about rebelling, and finally said, "The hell with it. Come in."

The door slid open to admit Dr. McCoy. "You look relieved, Jim."

"Maybe it's the sight of that bottle in your hand."

"This?" McCoy held it up. Brown liquid sloshed inside. "Just a product of the local culture."

He tossed it to Kirk, who only just managed to field it. He peered at the label. " 'Hagbard's Select'?"

"Literary reference, they tell me." McCoy went to the settee and sat down.

"The seal is broken," Kirk said, "and there appears to be some missing."

"Well, since the stuff is manufactured by a belligerent in a war you're trying to stop, it'd be a clear dereliction of duty for me to permit my captain to drink the stuff without subjecting it to rigorous scientific analysis first."

He rubbed his stomach. "It passed the taste test with flying colors. And it hasn't killed me yet. So I feel confident in pronouncing it fit even for a starship captain. Especially one with a load of travails."

"You can say that again." Kirk squinted at the bottle a little more closely. "Except—tell me one thing. Just what grows on this planet that somebody might be able to distill 'fine sipping whiskey' from?"

"Some things, Jim, a man isn't meant to know. Now drink, don't analyze. Prove you're a man instead of a Vulcan."

Kirk went to the sideboard, took out a couple of tumblers, and poured a couple of fingers in each. He handed one to the doctor.

"You first."

"What? You don't trust me?" He hoisted the glass. "To the wonders of modern medicine." He tossed it off, smacked his lips, and sighed. "Ah. Five or six more like that and I'll forget what it's like on that infernal Dutch oven of a planet."

Kirk sipped his cautiously. It rolled silkily over his tongue and down his throat—then seemed to ignite like a kerosene spill.

"My," he gasped, "that's—"

"Smooth. But beware the afterbite."

"I'll say." Kirk paused, sucking on his lips. "You know, a man could get accustomed to that."

"The way you sounded when I rang," McCoy said as Kirk poured himself another, "I figured you thought I was the Terror of Red Tape Mansion."

"She's still safely down on the planet, continuing

147

her own inquiries." Kirk sat in his desk chair. "For some reason the Susuru don't mind her staying on."

"She tells them what they want to hear. Also, I think their bosses, those 'forward walkers' or whatever you call 'em, are only too eager to give their shiny new ridge-headed friends anything their black hearts desire."

He looked closely at Kirk. "Funny you should use the word *safely* in this context. If I didn't know better, I'd swear that silver-tongued Klingon bastard is beating your time."

Kirk laughed weakly. "Do you really think that's likely, Bones?"

"Well, now, Klingons and humans are anatomically compatible, reproductively speaking, much as it might gripe them to admit it—"

"I mean—do you really think a woman in her position—"

McCoy was leaning back. "I think that Deputy Commissioner Wayne has so many demons crammed into her head there's no telling who's running the show at any given moment. By all accounts Daddy Cornelius was as tyrannical an old reptile as you'd care to run across. Moriah was his only child. Now, I'm a doctor, not a headshrinker, but I'd say that's a situation tailor-made to produce a confused overachiever who's always looking to please Daddy. And never, ever can."

Kirk stared into his glass. "You mean to say, you think her interest in me was based on a desire for a father figure?"

McCoy grinned.

"Bones, I'm a year or two older than she is, if that. And the idea of *Kain* as a father substitute—"

"The human mind is a wondrous contrivance," McCoy said. "Who knows what gyrations it's capable of?"

He crossed his legs and the two men drank in companionable silence. After a few moments Kirk went and retrieved the bottle.

"How did that Klingon son of a gun Kain get to be so damned smooth, anyway?" McCoy asked as Kirk poured. "Most Klingons think etiquette means you don't wipe your hands on your sash after you stab the person next to you at the dinner table. This boy's fit to be presented to the Queen of England. Most Klingons talk like a handful of gravel being shaken on a washboard. This one has a voice Wu Shanxi would kill for." He referred to the Federation's leading operatic baritone.

"He does show a lot of polish for a Klingon," Kirk said. "For example, you contradicted him over the similarity of Discord and his homeworld, and he didn't even try to kill you."

McCoy blinked and swallowed. "Yeah. Well, he sure doesn't come by it honestly."

"Oh, but he does, Bones. His father was a diplomat."

"A diplomat?" McCoy raised an eyebrow. "I didn't know the Klingons grew any of those."

"They don't, many. But even a fanatical warrior culture needs a negotiator sometimes. And given the stakes that're liable to be involved wherever Klingons are concerned, they tend to be good ones. That's how I met him, in fact—he accompanied his father to a conference I attended, when I was still at the Academy."

"Axanar."

"That's the one. His father was a big man, imposing, very dignified. To tell you the truth, aside from height, Kain doesn't look a thing like him. Krodan, we knew him as, though I guess his real name's more along the lines of QoDang."

He was slumping lower in his chair as the fierce Discordian whiskey relaxed him. "Want to know something ironic? I think that's why Kain is such a swashbuckler. He's trying to compensate for the dishonor of his father's occupation." He shook his head. "And in his heyday, Krodan was one of the four or five most powerful men in the Empire."

"From the way he was talking to you, you and he have some history beyond the Axanar talks."

"I guess so." Kirk shrugged. "He and I never saw each other. Planet called Endikon. I was still a lieutenant on *Farragut*—after Captain Garrovick died. We and the Klingons were vying for the right to trade for life-extending pharmaceuticals from yet another crabby, zealous race with bony heads. The Klingon captain sent a party down to steal a valuable holy relic to hold for ransom."

"What happened?"

"It—ahh—disappeared before they had the chance."

McCoy squinted at him. "Are you telling me you stole the relic yourself?"

"I thought of it as removing it for safekeeping."

The doctor roared. "Then what happened?"

"Somehow the local authorities had been tipped off. The Klingon group walked right into their arms. Repercussions blew them clean off the planet."

He tossed off the tag end of his drink. "I remember now, the party was commanded by a kid ensign. I guess that was Kain."

"Given the usual Klingon response to failure, that was a pretty rough trick to play on a kid."

"I suppose it was. That wasn't the kind of thing I thought about back then, when I was young and wild and full of beans."

"And now you're old and wild and full of beans."

Kirk stood, and swayed. "Who's old?"

"Ask the man in the mirror." McCoy leaned forward and held his glass between his knees. "I wonder what our friend Kain is doing wearing a *kligat.*"

Kirk looked at him. "The knife? It looks familiar, somehow."

McCoy laughed. "Are you getting old, or is the booze clouding your memory? That's a *kligat,* favored weapon of the inhabitants of Capella IV. One of whom just happens to be my godson."

"Teer Leonard James Akaar," Kirk said.

"Does have a bit of a ring to it, you gotta admit." McCoy rubbed the back of his neck. "Of course, I still have a knot on the back of my head left over from where his mom cold-cocked me with that rock. My old friends the Capellans are even crankier than Klingons —as that Klingon spy found out. What was his name, anyway?"

"Kras."

"Very conspirators he had talked into killing old Teer Akaar, Senior, whacked him out with one of those flying can openers . . . I wonder if Kain knows how to use his."

"Probably."

McCoy shook his head. "If they've got many more like him, we're in a peck of trouble."

"There's only one *Qeyn HoD wa'DIch,*" Kirk said, making fairly heavy weather of the Klingon, "in either the Empire or the Federation."

McCoy held up his glass. "Thank God for that!"

He chuckled. "Though I think our lovely commissioner may have a point. You *are* a pretty close counterpart . . . say, this thing's empty."

"So's the bottle."

McCoy eyed him blearily. "I still see before me a man in the throes of stress. As your physician, I prescribe more of the same medicine. What do you have in the cupboard?"

Kirk held up a brown glass bottle. "How does Saurian brandy sound?"

McCoy pursed his lips. "Extremely fancy. How come I rate a shot of it?"

"Well, I *was* saving it for a special occasion—"

"And?"

Kirk shrugged and poured two generous snifters. "It came," he said, "and went."

McCoy accepted the goblet and gazed into the depths of the liqueur. Then he looked up at Kirk.

"What if he's on the level, Jim?"

Kirk smiled. "What was that you said, about pigs having wings? *Prosit.*"

Where the deep submersible drove there were no lights except those she projected from her own stubby hull. Screens in the cramped interior offered views generated by a variety of sensors, including visual imaging of radar and sonar returns. Right now they were displaying a seafloor bare of vegetation, across which small, strange organisms crept.

"I admit to perplexity, Dr. Arkazha," said Spock.

The pilot glanced back over his shoulder. He was a curly-haired young man with plump red cheeks, wearing a mustard-yellow jump suit. He belonged to a

Gens of stature similar to the Micros, but chunky and round-faced, and tending to thickness around the middle. They called themselves Hobbits.

Mona Arkazha nodded her heavy head. Her mister was turned off, though water still circulated through the yoke that covered the gill slits in her neck. Her skin only required moistening in direct sunlight.

Spock looked to the screen. It showed what seemed to be a glow coming from the ocean floor itself. It was surrounded by an abundance of submarine vegetation, like an oasis in a desert.

"What is that, Doctor?"

"Volcanic vent. They provide the energy sufficient to run a tidy little ecosystem. Each is in effect its own little world. Right now, in fact, they are my main area of study."

The large gelatinous-looking eyes studied him for a moment. "But you asked about the war. We found no Susuru when we arrived, though we scarcely had the opportunity to make an exhaustive survey of the planet. We did not encounter them for some three local years—about twelve Terran years."

"How did the initial contact transpire?"

"A boatload of Swimmers noticed signs of activity on an island. Thinking there might be someone shipwrecked, they stood in to investigate. What they found were Susuru, who opened fire on them with projectile weapons."

Spock frowned. "Are you certain your people did nothing to incite them?"

"Mr. Spock, we Vares are a contentious lot, and frequently flamboyant. And I am sure you are aware that the fact of persecution does nothing of itself to render a group more tolerant; generally it has quite the opposite effect. But we tried our best to *learn* from our travails. We have never *wanted* to do to anyone what was done to us.

"More than that—do we strike you as people who would fear or hate something because it was *different?* I'm almost as alien to young Jason or Aileea as the Susuru are, no matter how human my genes are. Do you think we would reflexively attack them?"

"Why should they attack you?"

The pilot laughed bitterly. "If you learn the answer to that one, please let us know," he said. "When we capture Stilters, all they ever say is that we're a danger to them. And unless we catch them, they won't talk to us at all."

"Most odd. When we visited them, the Susuru seemed anything but a belligerent race."

The pilot turned a stunned look over his shoulder at the Vulcan. "But they shoot at us on sight!"

"Almost forty-two years have we lived on this planet," Arkazha said. "For thirty-nine of those years we have been at war. And never have we had any idea *why.*"

"Coming up on our objective, Mona," the pilot said.

"Thank you, Suleyman." Arkazha hunched her squat form around to better see the screen. Her body language bespoke excitement. "Look at this, now—look!"

The oasis surrounding the vent had fallen behind. The ocean floor spread flat and featureless below. Then a line appeared across the "horizon." It grew wider as the submersible approached, became a crack, a chasm, a canyon, and then what seemed a split in the world.

"Hellsgate Rift," Arkazha said. "Ten kilometers deep and more."

The submersible was over the abyss now. Even the small craft's artificial senses showed only blackness below.

"Bad waters," the Hobbit pilot grunted. "Craft disappear around here all the time. It's Leviathan takes them. We're precious near the lair of the Devil in the Sea."

"Superstition," scoffed Arkazha. "No one knows what's really down there, save volcanic vents in plenty. They roil the water so our sonar works poorly, and the strong electromagnetic activity associated with volcanism on this world befuddles our radar."

"Fascinating."

She nodded. "It is that, Spock." She placed greenish black fingertips on the screen. "I hope to help unlock the mysteries of Hellsgate. I've already glimpsed things down there—but I don't know if I can trust you."

Spock looked at her quizzically. "Why not, Doctor? I have dealt with you as openly as I am able. In fact, I must say, I've found our association . . . most congenial."

She smiled. "As have I, Spock, my friend. But I keep forgetting . . . you work for the State. For Leviathan —our ancient enemy, whatever form He takes. I just don't know if I can trust you."

"What does my employment with Starfleet have to do with my trustworthiness?"

"You owe a duty to your State and to your superiors. If they should decide to stick their boot on our necks, the way Commissioner Wayne wants to do, you will be bound to relay anything I tell you."

"It is difficult to see how what lies at the bottom of an oceanic trench might constitute usable intelligence."

She turned her head aside. Her rubbery lips twisted in a strange smile. "Ah, but you never know what might be down there. Perhaps even the lair of Leviathan."

Spock raised an eyebrow. Still, Dr. Arkazha possessed a most refreshingly logical mind for one of her species. He could not hold the occasional descent into fanciful thinking against her.

She could not help herself, after all. She was only human.

Chapter Fifteen

THE LITTLE AIRCRAFT flew two thousand meters above a sea like a sheet of sapphire with milk-white stars for wave crests.

"Aren't you worried about the Susuru ultimatum?" Kirk asked from the passenger seat on the cockpit's starboard side. "Three days left."

Aileea dinAthos snorted a laugh—unladylike but charming, he thought. "If they could have wiped us out, they would have done so forty years ago."

"They have help now."

"The *Kofirlar*." She sneered. "We can handle them, too, Captain, so long as they don't range their weapons of mass destruction against us."

She gave him a sideways glance. "Where do you stand? If their ship of space takes us under fire, what will you do?"

"Warn her," he said. A pause. "If she doesn't stop, I'll blast her out of orbit. That kind of intervention is way outside the rules, and the Klingons know it."

She flipped her head, clearing shag-cut hair from her forehead. "Then we will endure. Just the way we always have. We're good at enduring, Captain."

"Jim."

Aileea nodded. "There it is," she said, banking the aircraft to circle an assembly of three shiny metal cylinders fastened together in parallel, one above the other two, with an oval tower rising from one side and a white fiber-matted deck extending from the other. "My home float."

"*Your* home?" Kirk shook his head, puzzled. "I thought Dr. Arkazha said the Susuru sank your home."

Aileea looked at him from the pilot's seat and smiled thinly. "No. Mansur *submerged* it, to avoid the Stilter missiles." To his blank look she explained, "It's a submarine, too, you see. Practically every dwelling on Discord is. It's the only sure way to beat the real killer storms—though a big city can ride one out. That's one of the attractions to living in one."

"I thought you made your home in Discord City now."

"I'm *based* there. This is my home." She brought the craft level and began a descent. "Even now."

"So you're still a country girl at heart?" Kirk asked. He sat turned in his seat, with his left arm propped on the back.

She looked at him with a slight frown of incomprehension pulling her brows together. With her green bangs hanging almost to her eyes she looked quite cute—despite the ominous mass of the pistol hung to a nicely rounded hip.

Watch yourself, he thought. *This trip is purely business.* Which wasn't entirely true; Bones had threatened to write him up unless he found time to get a little R and R himself. With the clock running out on planetwide escalation, it seemed strange to be beaming down for shore leave. Yet with the Susuru stonewalling the very concept of peace talks, Kirk could find no excuse not to go along when dinAthos asked him if he wanted to see what life on a Discordian sea ranch was like. There was nothing to do that he hadn't already done.

Her face brightened. "I understand," she said. "You mean my heart and soul still belong on the ranch. That's true."

He nodded. "Thought so. I'm an old Iowa farm boy myself. I know all the symptoms."

She nodded absently, speaking into the microphone of her lightweight headset. Wallowing in the surface chop, the craft slowed. With a creaking sound the high-mounted wings rotated upward, allowing the broad props to hold it up instead of the airfoils. Aileea held the ship steady, then steered it expertly over a round platform floating beside the main house, hovered briefly, and settled down to an easy landing.

Kirk made an appreciative face. He was a Navy man, not a flyboy; as her name implied, *Enterprise* bore a much closer relationship to an old Earth aircraft carrier than the craft that flew from its decks. But he knew neat piloting when he saw it.

He carefully said nothing. His hostess's prickly pride might interpret a compliment as condescension when it concerned such a workaday task. Starting with nothing but will, resourcefulness, and the equipment they had been able to carry on board their sleeper ship—which Kirk knew must have been next to nothing, given the space the cryosleep units and crude warp drive took up—the colonists had done a magnificent job of building a technic civilization. Nonetheless they were markedly less advanced than the Federation, and inclined to be defensive.

Aileea hopped out, to be met by a pair of meter-tall women with short hair and round faces, stockier in build than the Micros. They traded hugs with the tall woman, then helped her make the aircraft fast to the pad and cover it with a tarp as Kirk stood by with his seabag over his shoulder, wanting to help but feeling as if he'd only get in the way.

"This is Captain Kirk," Aileea told the two. "He's one of the men from Earth everyone's talking about. Captain, these are Ranit and Yuki. They've been with us for years."

"He's very handsome," said Yuki.

The other looked skeptical. "Is it true that you'll try to make us leave Discord, Captain?" she asked. "Where would we go?"

"I don't want to move anyone anywhere. I want to bring peace."

The two laughed. It was not a cheerful sound.

He followed Aileea across a short floating walkway that bobbed alarmingly underfoot. She was wearing white shorts and a short loose top that left her flat tanned stomach bare. He reminded himself of how it would look to a board of inquiry if he got too intimately involved with one of the very people he was supposed to be seeing off the planet with all deliberate speed.

Kirk stepped aboard the float proper and stopped. Jutting above the topmost cylinder of the ranch house was a rack of tubes tipped with sharp cones.

"What're those?" he asked.

160

"Koman ship-killer missiles," she said with grim satisfaction. "Supersonic, hundred-kilometer range. They guide on data provided by our wranglers. A solid hit with one can sink the biggest ship the Stilters have."

She glanced at him sidelong. "They're just installed —we haven't got the protective shrouds up yet. The Stilters won't find us such an easy mark next time, Captain."

"I see." Aware that she was gauging his reaction, he paused a moment, staring up at the ominous shapes, their white noses ringed in yellow. They seemed to serve as a reminder of just how tough the task facing him was. He allowed himself to show her a frown of concern.

She led him into the house. Inside it was climate-conditioned to perfect comfort—by Discordian standards. That meant only moderately sweltering, though for the moment, out of the unforgiving eye of Eris, it felt blessedly cool, in fact.

He was skeptical as to how roomy the ranch house could be. The main cylinders were twenty-five meters long and six across, which didn't seem to offer much space for the twenty or so people Kirk understood lived and worked there. Then Aileea led him down a circular stairway, and he realized that, like an iceberg, much of the house lay under water.

In a narrow passageway with exposed pipes in red and yellow and white running overhead a couple of cylinders down, Aileea pushed open a door. "This'll be your cabin, Captain. It's probably nowhere near as grand as you're used to, of course."

It was a small chamber, with a bed that seemed to be built into the curving hull. It was clean and well lit.

A port showed seawater surging without, with shafts of white sunlight falling through like searchlight beams. It felt like a Turkish bath.

He smiled. "This will do nicely indeed, Ms. dinAthos."

"Aileea, Captain."

"Agreed—if you call me Jim."

She grinned. "It's a deal. Would you like something to eat before we see how the ranch works?"

"I feel as if I could eat a whale."

"No whales on Discord, Jim. But wait until you see our prawns."

The upper cylinder served as mess hall. A long table ran down the center. Extensive ports looked out over the deck on the one hand and the sea on the other.

A giant Grunt in a white apron served them dishes of stew—of sea pulses steamed with shellfish—with hard-crusted bread on the side. He acknowledged Aileea's introduction of Kirk with a ponderous nod and left without speaking.

"That's Mansur," Aileea said. "He hasn't been with us all that long—three or four years. He came here not long before I went off to school. But he's the backbone of the ranch. He pretty much runs things now."

"And he's the cook?"

"He enjoys it. A Grunt needs something to do with his hands or he fidgets himself crazy."

"I guess the way you live is determined to a great extent by what Gens you belong to."

She stopped with her spoon halfway to her mouth. "No. The way we live is *influenced* by our genes, same as everybody else. We're aware of our differences— Eris, we cherish them. But it's up to us to choose our lives. Our chance—and our responsibility."

162

The hatch to the outside opened, allowing a dragon's breath of the metal-smelling sea air inside. Three ranch hands came in, two men and a woman, to greet Aileea with happy cries and a back-thumping group hug. Aileea introduced them as Haidar, Krysztof, and Jasmine. They went and drew bowls of stew from the counter at one end of the mess and joined the two at the table.

"We have to thank you for bringing our Aili back to us," said Haidar. He was a short brown young man with a shock of straight black hair and a round face that reminded Kirk of Chekov. He had more than a little of the *Enterprise* navigator's ebullience, too, though from the tiny network of wrinkles at the outsides of his pitch-black eyes it was clear he was older than Chekov.

"We see her all too little since she went away," said Jasmine. She was a brown-haired, brown-skinned Swimmer woman of early middle years, with amber eyes and a long, somewhat sad mouth. She gave the appearance of having faded from spectacular youthful beauty to a wiry, weary handsomeness. Like the other two hands she was dressed only in brief swim trunks and a utility belt supporting, among other implements, a holstered sidearm. "We feared to see her even less after the attack."

"This will always be my home, Mina," Aileea said in a subdued voice.

"And now our Aili's gone and lured lovely Gita off to the city to join her company," Haidar said. "We have to wonder who'll go next."

"Haidar," said Krysztof sternly. The third outrider was a large man with a craggy, sharp-nosed face, wild and wiry blond hair and beard, and an impressive blond-haired paunch. Like Haidar he showed no outward sign of modification. He might have been a Norm, who in fact had none.

Realizing that his remark wasn't in the best of taste, given the death of Aileea's father, Haidar flushed and paid close attention to his stew.

"I know you work for some kind of security company, Aileea," Kirk said. "But I don't actually know what you do."

Aileea looked away. "Aili, listen," Jasmine said. "What you do is no disgrace. *We* won't hold it against you. Your handsome guest won't either."

She looked at Kirk. When something engaged her interest, her eyes were lively bright. "That spaceship of yours—she's a warship, is she not?"

Kirk nodded. "I don't really like to think of her that way. *Enterprise*'s primary mission is exploration. But she's pretty well armed, and I do draw my pay from an outfit called Starfleet."

"See?" Jasmine said to Aileea.

The green-haired woman nodded. "All right. I'm a soldier, Captain—a professional warrior."

Kirk frowned. "But you work for a security company."

"Our Aili commands a squadron of one thousand," Haidar said proudly. "She holds the rank of colonel."

"We don't have standing armies on Discord, Captain—Jim. And we've been fighting a long time. We have two types of warriors, volunteers and professionals. I'm a professional, under contract to the Discord City Service Corporate."

"She's a wizard pilot and a dead-eye shot," said Haidar. "Even before she went off to get trained, she was as good as the best."

"Not quite, Haidar," Aileea said. "And in the raid, it was Gita who played the heroine."

"That's why you took her from us," said Krysztof.

"She's freeborn, 'Sztof," Jasmine said sternly. "She makes her own destiny, like all Discordians."

"You take your individualism seriously, don't you?" Kirk asked.

"It's one of the reasons our ancestors left Earth," Haidar said. "Along with the fact that the place was busy blowing itself up at the time."

"I'm surprised to see you eating in a communal setting," Kirk said. "It seems to run contrary to your individualist natures."

Haidar laughed. "Do we look as if we dislike each other? We are all free, we are all ourselves, and we live as we choose. But being individuals doesn't mean we cannot work together. The ranch, our profits, our very lives depend on our cooperating. Neither does it mean we cannot enjoy spending time together."

"Sometimes," Krysztof said.

"When we want privacy," Jasmine said, "we have our quarters. And we always have the sea."

Like a moving island, the prawn undulated through clear sun-shot water. Kirk propelled himself alongside the dark metallic bulk of the beast with strokes of the fins strapped to his feet. He hoped he didn't look *too* hurried in his attempt to keep pace with his hostess.

He was bucking the surge of water displaced by the prawn's two hundred-tonne bulk, a slow tidal push, and the pulse of the propulsor membranes, which ran like ribbons along either side of the underside of her carapace, rippling like peristalsis. Moving like a slim fish, silver with sun under water, Aileea swam right up to the creature near the stylized wave brand and patted its shell.

Kirk followed, bubbles from his respirator mask

rising in tickling clouds past his ears. He felt naked beside that armored vastness. He nearly *was*—in the womb-warm ocean of Discord there was no need to wear more than the almost indecently brief trunks Aileea had lent him. There was tension in his guts and throat; no mistaking the fact that the merest accidental twitch by the monster would break him like a cheap toy. But that was wariness, not fear. What he really felt was *awe*.

He reached to touch the shell. It was cool and hard as a starship's hull. "You *eat* these things?" he asked. The button mike glued over his trachea picked up his words without his needing even to vocalize and transmitted them to the bone-conduction speaker behind Aileea's right ear. "Now, this is what I call a jumbo shrimp."

Aileea laughed. "We won't eat Old Lucy. As near as our biologists can reckon, she's over a hundred of our years old. She'd be pretty tough, wouldn't you think?"

"She'd take a lot of cocktail sauce, that's for sure."

He did his best not to sound breathless. He was swimming nearly flat out to keep pace with the giant's unhurried roll. Even Aileea seemed to be exerting herself—a little bit, anyway.

His hostess eased off, let the creature gain way on them. Kirk became aware of the rest of the pod at graze about them, from infants no larger than he was to monsters nearly as intimidating as the matriarch. The microscopic sea life that they sucked into wide funnel-shaped mouths shimmered like fairy dust in the water around them.

"She still lays eggs, though not as often as a younger prawn would," Aileea said. "They're our main stock. We eat the eggs, and we eat the younger prawns. They also exude a waxy substance between the scutes of

166

their belly. We scrape that off and sell it. It's very valuable—it's used in a number of pharmaceuticals and cosmetics."

"You must get a lot out of Old Lucy," Kirk said.

"We do." She grinned at him. *She,* of course, wore no mask. The gills along her neck pulsed to a leisurely rhythm. In her own environment, to which the Discordians' outlaw science had fitted her, Aileea did not seem at all exotic. She seemed as natural—and as beautiful—as the sea life that teemed around them at a respectful distance from the prawns.

If only Moriah could see her like this, Kirk thought. With a pang he realized that would do no good; the deputy commissioner would never see past the woman's differences—and their source. It made him uneasy to think that a woman he felt such honest respect and affection for—a woman with whom he had been more than slightly intimate—could be so blind.

"She's really more the ranch than we are," Aileea was saying. "She's been alive since long before humans got here, and she'll still be swimming long after all of us are dead."

"Those are impressive," Kirk said, eyeing the three-meter dragonflies that hovered over the raft. They had six wings like ruby sheets. Their armor showed blue tiger striping over dull scarlet bellies.

Aileea had the scooter heeled well over to port to circle the thick seaweed mat. Spray raised by their booming passage through the waves misted the left side of Kirk's face and body. Miraculously, it felt *cool.*

"We call them Hinds," she said. "I'm not really sure where that comes from. I think it has something to do with the time our people were in Russia, after the

Soviets captured SS General Prester and his gene-engineering project from the Nazis at the end of the Great Patriotic War."

World War II, he translated mentally. While the Vares came from all races of Earth, ethnic Russians, Pacific Rim Asians, and Polynesians predominated. Mona Arkazha's birth city of Exile in the far south was as thoroughly Russian as contemporary Volgograd—to the delight of Chekov, who was fit to bust waiting for the rotation to allow him to beam down on shore leave. Discordian cultural referents tended to be a lot like the ensign's.

"How does a beast that huge fly?" Kirk asked. They still wore their communicator patches, allowing him to make himself heard above the rush of air and water without shouting.

"High metabolic rate. Discord's a fantastically high-energy ecosystem, Jim, what with all the high-frequency photons Eris puts out. The air those bugs pump out through their exhaust spiracules is only slightly cooler than live steam. We have to put computer filters on our heat-seeker rockets to keep them from locking onto the Hinds."

Kirk grimaced. That was another facet of Discordian life—talk of weaponry was never absent long.

"What do they eat?" he asked.

As if in reply a Hind dipped down to the mat and rose up again clutching a wildly waving joint-legged thing in its chitin-covered palps. "They'll eat *you*, if you give them half a chance, though they couldn't lift a full-grown Micro. There are *reasons* we carry guns, James Kirk, and not just what your delightful Doctor McCoy would call our cussedness. Hang on."

The clear metal-crystal canopy sealed itself above

them, cutting off the spray and the sound of their passage. The scooter nosed down; the sea bubbled up at Kirk's face, and then they were flying underwater, beneath the raft. He marveled at the life-forms that thronged around, and in its shaggy green underside: steel-spined worms like demon caterpillars; moving blobs of brightly colored jelly; things like rolling tangles of knotted gray string, strung with plump yellow nodules. Three-eyed raft-dodger fish, fat and agile, played tag with the scooter.

The scooter was not properly a two-person vehicle. Aileea had adjusted her padded pilot seat so that Kirk could slide in between her and the back, where he got to ride about the sea at alarming speed, clutching handrails down by his thighs. With the craft sealed off like this it was even harder than before not to be aware of the fact that he had a beautiful, virtually naked woman pressed against the front of him.

He forced his mind off the subject. Aileea drove too fast for his comfort, but he had to admit that Haidar was right about her piloting skills. They flew among schools of eels like animated ribbons, giant swimming insects holding serious-looking pincers before them, clouds of colorful fish that looked a lot like . . . well, *fish*.

"If it wouldn't cost you time in our decompression chamber, I'd take you to see the bottom," Aileea said. "It's only three hundred meters down here. Our seas are mostly shallow—though Hellsgate Rift is ten klicks deep in places, and more."

The canopy shook. A sound like thunder reached Kirk's ears and shivered in his marrow. "What was that?"

"Detonations."

"Are you under attack?" Visions of himself getting

169

caught up in a battle flooded his mind like water through a breached hull. He could imagine what Commissioner Wayne would make of *that* when they got back to the Federation. He realized in a rueful flash that he had begun thinking of her as an adversary. It was an uncomfortable transition to have to face.

Aileea was shaking her head. "That's Lev and the new 'rider, Magda, trying to drive off predators with rockets. Our wrangler robots project sonic vibrations to keep predators out and our stock in, but sometimes predators sound beneath the coverage—or just come through regardless."

"What kind of predators do you need to hunt with rockets?" Kirk asked, looking around the ocean with a whole new interest.

"Sea dragons, *akyula, volk,* kraken. They are—let me remember my lessons of Earth—similar to plesiosaurs, sharks, reptilian orcas, and giant squid."

"They prey on the likes of Old Lucy?"

She laughed. "We ranch fish and other sea creatures a lot less spectacular than the prawns. With the prawns our main problem is parasites. Not even a big kraken would dare try to drag Old Lucy down. Unless the legends are true."

"Legends?"

She glanced back. "Are you easily alarmed, Captain?"

His turn to laugh. "I guess not. Any creature big enough to eat Old Lucy, we wouldn't make a decent *hors d'oeuvre* for."

"Good saying, Captain. Our legends speak of the mightiest of all kraken: Leviathan, the Devil in the Sea."

"I wouldn't want to meet him. Or her."

A shrug. "I wouldn't worry. Leviathan doesn't really exist. He's just a story we use to scare ourselves with—and a personification of the all-powerful State we all fear. Thomas Hobbes, and all that."

"They teach you a lot about Earth in school."

"We remember where we came from. Terra rejected us, not vice versa."

When they returned to the float the sun was already low—that short rotation period again. The eastern horizon was weighed down under towers of white cloud that bulked upward until the jet stream shaved their heads off flat.

Aileea froze on the deck, shading her eyes to stare off to the east. Kirk looked that way, and shortly made out a tiny black fleck sliding across the sky. It slowly grew larger.

She lifted a communicator from her belt and called the tower. "Mansur," she said, "are we expecting company?"

The gray giant had a voice like a wire brush skimming steel. "The aircraft is friendly. Do not be afraid."

She looked at the communicator. "That's all he's going to say, isn't it?" She stuck the unit back on her belt and stood watching the sky.

It seemed natural to Kirk to come and stand right behind her right shoulder. She did not move away.

"Storm coming," was all she said.

The fleck grew larger, became another verti like the one Aileea and Kirk had flown out in, with similar bulky pods affixed to the sides of the fuselage. As it rotated its wings upright to hover, Aileea gestured

Kirk back against the ranch house. With the floating pad occupied, the only place for the craft to touch down was on the deck itself.

It landed in a whirlwind of furnace-hot air. The hatch on the pilot side opened and a young woman dropped lightly to the mat. She was shorter than Aileea and emphatically rounder in a loose white blouse and blue and red pantaloons. Her skin was cinnamon, her hair a luxuriant dark blue mane.

Aileea ran to her and hugged her. The two waltzed each other in a laughing circle. "Gita!" Aileea said. "What a wonderful surprise to see you!"

"Yes," the newcomer said in one of those contraltos that ran down your spine. "It's been all of three days since I saw you last."

"I still haven't gotten used to having you around all the time."

Holding her arm around the shorter woman's waist, Aileea steered her toward Kirk. "Jim, there's someone I'd like you to meet. Her name's Gita. She's my oldest friend, not to mention the newest recruit in my unit."

Gita stepped forward, away from Aileea, and walked right up to Kirk. She had a long straight nose and black eyes deep as Hellsgate Rift. At close range she had the same sort of brute-force sultriness of an Orion slave dancer, except she wasn't green.

"So this is your starman, Aili," she said, reaching out a fingernail to run down the center of Kirk's chest.

Over her shoulder he saw Aileea droop. The proud and competent warrior suddenly looked like a wet, sad bird. *What's going on?*

Gita spun to face her friend. "Well, guess what? I couldn't let you outdo me. So I brought home one of my own!"

Around the snout of the aircraft came a compact

172

figure wearing a Hawaiian shirt, a Panama hat, and swim trunks. It held a seabag just like Kirk's over its shoulder. It stopped.

"Captain?"

"Mr. Sulu?"

The helmsman faltered. "Um, Gita—maybe this isn't such a hot idea—"

"Nonsense, Mr. Sulu. At ease. Man does not live by slime mold alone."

Gita went to Sulu's side. He slid a hard brown arm around her.

"I'll say," he said.

Chapter Sixteen

CAPTAIN KAIN held up the glass of heavy but expertly cut crystal so that the green liquid within caught the torchlight and seemed to sparkle. "To the success of your mission," he said, "and the return of peace to this planet."

His black eyes met the green eyes of Moriah Wayne. They drank.

The Klingon mission was headquartered in bunkers blasted out of the lava of cliffs on the coast not far from Swift's capital. Klingon doctrine preached austerity and resistance to discomfort, but the Klingons weren't deranged on the subject. Or at least Kain wasn't. He kept the rock-walled bunkers air-conditioned to approach the norm of the Klingon homeworld.

Several hours before he had had the climate controls adjusted so that this chamber actually warmed a few degrees, to a temperature an Earther would find pleasant. Kain was a most considerate host.

Wayne looked at her glass. "Wonderful vintage, Captain. It's tart, but marvelously refreshing. It tastes —it tastes like spring somehow. Is it Klingon?"

He shook his head. "No. It is a Susuru beverage, fermented from a fruit they brought with them—" He paused, scowled.

"Brought with them—" Wayne prompted.

"From a distant archipelago, on the other side of the world. It's, ah, it's extinct there now, of course. The Earther intruders clear-cut the island where the treasure fruit grew, left the ecosystem so devastated it could never recover."

"Really? How tragic." She shook her head. Tonight she wore a sheer green off-the-shoulder gown. Her hair was done up in an intricate knot, and the torches burning in black iron sconces on the walls sent highlights chasing each other through it like tiny flames. "And the settlers claim they don't use the land for anything at all."

A rich laugh rumbled up from Kain's chest. He had a greyhound build, long-legged, narrow at hip and belly, big in the chest and shoulders.

"In your experience, Commissioner," he asked, "are your people generally addicted to truthfulness?"

"My people are addicted to many vices, Captain," she said, "but telling the truth isn't one of them."

"What about indiscipline. Is that one of them, perhaps?"

She dropped her eyes to her plate. The meal was steamed sweet grasses and broiled fillets of the white flesh of some sea beast, served with an astringent green sauce that reminded her of Japanese mustard. It was an excellent meal. It did not accord with the reputation Klingon cuisine enjoyed in the Federation for being as fierce as the warriors who ate it.

Should I be surprised? she thought. *Captain Kain is living refutation of most of our stereotypes.*

"Captain Kirk is a man who believes in doing the right thing," she said softly, "just as you do."

"Is it right to defy the orders of one's superiors?"

"I'm not really in his chain of command, after all. I'm only a civilian."

Why am I defending him? she wondered. *He's ready to sell justice down the river for his Earth human prejudices.*

But something compelled her to take Kirk's part. As something had compelled her to defend her father against those who said he was tyrannical and over-bearing, that his personal ambition and lust for power had done damage to the Federation.

"It isn't just that he disrespects you, Moriah."

She looked up sharply. His one good eye was looking at her in just the right way—forthright, challenging, yet not judgmental.

"Does he not also defy his own superiors of Starfleet?"

She dropped her eyes again. "Yes," she almost whispered.

"The duty of the warrior," Kain said, "is to serve. To obey, in the interests of the greater good. Or is it otherwise in the Federation?"

"We permit the individual greater rein," she said brittlely. "Too great. Everyone thinks he has the right to pass judgment for himself on any issue—that his conscience outweighs the voice of the community."

"Does that make you strong?" He turned the wine-glass in fingers that seemed to her capable of crushing it at a squeeze. She had never known a man as powerful as this. Not even her father.

"It divides us. Makes us weak, makes us a pack of

self-absorbed, self-interested"—she groped for a word—"thrill seekers. The lust for personal gratification overwhelms everything."

"We Klingons practice abnegation of the self in service of the whole." He smiled. "Doubtless you are more advanced than we."

"No." She shook her head. "It's you who are the wiser."

He sat back in his chair and studied her. At length his shook his splendid black-maned head.

"Moriah, Moriah. How long are you going to let him do this to you?"

"He is strong," she almost whispered. "Willful. He's blind to what's happening here, he's deaf to my words."

"An ancient Earther philosopher said there are none so blind as those who will not see."

A tremor ran through the subterranean chamber, a whisper of the song of sliding crystal plates way off across the ocean floor. Such microshocks had rattled the tableware on and off throughout the meal. Kain held up a finger.

"Listen. Do you not hear the planet itself crying out for requital? You are not deaf. Nor are you blind."

She stared at her plate. "In three days the Susuru launch their offensive. Maybe they'll settle the issue."

Kain's lips curved in a bitter smile. "The Susuru are peaceful folk, as you have seen—they have no skill at bloodletting. We are mighty warriors, but we are also few. The settlers are violent criminals. They all have arms, and they have no scruples about using them." He shook his head. "All that is certain is that the seas of Island will run red with blood."

"What can I *do?"* She shook her head, a desperate look on her face. "It's his ship, his crew. I've sent countless requests to Starfleet for support, but the subspace delay is so great out here, and who knows what his cronies in the military hierarchy might do to cover up his insubordination."

"You can act," Kain said, and his voice rang with the steel of command. "You can first master yourself —stop this self-pity and confusion. You are stronger than that, Moriah."

She looked at him with huge and wondering eyes. "Do you really think so?"

He nodded. "I know so. And after you have mastered yourself—and only then—you can master the situation."

She bit her lip. "But I don't see what I can do. Everything's so confused."

"Didn't your father teach you self-discipline?" His voice was low. She snapped her head back as if he had slapped her.

"That's better," he said. "Your spirit shines through your eyes. When that occurs, I can *see* the strength in you."

He rose. "The time will come when I can offer concrete assistance, Moriah. But you must be prepared to assist me in return."

She stood up slowly. "I can't do anything—that is, your people and mine are enemies. At least on paper."

"I will ask you to do nothing that isn't *right*," he said, and his lone eye bored through her like a neutronium drill. "Everything I do, I do for the good of this world, and the Susuru to whom it belongs."

She shook her head in confusion. He came forward, extending a hand.

"Come. There is an observation port with armored glass overlooking the bay. We can watch the fury of the storm spend itself on the rocks below and revel in the wild power of this world."

He took her by the arms. For a moment she stood there, quivering, seeming small and frail next to him. Then she tore herself away. "I—can't. I really must be getting back to the ship."

She wore a communicator hung from a loose elastic band around her right wrist. She flipped it open. "This is Commissioner Wayne calling *Enterprise*."

"*Enterprise*. Lieutenant Kyle here, Commissioner."

"Lock onto my coordinates and beam me aboard at once."

"Yes, Commissioner."

Kain held his hands out to his sides. "Run away, little girl," he said, almost gently. "Run away at the speed of light. You'll find you cannot escape yourself."

She gave him a lambent look. She became gold light, became a shimmer and a trill, and then became nothing at all. He stood looking at the place where she had been. Then he threw his head back and laughed. It was not the polite laugh he showed the Earthers, hearty as it seemed to them. It was a full-throated Klingon laugh, wild and raw, like the roar of an elemental beast.

He heard the rasp of a boot sole on the stone behind him. He turned. His aide stood behind him.

"*luHoHta' Sogh nuqneH,*" he snarled. (*Lieutenant Lu Kok Tak, what do you want?*)

"*Qeyn HoD wa'DIch,*" she replied, speaking his name and rank and offering the appropriate salute.

She was a tall young woman, who bore the insignia of a senior lieutenant. She had a straight nose and high, slanting cheekbones. Most Klingons would have called her features overfine—indeed, insipid. Kain found her quite appealing. But then, everybody said he had degenerate tastes, from long contact with Earthers.

Her name had the meaning—poetic and evocative to Klingon ears—of *They killed him.* It hearkened back to the upshot of a particularly glorious episode in the long history of her clan.

"The monitors functioned perfectly," she said. "The whole disgusting scene is recorded."

"maj," he said, expressing satisfaction.

She stood beside the table, distaste twisting her face.

"You're still here," Kain said.

She reached out and picked up a plate. "Why do you subject yourself to such insipid filth? Where is the pipius claw, where the good serpent worm? The *thlIngan* food?"

She spilled the food deliberately onto the white cloth that had been laid across the table of native hardwood. "Do you now find pale *tera'ngan* meat more to your liking?"

He looked at her. She took a step back and set down the plate.

"Lieutenant, you are an exemplary officer and have made yourself highly useful to me. You are of the lineage of *tlheDon,* my first captain, to whom I owe a heavy debt of blood. Still, do not take it upon yourself to presume too much upon my tolerance, *luHoHta'."*

She lowered her head, but her strong jaw worked. Kain walked to her, put his hand under her chin, and raised her face.

"What?"

Her eyes blazed up at him. "Why do you degrade yourself, catering to this foolish Earther woman? She is no part of the plan."

He scowled. She did not give ground.

"It is *my* plan," he said. "It was my conception. It is mine to implement."

"But—but what of your *vengeance?*"

Kain raised his head. "It, too, must wait."

Lu Kok Tak's jaw dropped. For all that they were bound by an iron discipline that knew neither mercy nor exception, it was unheard of for a Klingon to place anything in the way of revenge. Not even duty.

"But—" she began.

He walked to the far end of the table, turned, and looked at her. "Who are you to talk of my vengeance? *Who?*"

The last word was a bark that rocked her back on her boot heels.

"Do you think I do not *know* what Kirk has cost me? When my mission failed on Endikon, and my party was discovered and trapped by the local authorities, it was my captain on whom the bulk of the blame fell. Your grandfather, Kledon. A superior is responsible for the failures of his underlings. Mine cost him his life."

He touched the scar above his missing left eye. "I was permitted to atone by putting out my own eye with a red-hot dagger."

The lieutenant stood listening with head bowed. She had heard this story before. But a Klingon did not interrupt her superior officer. Especially when he was *Qeyn,* and when this mood was on him.

"That was the first debt I owe to James Kirk." He dropped his hand to the *kligat* hilt. "And then, two years ago, his allies on Capella Four murdered *QaS,* my brother, with this very weapon!"

"Then why do you delay, my captain?" blurted Lu Kok Tak.

"bortaS bIr jablu'DI'reH QaQqu' nay," Kain quoted. "'Revenge is a dish that is best served cold.'"

"My grandfather is twenty years cold," Lu Kok Tak said. "Your eye is twenty years gone. How much colder must your vengeance be before you dine?"

Kain advanced and raised a hand. She still did not turn away. Slowly he lowered his fist and walked away from her.

"There is more at stake here," he said. "Much more. This planet is rich beyond imagining in resources. Our empire is poor. Our enemies are richer than we and more numerous. This planet is not merely an instrument in my hands"—he made a gesture first of scooping, then of crushing—"that I can use up in the fulfillment of my vengeance and toss away like an empty wrapper. It is a treasure, which must be secured for the Empire. As for my revenge—"

He turned to her with a smile. "It will come, Lieutenant, it will come. But how much sweeter will the destruction of *Enterprise* and her captain James Kirk taste, when captain and ship have disgraced themselves and their Federation by playing party to the destruction of a colony of their own precious Earthers?"

Chapter Seventeen

FOR DINNER Mansur set up a table in the observation dome atop the tower. They ate to the accompaniment of a fabulous display of lightning, lancing and pulsing overhead.

"What happens if the Susuru attack?" Sulu asked, nervously eyeing the unattended sensor displays and control consoles.

"They wouldn't dare," Gita scoffed. *"We* wouldn't, and they're not as good on the sea as we are."

"It doesn't matter, anyway," Aileea said. "There's always somebody monitoring the Command Center, which is way below the waterline. That's where the house is fought from."

As she spoke she sidled over closer to Kirk. She had put on a flimsy white smock that came down to her hips for dinner. He was both relieved and disappointed.

The meal was excellent, paced to the slow roll of the sea. Gyros and computerized ballast management damped the rocking imparted by the waves, but did not try to suppress it altogether. Discordians preferred to live with the feel of the rhythms of their ocean home.

The soft, flickering amber instrument glow wasn't romantic candlelight, but it would do in a pinch. Kirk enjoyed the sense of easy camaraderie he felt with Sulu. It wasn't something he experienced often, except perhaps with Spock and Bones, his two best friends. The invisible barrier of *command* lay between him and the rest of his crew—even the bridge complement.

Not that Sulu paid much attention to him. The helmsman spent most of the evening conversing with his escort in whispers and giggles.

At one point Kirk noticed Aileea studying Gita across the table with a curiously blank expression. Her voluptuous friend was engrossed in Sulu and didn't notice the scrutiny. Clearly rivalry passed between these women as well as friendship. Kirk suddenly realized why Aileea had seemed deflated by Gita's arrival: She assumed Kirk would make a dive for her old friend's rather more obvious charms.

It's nice to know she cares.

He was awakened by almost being tossed from his bunk, even though it was mounted on gimbals. He flailed an arm, found the lamp mounted on the wall by the bed, and flipped it on. Pulling on a shirt and trousers, he staggered across the pitching floor and out into the hall.

Aileea was already there, dressed in a light robe. "I was coming for you."

"I guess the storm has caught up with us for real," he said, as the hull reverberated to a crash of thunder.

She nodded. "Come with me."

She led him up the circular stair, which seemed to be trying to buck him off. The added gravity load was only 20 percent, but with the storm rocking the ranch house wildly it felt as if he had a full-grown man strapped on his back and cackling in his ear. Somehow he fought his way to the mess.

Gita and Sulu were already there, with the ports unshuttered and the lights out. The sky was a constant blaze of lightning. Black waves washed over the deck and reached black tentacles for the uppermost cylinder. The float lurched in random directions like a drunk trying to balance on a medicine ball.

"It's a little unnerving, isn't it, Captain," Sulu said, "to know that if something goes wrong we can't beam out of here because of the storm."

Kirk stared out at the storm. "You have a talent for looking at the bright side of things, Mr. Sulu."

"I'm sure everything will work out fine, Captain."

"No worries," Gita said serenely.

Aileea had been speaking into an intercom. Now she came and stood beside Kirk. It seemed natural to put his arm around her. She leaned against him.

"Watch," she said.

The plunging of the float eased, even though the waves rose up higher and higher. "Captain, we're sinking!" Sulu exclaimed. He gazed wildly around, eyes agleam in the lightning glow.

"It's all right, Mr. Sulu. It's intentional—I think."

Aileea nodded. "This one's too bad to ride out. We're going under till it passes."

The water rose up in a black froth, seeming to wash the pandemonium of the storm up and away. Then they were floating in peace, surrounded by the weird blue-fluorescing undersea life of Discord.

In time Kirk noticed that Sulu and Gita had slipped away. He hugged Aileea close to him. Then he kissed her hair and went away to bed alone, feeling no end of virtuous, and a fool.

"Uh-oh," Aileea said. Her fingers stabbed at the controls of her aircraft radio.

The storm had passed, leaving no trace. The sky was clear, except for a few stringy clouds like egg white trailed in hot grease. Waverider Ranch had surfaced again, none the worse for wear. Kirk had the option of beaming straight back up to the *Enterprise,* but out of consideration for his hostess he was making the long ride back to Discord City with her.

Aileea listened, her body taut, then spoke into her headset microphone, too low for Kirk to hear. She punched the computer keypad, sucked her lower lip, and nodded. Then she pulled off her headset and looked at Kirk.

"Stilters in small boats, attacking a Harmony harvest ship forty klicks from here."

"What are you going to do?"

The banking of the aircraft wings answered him. "I'm going to help. Those silly Harmonians are the next thing to pacifists. The Stilters will tear them apart."

She glanced at Kirk. "The storm is over," she said. "You can beam back up to your ship if you're worried about your neutrality." She could not keep a tincture of bitterness out of her voice.

"No. I should see this."

"You're armed," she said, with a nod toward the phaser he wore at his belt. "Will you fight?"

"I can't."

She showed her teeth and said no more.

In a few minutes Kirk could see the wakes, white lines on blue, and then he made out the mass of the seaweed harvester, and finally the Susuru boats, circling like Orcas attacking a blue whale.

"I've called the ranch," Aileea said. "Gita will be here as soon as she can."

"Sulu—"

"Will he fight?"

Kirk looked grim. "I'm sure he would, if he had any choice. But he doesn't."

Aileea looked at him. "But you, as captain, have the privilege of following your conscience and defying your commissioner with impunity."

"Not exactly with impunity."

She shook her head. "It's a hell of a system you live under."

As she spoke she had descended until the belly of the craft was almost brushing the waves, which a fresh breeze blowing counter to the current was whipping into a chop.

A pink flash from ahead—another. Aileea made an exasperated sound at the base of her throat. "There go the Harmonians. Missing again."

"You have lasers?" Kirk asked.

"A few. I put my trust in bullet launchers. Lasers're energy hogs, and as much energy as we've got access to, it's tough to make it portable enough to make them useful."

She looked at him. "I suppose you've solved that problem, with those phasers of yours. You and the Klingons."

He nodded.

He goggled then, because they were closing at a fantastic rate with a small boat, from the fan deck of which a pair of heavy machine guns were raking the

187

harvester. From this angle it looked as if a head-on collision were imminent.

Aileea flipped a cover up on the top of her stick and rested her thumb against a button. Cross hairs appeared on the windscreen in front of her. She adjusted the bank of the aircraft and hit the button briefly.

A snarl. The aircraft decelerated. Kirk saw splinters fly white from the bow of the Susuru boat. It instantly lost way and was settling by the bows as Aileea pulled up her nose to flash overhead.

"Chin Gatling," she said. "One down, five to go." Then: "Draft them all, anyway. They're boarding!"

Kirk looked quickly and saw two of the boats bobbing unattended, one to either side of the tender's broad, flat stern.

"No time to mess with these fools," Aileea said. She zoomed a hundred meters and hit the controls that changed the wing aspect from horizontal to vertical. The verti lost speed as if the air had suddenly gotten thicker.

The aircraft vibrated. Kirk glanced out his window and noticed a line of holes in the starboard wing.

"Those are—"

"Bullet holes," Aileea said, pivoting the aircraft to face back toward the ship. "We're low and slow. We're a good target right about now."

Before he could react to that good news she pressed another button. Fire and smoke rippled into Kirk's right peripheral vision. Explosions fountained water next to the slab-sided hull of the Harmonian vessel. A Susuru boat burst through the spray curtain on its side and struck the ocean upside down, plowing a great white furrow in the water.

"Strapped-on rocket pods," Aileea said. "Where're the other two boats?"

Kirk pointed. He opened his mouth. It took him a moment to find his voice.

"Running," he said.

She nodded. "Good. Good boys. They've got the idea."

Like a giant predatory insect the verti dropped its nose and swept forward. Brown Susuru bobbed in the water ahead, their ruffs matted miserably. Kirk tensed, fearing his escort would machine gun the helpless beings in the water. He wasn't prepared to sit still for that.

But what am I going to do? he wondered. *Stun her with my phaser? She's* driving.

She passed over the swimmers without a glance, flying toward the harvest ship itself. A gun battle raged on the deck. Several figures lay still or kicking on the open afterdeck. Others fired automatic weapons from the stern and a tangle of machinery amidships, attacking the tall superstructure forward. Kirk thought he could count at least twenty figures in the boarding party. Not all of them had the attenuated oddly proportioned outlines of Susuru.

"This is bad," Aileea said. As she came alongside the ship she was pivoting again, clockwise, so that her gun bore along the vessel's beam. A rush of Susuru was just crossing the afterdeck. Several quick pulses of Gatling fire swept them away.

Kirk wasn't watching the carnage on the deck. He was watching Aileea's face. He saw no pleasure there, no exaltation—merely a drawn-back grimace, as if she were doing something necessary but unpleasant.

The ship stopped and hovered. From amid the metallic tangle a pale flash. The windscreen starred between Aileea and Kirk. Kirk ducked as metal-crystal flakes showered him like snow.

"Surrender, you stilt-legged idiots," Aileea snarled. "I've got the drop on you!"

More shots reached out for them. An incautious Susuru blasted away at them from the rail aft. With apparent reluctance Aileea twitched the nose that way and blew him apart with a short burst.

"You don't like killing them!" Kirk said, shouting over engine whine and gunfire.

"No! It's not a challenge. It's just sad."

She tweaked the collective for her left and right engines, making the aircraft dip and bob. She searched for clear targets. Muzzle flashes winked among the machinery. Aileea fired a burst amidships, spinning a cloud of debris into the air.

"No," she said angrily. "I can't just shoot up the ship at random."

She reached behind her seat and came up with a stubby machine pistol with a curved feed device in front of the handgrip. "Forgive me for what I'm about to do," she said.

The aircraft darted forward and dropped onto the afterdeck. The engine noise whined down the scale as Aileea dove clear of the aircraft, hit the deck, rolled, and came up shooting. Kirk twisted in his seat. A pair of Susuru in the stern dropped their own machine pistols and dove over the rail.

He already knew the aircraft wasn't bulletproof. It was, however, an excellent target. And even if no one wanted to shoot at it per se, it was still big and in the way. Kirk jerked open his own door and threw himself down on the ubiquitous fiber mat that covered the deck.

Aileea ran toward the amidships jumble. A pair of Susuru stood up and opened fire on her. Screaming, she held up her weapon and swung it side to side, spraying them. The one on her right went down under repeated hits. The other threw his piece down and fled.

Bullets gouged the matting by the heel of Kirk's right boot. He didn't know who was shooting at him. Under the circumstances, he didn't care. He tried to spring up. Unaccustomed gravity staggered him. He got to all fours and scrambled forward.

He started to lunge into an alcove surrounded by comfortably solid-looking housings. A brown furry figure blocked him—a Susuru clutching some kind of short two-handed gun. It shied away and started to point the weapon at Kirk. He punched it in the nose. It collapsed onto the backward-angled knees of its forelimbs, covered its snout with its hands, and began to cry.

Kirk stepped back. *What the hell am I doing here?* He felt like a bully.

Bullets from somewhere cracked past his head. He dove willy-nilly into the machinery, managing to avoid running into any more lurking foes or busting a shin on anything. He ducked under a foot-thick conduit and took stock of the situation.

Aileea was rampaging around the metal jungle somewhere. He heard her hollering and shooting. Shots were still cracking off in various directions, bullets striking metal and tumbling off with nasty little supersonic-edged whines. He felt the weight of the hand phaser at his belt, longed to draw it; he was at the mercy of anyone who stumbled across him. But he did not dare draw a weapon unless he was prepared to stun anybody he saw with a gun, Aileea included. And he was unwilling to drop her and allow the Susuru to take the ship by default.

It was a strange sensation, tasting of copper in his

mouth like the trace-element tang of Discordian food. He was *Kirk,* the fearless starship captain, always in the first party to beam down into the unknown, always the first to seize control of any situation. *And he couldn't do a thing.* Enforced passivity made him itch all over, as if he had been sprinkled with tiny metal shavings.

Nor was he impartial as he should have been. He ached to do something for Aileea. She was obviously good at this. And the Susuru's morale was just as obviously not good. But a lone woman, however formidable, against twelve or twenty well-armed foes was not sane odds. Sooner or later the Susuru were bound to get bold, or lucky.

A noise like a giant pillowcase ripping. A ringing boom, and a ball of yellow flame rolled up above the portside rail aft. Then Gita's verti roared overhead, residual smoke drooling from the rocket pod with which it had just exploded one of the Susuru boats moored at the harvester's stern.

Kirk heard shrill despairing yips. Then he heard heavy muffled thumps as Susuru began to toss their weapons out on the mat. He saw one step out with hands clasped over the small of its back in an unmistakable sign of surrender.

"You can come out, now, Captain," he heard Aileea call. "It's over."

Frowning, he emerged to find the green-haired Discordian herding Susuru into a disconsolate huddle under the wing of her aircraft. Blood streamed down the right side of her face.

His heart in his throat, he started forward. "You're shot," he said.

"No. Just clumsy. I banged my head on a flange."

"So what happens now?"

"We don't make a practice of feeding prisoners," Aileea said. Kirk's eyes got bleak. "So first we get Gita and some boats out to pick up survivors from the boats I sank, and then we find some scow to ship these critters home to their pals in."

"You just . . . let them go?"

"As I said, we don't want to feed them." She grinned. "Besides, it drives their High Command insane, figuring out what to do with them. Their morale's shaky enough without survivors coming back to spread tales of defeat."

"You don't hate them?"

She looked at the prisoners, sad slumps of dejection. It was impossible to imagine them offering anybody harm again.

"But they killed your father," he said, not because he wanted to reopen a wound, but because he could not fathom how this young woman, so passionately devoted to defending her sense of self, could not want vengeance on those who had aggressed against her and hers.

Her response caught him completely by surprise. She spun toward him, bringing up her machine pistol one-handed. Her face was twisted into the purest look of rage he had ever seen.

Too stunned by her abrupt betrayal to respond, he watched as her finger tightened on the trigger, saw the muzzle flare dance, and felt impacts along his rib cage.

But they were feather pats, shockwaves from the mini-sonic booms the bullets made in passing. Beside Kirk's right boot a patch of deck glowed pink and vanished.

Kirk wheeled. A young Klingon with an ensign's emblem on his sash and blood streaming down his face from a gouge on his cranial crest staggered back with half a dozen holes in his chest. A phaser dropped from his hand. He clutched at himself and collapsed to the deck.

"You know who killed my father, Captain?" Aileea called. "It was them. The ridgeheads, the *Kofirlar*. For forty years we fought the Stilters. For forty years we always beat them. They never hurt us so badly that we really felt the sting.

"Now these Klingons have come, and everything has changed. They're promising the Stilters the means to wipe us off the planet—if they can't get you to do the job for them."

She ejected the spent magazine onto the deck.

"Now we have somebody to hate."

Chapter Eighteen

"AH, EXILE," Chekov was sighing when Kirk returned to the bridge. The young ensign had just returned from his own leave rotation on the surface and was regaling Lieutenant Kyle with his adventures. "They stuffed me with beef stroganoff and wodka until I could barely move. And the *women—*"

Kyle gave him a skeptical look. "What were they doing *giving* all this away? I thought that lot were fanatical laissez-faire capitalist types."

"That does not mean they don't know how to be hospitable," Chekov said. "They wanted me to tell them stories and more stories of life in the Federation, and the strange and wonderful planets I've seen."

"And they didn't present you the check when you left?"

Chekov shook his head. "It was walue for walue," he said. "They said the entertainment I gave them more than paid for my room and board."

"Rum lot of capitalists, if you ask me."

"Bah. Don't talk to me of capitalism. We Russians *inwented* capitalism."

With a sigh of satisfaction Kirk settled into his command chair. He was back where he belonged. The temperature was normal, the gravity was normal, and the very light didn't make him itch as if he were receiving a lethal dose of radiation.

There were plenty of unpleasant ramifications of the encounter he'd been embroiled in earlier to ponder. He would ponder them later. Right now he was filled with the rather foolish elation of once more having been shot at and survived.

He nodded to Chekov at the helmsman's station, then looked at his communications officer. "Lieutenant," he said, "you're looking especially radiant today."

"Why, thank you, Captain," Uhura said.

"Is there something—different—about your appearance?"

She turned her head to display an orange flower behind her ear. "Jason gave it to me, sir. It's called a passion bloom."

"Well, it's hardly regulation, Lieutenant—but under the circumstances I suppose we can overlook it."

"Thank you, Captain."

"Status report, Mr. Chekov."

"Captain, all systems are fully functional. We have no personnel in the brig. As of this moment, we have one hundred and seven crew taking shore leave on the surface of the planet, including Mr. Spock, who is at a deep-sea research station in the southern hemisphere, near the oceanic trench the human colonists call Hellsgate Rift, and Mr. Sulu, who is—"

"In capable hands, I know, Ensign. What about Commissioner Wayne?"

"She beamed aboard at twenty-three seventeen ship's time last night, sir. She remains on board—"

"Captain," Uhura said, "I'm receiving a coded subspace communication from Starfleet. It's directed to your personal attention. I—I'm getting one for Commissioner Wayne, too."

"Forward hers to her quarters, Lieutenant," he said. "I'll take mine in the briefing room. And kindly pass the word for Mr. Spock to beam up as soon as possible."

"Yes, sir."

Concern made Admiral Douglas Satanta's prerecorded face heavier than usual. "Captain, Deputy Commissioner Wayne says you've been refusing to carry out your orders. She's been raising seven kinds of hell with Starfleet Command. She's got Commissioner Hightower camped out on the front steps of the Federation Council.

"You may not realize just how powerful Interspecies Affairs has gotten. Starfleet has been receiving a lot of heat recently, about so-called human 'cultural imperialism' and domination of nonhuman sentients. Hightower's been capitalizing on that to increase his own power—and Wayne's his fair-haired lass. The two of them are making you out as accomplice to the rape of the Susuru. And the Council's buying it."

For a moment he just looked out of the screen. Kirk felt a crawling sensation at the pit of his belly. There were few things in this universe Douglas Satanta was afraid to confront. Even the truth.

"I don't know what you're doing out there, Jim. I'm sure it's what you think best. But it's past the time for that now.

"A fleet of transports just left this Starbase. Its commander has orders to bring back the human colonists from Okeanos. If you don't have them ready to leave at that point, he has orders to bring you back in irons."

He spread his big, capable hands. "Jim, I've done all I can to run interference for you. But it's out of my hands now."

The screen went blank. Kirk sat back in his chair and stared at it for a long time.

"That's the trouble with feeling as if you're on top of the world," he finally said. "It's always a sure sign you and it are about to swap places."

He got up and walked back to the bridge.

Uhura was working her console again. "Captain, a message from the surface. It's the Susuru leader, sir."

He waved. "Main screen, Lieutenant."

The face of Swift appeared. "Captain," he said, "your delays have become insufferable. You clearly intend to take no measures to remove your people from our world."

Kirk took a deep breath. "Lead Walker, I have told you I would take no action until you and the Discordians had gotten together at the negotiation table. At this point, it's you who's doing the delaying."

The Susuru made a chopping gesture, inward toward its keellike breastbone. "There will be no negotiation. There must be an end. Therefore, I have ordered my forces to prepare to launch nuclear-tipped rockets at the Discordian cities when my deadline expires, two days hence."

"No," Kirk said softly.

The ears tipped forward. "I beg your pardon, Captain?"

"No. You are not going to do that. Because if you do—if you *try*—I will blast every stick of your military equipment that's bigger than a rifle into slag. I'll sink your ships. I'll ground your aircraft. I'll bring your commerce to a halt."

Swift's ruff stood on end. "Captain, you cannot—"

"Oh, but I can," Kirk said, leaning forward. "Just try me, Swift."

"I invoke the Prime Directive!" the Susuru said. "You cannot intervene."

Kirk smiled. "It won't fly, Swift. You invited us in here. You insisted that we come and involve ourselves in the affairs of your planet. Indeed, you said we couldn't refuse, because your enemies were our people and therefore our responsibility. Yes, the Prime Directive exists, Lead Walker, and it exists to prevent starship officers like me from interfering in the affairs of planets like yours. But guess what? *You waived it when you asked us in here.*"

"This is an intolerable breach of our sovereignty!"

"No, it isn't. If you want to see one, though, make one move I can even *possibly* interpret as leading up to a nuclear attack on the Discordians. Kirk out!"

He sighed. "What else could go wrong?"

The turbolift door hissed open. "What is going on here?" the voice of Commissioner Wayne demanded.

"I should know better than to ever ask that question," Kirk said.

"What?" Wayne said, coming forward.

"Nothing, Commissioner."

She smiled. "I take it you've heard the news from Starfleet?" she said. Her cheeks were flushed, her eyes glittered with triumphant malice.

"I have."

"So now you will naturally comply with your orders."

Mr. Spock stepped onto the bridge. "Captain, I understand you summoned me."

"Yes, Mr. Spock, I did. I just received two disturbing pieces of news."

He saw Wayne frown, perplexed. "First, I am informed that Starfleet has dispatched a fleet of transports to remove the Discordians. I'm to have the colonists ready to depart by the time they arrive."

A flicker of concern passed over the aquiline face and was quickly suppressed. "Perhaps that should not surprise us, Captain."

"Perhaps it should not. Second, the Susuru have just announced that they intend to wage nuclear war upon their neighbors."

"We cannot certainly permit that, Captain."

"I've already made that abundantly clear to Lead Walker Swift."

"What did you tell him?" Wayne asked. Her eyes were strangely bright, and her cheeks were flushed. Spock looked at her intently.

"I told him if he tried it, I'd phaser his war machine into the middle of next week," Kirk said. "He seemed to get the message, but he wasn't happy about it."

"So you continue to intervene on behalf of the intruders," Wayne said.

Kirk stared at her, momentarily unable to believe what he'd heard. "Commissioner," he finally managed, "what exactly are you saying?"

"That you'll do anything to help the invaders against the native people. Simply because they're human."

"The use of nuclear weapons is strongly proscribed by the Federation," Spock said.

"As your captain's friends down there love to tell us, this isn't the Federation. You have no right to intervene."

"But we are here acting as representatives of the Federation," Kirk said. "If the transport fleet arrives to discover we have permitted the inhabitants of Okeanos to use nuclear weapons on one another, you and I will both be sharing the wrong end of a capital court-martial for genocide."

Her answer was a defiant head-flip, clearing red bangs from her eyes.

"The issue would appear to be moot," Spock said. "Lead Walker has achieved his objective. Starfleet has sent a transport convoy to remove the Discordians."

Wayne drew in a deep breath. Her shoulders sagged as she let it out again. "You're right, Mr. Spock. It was the principle I was concerned with."

Kirk and Spock exchanged glances.

"Captain," Wayne said, "I'm beaming down to the planet surface. There are matters I need to attend to."

Kirk spread his hands. Wayne left.

The bridge crew stared at Kirk. "Captain," Uhura said hesitantly, "was the commissioner actually saying she might let the Susuru use nuclear weapons?"

"Either that or we're both hallucinating, Lieutenant."

"Captain," Spock said, "Deputy Commissioner Wayne has begun to behave in a most erratic manner."

"You've noticed."

The irony was lost on Spock. "I have taken the liberty of reviewing the commissioner's records. They

201

seem unduly cursory. She does seem to have left behind her a string of complaints for high-handed and impulsive behavior. In all instances, however, she was found to have acted correctly."

"By Commissioner Hightower?"

"The records do not say. I would estimate the probability as high."

He seemed about to continue. Kirk held up a hand. "Spare me the exact percentage, Spock. I'll take your word for this one."

Spock nodded imperturbably. "If you will not be needing me, I should prefer to return to the research station. Dr. Arkazha claims she has something of great interest to show me in the region of the Hellsgate Rift."

Kirk waved a hand. "Go, Spock. Might as well gather ye rosebuds while ye may."

Spock cocked an eyebrow at him and left. Kirk rose. "Uhura, contact sickbay," he said. "Pass the word for Dr. McCoy to meet me in my quarters immediately, if you please."

"She refuses to let me examine her, Jim," McCoy said. He stood with his back to the bulkhead and his arms folded, beside the niche which contained the model of the *Constitution*. "Since she's a civilian, I can't insist."

Kirk paced. "What about her medical records?"

"She has no organic condition which might account for her increasingly irrational behavior," McCoy said. "Her psychological records were not downloaded in the ship's computer."

Kirk stopped and stared at him. "Isn't that unusual, Bones?"

"Not really. She's a highly placed civilian official.

It's considered an invasion of privacy for the likes of you and me to be prying into such confidential information."

Kirk grimaced and went back to pacing.

"I'm just a country doctor, Jim," McCoy said, "and not a headshrinker by any means. But I can offer a possible explanation."

"Shoot."

"Now, this can't leave this room; I'm way outside my field, and it borders on the unethical to diagnose a patient I haven't examined. You can't take any of this as constituting an official opinion—"

Kirk made a chopping gesture. "All *right,* Bones."

"To me, Commissioner Wayne seems to show all the signs of being an abuse survivor who never dealt with the fact."

Kirk frowned. "You mean her father—"

"Was an overweening old bastard. Imagine what it was like growing up as his kid?"

"You actually think he beat her?"

"I can't say, Jim; I didn't examine him, either. As another utterly unqualified guess, I'd say it's damned likely. But systematic psychological abuse leaves scars that are just as deep, even if they aren't as visible."

"Why hasn't all this surfaced before?"

McCoy shrugged. "Maybe it has, Jim. But probably not in such a severe manner."

"What do you mean?"

"She's under enormous stress out here. A virgin planet, a previously unknown alien race in conflict with human settlers—to her it seems a textbook example of the sort of abuses Interspecies Affairs was created to correct. And she feels both a strong psychological identification with the Susuru, and a strong antipathy toward the Discordians."

203

"Don't I know it."

"Then there's the Klingon presence to complicate matters. More to the point, there's you and Kain."

Kirk looked at him sharply. "Explain yourself, Doctor."

"I'd say the poor child finds herself caught in a conflict of father figures. Combined with all the other stressors, it's causing her to come apart."

Kirk stared at his friend. He felt his face grow warm. "But I keep telling you I'm only a year or two older—"

McCoy shook his head. "Doesn't make a bit of difference, Jim. You're the man in command, and that's not just a matter of the color shirt you wear. You're a strong man, a strong personality type. You stamp your mark on any situation you come in contact with. You press all her daddy buttons at once.

"And so does this Klingon devil Kain."

Kirk took a deep breath. "If this is true, why has she been entrusted with so much responsibility?"

"Good heavens, Jim! The Federation can't discriminate against someone simply because of the way he or she was raised. Child abuse isn't as prevalent as it was a couple of centuries ago, but it still goes on. It isn't her fault; she's obviously a very intelligent and capable woman, who deserves the chance to rise as high as her abilities will carry her."

"What about the fact that she hasn't dealt with her past? Assuming that all of this bears any relationship to reality."

"I warned you this was all liable to be spun sugar and moonshine, Jim."

"And that's never stopped you before, Doctor."

McCoy started to glower, then turned it into a grin

that vanished as quickly as it had come. "And I won't let it stop me now. Dealing with a history of abuse is a highly personal matter, Jim. It's not something any-one outside you can force; intervention is just flat counterproductive."

"But she's vulnerable."

"Everybody's vulnerable, one way or another. Can't hold it against us."

"I guess not." Kirk stopped, stood staring down at his model sailing ship, as if imagining himself riding its decks, through seas less poisonous and strange than those of Discord.

"Besides, it's all academic now, anyway, from what you tell me," McCoy said. "She's got what she wanted."

Kirk reached a finger to touch the rigging. "Yes." He turned to the doctor. "What would it take to get hold of her psychological records, Bones?"

"A request from me to Starfleet, countersigned by you as the captain." The seams of his face deepened in a frown. "Jim, a request like that won't look too good on your record at a Court of Inquiry. It'll look like some kind of petty revenge for her going over your head to Starfleet."

"Send it anyway. Might as well be hanged for a sheep as a lamb." He snorted a laugh. "Haven't you always wondered just what that expression means?"

"Good thing Spock's not here," McCoy said gruffly. "He'd probably tell us."

Kirk started for the door. McCoy hung back. "Do it, Bones," the captain said. "I just have to know. Even though there's nothing more she can do."

"And so we've won, Captain Kain," Moriah Wayne said. She sat by the great hardwood table in the

Klingon's underground chamber. She was speaking somewhat too brightly, like a chattering bird. "Starfleet's sending transports to take the colonists off Island. We've got what we wanted."

Kain stood beside the table with one arm folded across his chest, the other elbow propped upon it, the palm cupping his chin. He studied Wayne with his single eye. Then he shook his head.

"Moriah, Moriah," he said sadly. "How you disappoint me."

"What?" she cried.

"Surely you're not that naïve, to believe you've bested James Kirk so easily."

She jumped to her feet. "But he'll have no choice! There'll be an admiral with the fleet. He'll make Kirk obey—or relieve him."

"Kirk has slipped the noose before," Kain said, "time and time again. What makes you think he won't do so this time? He's a hero to the warmongers of Starfleet. Do you really expect them to act against him?"

In her agitation Wayne kept walking several steps one way, then several steps the other. "But—"

Kain shook his head. "This will end as so many similar episodes have ended—with more Earther perfidy. Another helpless native race beaten down by human arrogance, another planet falling victim to human greed. A piquant irony, don't you think—that your human-dominated Federation favors even its outlaws over the natives they exploit."

She covered her face with her hands and pulled them slowly downward as if trying to scour away self-doubt. "Not again. Oh, Earth Mother, I can't let it happen again."

"The men of Starfleet stick together. It's just a fact of life."

"He's going to get away with it, isn't he?"

Kain smiled. "Not if you don't let him."

Yeoman Robison nodded politely as Commissioner Wayne stepped off the transporter stage. She walked purposefully around the control console to where he stood.

"Can I help you, Commissioner?" he asked cautiously. He was a properly respectful young man, but he wasn't about to let any civilian, no matter how top-lofty, go poking at his board without due authorization.

She smiled a warm smile—thrilling, even. Smiling like that the commissioner was really something to look at, not at all the dragon scuttlebutt made her out to be.

"Why, yes, Yeoman. I felt a strange kind of dislocation as I beamed up—something like nausea. I wondered if everything was adjusted right."

Of course it was, but he looked the slide controls over again, just to make sure.

"Well, Commissioner," he said, trying not to sound too condescending, "the fact is you can't feel much of anything in the dissociated state—"

Concentrating on his console, he did not see the commissioner bring her hand out from behind her hip and press a small gold tube to the side of his neck. And then he didn't see anything at all.

Her heart in her throat, Wayne stood watching the young man in the red shirt. *Surely it hadn't worked, surely he was still awake—*

She waved a hand in front of his face. His eyes did

not move to track the motion, nor did he blink. He did not seem to breathe.

It was as she had been told to expect. The *'ur'*, a spiny rock lizard from a little-visited world of the Klingon Empire, produced a neurotoxin that had the property of putting all its victim's physical processes on hold. She had one hundred seconds; then the handsome young yeoman would begin to function again, with no memory of any interruption—or of the preceding few minutes.

Being careful not to come in contact with the youth—she couldn't bring herself to believe entirely in the toxin's effectiveness—she manipulated the controls, locking the transporter beam onto the first set of coordinates she had memorized. She had no experience of working a transporter unit, but the steps were simple and she had committed them to memory. Her father had made sure she knew how to memorize things, quickly and infallibly.

She energized the beam. A trill, a sparkle, and a dark metallic cylinder squatted on the central disk.

She left the console and jumped lithely onto the platform to bend over the cylinder and press a relay. A red light glowed alive on top of the cylinder. Unreadable characters began to flicker green on a small panel beside the pilot light.

Making herself breathe slowly and move without haste, Wayne returned to the console and set the controls to a different set of coordinates. *Plenty of time,* she told herself. *Nothing to fear. Nothing in the world.*

She pressed the button once more. The cylinder turned to light, wavered, and vanished.

Moriah Wayne shuddered. Then she composed

herself and walked quickly from the transporter room.

Yeoman Robison blinked and shook himself.
"Whoa," he said. "I must've been daydreaming there."
He rubbed his eyes. "Just zoned out there for a moment," he told himself aloud. "Good thing Lieutenant Commander Scott didn't wander in to check up on me."

From his seat in the glassed-in control room poised above the fusion bottle that provided power to Harmony, Sonny Puleomua was talking to his cousin Hannes in Storm. "No, there's been nothing exciting going on around here except for the visit by the space people. Didn't even know they'd been here myself—nobody tells me anything, and I was onshift, and anyway I heard they were being shown around by some of those snotty Discord City types. I'll tell you one thing—hey!"
The readouts on his panels had gone crazy. Interference lines crackled over his cousin's face on the telephone screen.
"What the hell's going on here?" he demanded. "My displays are all dancing around like spackle bugs in swarming season!"
He broke off, half rose, and leaned forward to stare through the observation window. "There's some kind of yellow light flickering down on the floor," he said.
Something dark and heavy-looking had simply appeared next to the foamed-cement containment bottle. "Holy Mother Eris!" he exclaimed. "What's—"

* * *

"Captain!" Ensign Chekov exclaimed. "Our sensors are showing something that cannot be!"

Kirk sat up straight in his chair. "What is it, Ensign?"

"I'm detecting what looks like a thermonuclear explosion of approximately one-half megaton in the city of Harmony!"

Chapter Nineteen

SPOCK SAT IN THE CABIN that had been lent him in Deep-Sea Research Station Five, anchored at a depth of five hundred meters beneath the Southern Ocean, not far from Hellsgate Rift. He gazed at a computer monitor. In his hand was a control. To the twitching of his forefinger screens full of data flashed by his eyes as quickly as cards being dealt from a bottomless deck.

The things Mona Arkazha had shown him were fascinating, from a scientific viewpoint. From one perspective Discord was a violent world, but from another its energetic ecosystem produced a dynamism among its life-forms that was unparalleled in the galaxy, to his extensive knowledge. And he was not prepared to totally discount Arkazha's hints of some greater discovery that she was not yet ready to share with him. But the information he was scanning had nothing to do with the undersea life of Discord.

It had nothing to do with native life-forms at all. Or so he was coming to believe.

The door opened. He glanced up.

Two Vares, a man and a woman, stepped quickly into the room and split to stand flanking the door. Both were Micros; each pointed a machine pistol at him. In the doorway stood Mona Arkazha. The gray bulk of a Grunt loomed in the passageway behind her.

"I fear I must ask you to surrender your hand phaser, your communicator, and that marvelous tricorder of yours, Spock."

Spock looked from her to the Micros. Their reaction time was quicker than his, he knew. They handled the firearms as if they knew how to use them— and were ready to. Resistance was therefore illogical.

Deliberately he unfastened his belt and laid it across the end of the desk he was working on. The nearer Micro moved away from the wall, sidled to the desk, snatched the belt, and danced back, being careful to stay out of Spock's reach should he be inclined to try anything melodramatic. Which, of course, he was not.

"You not long ago broached the subject of trust, Doctor," he said. "It would appear that you were demanding of me something that you yourself did not merit."

Was that a ripple of pain across the amphibian features? He had a hard enough time reading the facial nuances of normal humans. He had no idea what hers might signify.

"Soon we will find out who has kept faith and who has been faithless," Arkazha said. "In the meantime, you must come with me."

"—reports seeing possible survivors—"
"—floating debris at twenty-one forty-one north, fifty-five thirty west—"

"—my God, it's gone, the city's just . . . gone."

Kirk closed his eyes. Sulu was back at his station, monitoring surface traffic. The picture it painted was far from complete, but it showed Kirk far more than he cared to know.

"What about Mr. Spock, Sulu? Any chance of beaming him up yet?"

"Negative, sir. The storm has settled right over the research station, and it shows no sign of breaking up. It's not safe to try to use the transporters."

Kirk thought of the few terrible times he'd seen the results of interference in a transporter beam, and his stomach did a barrel roll. Spock was his friend as well as his first officer. The situation was not urgent enough to demand that Kirk risk doing *that* to him. Yet.

The transporters were working overtime as it was, trying to bring the *Enterprise*'s current leave rotation home as quickly as possible. He had as yet no idea of the source of the blast that had destroyed Harmony and most, if not all, of her three-quarters of a million occupants. The ship's computer had reviewed his last exchange with Swift exhaustively and confirmed the Universal Translator routine's rendering of his words: He had clearly been referring to fission weapons, not a fusion device. And the destruction of Harmony had unmistakably been accomplished by a runaway fusion reaction—a hydrogen bomb.

So he didn't *know* that the war for Okeanos had escalated catastrophically. But on general principles he wanted to get the *Enterprise*'s strayed sheep back in the fold with all deliberate speed.

Especially since it seemed increasingly certain that five of his people would never be coming back. Fortunately most of the crew had at least begun their leaves in Discord City, where the first contact had

213

been made. Discord Citians—the term *citizens* made them cranky—did not get along all that well with Harmonians. The crew members who made contacts elsewhere had mostly gone to Storm or Serendip or Qara-Qitay. But five had apparently wound up in Harmony.

Kirk listened to the broadcasts from volunteer rescue flights and boats in part to learn as much as he could about what had happened, in part to see if there was any way *Enterprise* could help the survivors. But mostly it was against the chance, thin as a monomolecular line, that some or all of the five had managed to survive.

"Captain," Uhura said, "a call coming through for you from Discord City."

"Put it on, Lieutenant."

The face of Aileea dinAthos filled the screen. Kirk managed a strained smile. "Aileea, let me say—"

"Captain Kirk," she said, as if she hadn't heard. "How could you?"

Her image flickered. An electric storm squatted on top of Discord City, too. It wasn't the same as the one over Deep-Sea Five, a whole world away.

"What?" he asked, utterly confused.

"I know that you're a statist, but in spite of that I thought you were a good man. Now I know otherwise."

"What are you talking about, Aileea? What have I done?"

Her cheeks rode up and turned her eyes to jade crescents. "Is this how it's going to be? You're just going to deny knowing that someone beamed down from your ship and sabotaged the Harmony power plant?"

"What?"

"Our power plants are linked together by data networks," Aileea said, "so that in case of disaster at one the others will at least know how it came about. The instrumentation at the Harmony bottle showed interference of the same pattern caused by your transporter beams right before the blast."

She drew a breath. "Also, the chief technician on duty at the plant was talking to a relative by phone at the time. He spoke of interference, then of something metallic-looking appearing in a flicker of yellow light."

A tear ran down her cheek. "Why, Jim? Why?"

He raised his hands and opened his mouth. It took all his will to force out words.

"Aileea, you have to believe me—*it wasn't us.*"

The intercom chimed. "Transporter room to bridge," said Mr. Scott's voice.

"Just a minute, Scotty," Kirk said aside, "I—"

"Captain, we've lost track of our people remaining on yon planet. We cannae beam anyone else aboard!"

"We—we find violation of the sacred rules of hospitality repugnant," Aileea was saying. "But you have a preponderance of power and we must protect ourselves. Therefore, we have taken those of your people who remain upon our planet into custody, and relieved them of weapons, communicators, and other items that might enable you to trace them. Even as we speak they are being dispersed across all of Discord."

"Aileea?"

"Your people are now our hostages. There will not be another Harmony." She vanished.

"Take the offensive," Moriah Wayne said.

"I beg your pardon?" Kirk said.

"It's time to crack down, Captain. You have enormous firepower on board; isn't it time to use it? If you're concerned about preserving the lives of these criminals, then try destroying some of the property they hold so dear. Discord City might be a place to start."

He looked at her. The regular bridge crew was gathered in the briefing room to assess the situation. It was bad. Few survivors of Harmony had been located, and some forty-one *Enterprise* crew members remained unaccounted for, including the five almost certainly lost in the explosion. The prevailing mood was shock, but grief and confusion and fear were beginning to vent in spikes of anger.

He tried to swallow an anger spike of his own. "Commissioner, this is no time for jokes."

"I'm not joking," the commissioner said lightly. She alone failed to share the grim mood. She seemed elevated, almost manic. "You tried coddling your precious human settlers, and look where it got you."

"We don't know what's gotten us here, Commissioner," Sulu said.

"We're not even sure where 'here' *is*," added Dr. McCoy. "We don't know who set the bomb, or why."

"What about the Discordians' charge that someone beaming down from the *Enterprise* placed the bomb?" Uhura asked.

"Yeoman Robison was on duty at the time," said Scott. "He swears nothing was transported down at all. Sean's a good lad—I trained him on the board myself. And you must admit, someone beaming a bomb down to the planet would be a wee bit hard to miss."

"The one thing we *do* know," Wayne said, "is that the self-proclaimed Discordians have taken members of this crew hostage." She leaned forward and propped her arms on the table. Her eyes moved from face to haggard face.

"I'm surprised," she said quietly. "Where is the military outrage, the fury at the fact that your comrades-in-arms have been treacherously imprisoned by their hosts? I'd think you'd all have blood in your eye. Are you willing to let these people *do* this to you?"

"No." All heads turned toward the head of the table; it was Kirk who had spoken. "No, we cannot let them do this to us. No matter what we may have felt about the Discordians, as a group or individually, we cannot tolerate having our people held hostage. I *refuse* to tolerate it."

"What can we do, Jim?" McCoy asked.

"I've already told you what to do," Wayne said airily. "Sooner or later, you people are going to have to start listening to me."

"Confound it, woman, hasn't there been enough destruction already?" McCoy exclaimed.

"There's a bigger problem," Kirk said. "How can I attack a city without risking more of my own crew? We don't know where they're being kept."

"Isn't it past the time for niceties like that?" Wayne asked. "A strong commander knows when to write people off and get on with the campaign."

"'He jests at scars that never felt a wound,'" McCoy quoted bitterly. "You speak of military matters very confidently for a woman who knows nothing of the military beyond the fact that she doesn't like it."

"If that's strength," Kirk said, standing up, "then I am weak, and proud of it. I write no one off, Commissioner, until I see the body, or until the danger to the living becomes too great to press the issue—and even then, I'll find a way to get back and perform a rescue if I can. Lives must sometimes be expended, yes. But no life is *expendable*."

"So you will take your customary action," Wayne said. "Which is to say, *nothing*."

"I will act when I find a sensible action to take."

She nodded, as if pronouncing judgment. "Then it's on your head," she said, and left.

"Now what was that supposed to mean?" McCoy asked.

Kirk strode down the corridor and headed for the transporter room. There was no easily discernible purpose to be served by the trip—Sulu's sensors couldn't locate Spock or the other hostages from the bridge, so there was little chance of detecting them down there. But at just this moment there was nothing he could accomplish on the bridge. At least the movement was action, of a sort.

Besides, something was nagging at him, from the back of his skull. He had the notion that a trip to the transporter might jog it loose from his preconscious.

Thus distracted, he turned a corner and bumped into a strikingly lovely young woman. He stepped back. "Oh, excuse me—I'm very sorry—"

Then he noticed she was a Klingon.

He snatched for his hand phaser. She was faster.

He saw a flash of red. Then black.

Chapter Twenty

"DR. ARKAZHA," Spock said, "your course of action is entirely illogical."

Down and down the submersible went toward the center of the planet—or at least the molten mantle. The depths of Hellsgate Rift were a black more absolute than space. The Rift embraced no stars.

Mona Arkazha piloted the craft herself. She respected her captive greatly. She did not want another to witness what she hoped—and thought—would happen.

"You cannot hope to defeat the Federation in an open confrontation," Spock continued. "Yet by your very actions you are mobilizing the full might of the *Enterprise*—and, eventually, of the Federation itself—against you. I do not understand what stands to be gained."

"Then consider what stands to be lost. If we fight, we die—but we die both proud and free. If we give in, we stand to lose freedom, pride, our homes. We lose the right to control our biological destiny. We become again the helpless property of a compassionate and caring state—too compassionate to kill us, too caring to let us walk among its people, who might be offended at our strangeness. Is that logical, Spock?"

"While life remains, so also does the possibility of altering circumstances for the better."

She showed him teeth. "We have you captive," she said, "and life remains."

"What will you do with us?"

"Care for you. Indeed, make plans to make restitution to you, if we can—for we know what has been done is unlikely to be the work of any who were guesting among us. You are victims, and we will not hide from the fact."

"If your intention is to care for me, why is it necessary to convey me to the bottom of a ten-thousand-meter-deep trench?"

"Because, Spock my friend," she said with her eyes gleaming, "there's something down there that you must see."

Rather to his own surprise, Kirk came back to himself lying on the deck. Voices bounced off the walls of a confined space and into his ears and made his head seem to bulge. Familiar voices. Unfortunately.

In the normal course of events, if he were strolling through his ship and happened to bump into a Klingon, who shot him, he would have to figure that was it. But this clearly wasn't it, unless he was destined to spend his afterlife in a place that also harbored both Moriah Wayne and a pack of surly Klingons. He refused even to contemplate the theo-

220

logical ramifications of that, and decided he must be alive.

It wasn't a fact he was necessarily happy with. He knew somehow that he hadn't been out long, which meant the phaser had been set on the lightest possible "stun." But the crude calibration of Klingon weaponry meant he'd still taken a pretty hefty jolt. His head felt as if somebody had drilled holes in both temples to see if there really were little men in there or what, and his stomach felt as if the little men were actually in *it*—bouncing on a trampoline.

He turned and vomited. "I'm sorry you did that, Jim," Moriah Wayne said. "It's going to get a little close for you, locked in here with it."

He looked at her blearily and tried to get to his feet. He was in a small storage compartment, he realized. The flower of Klingon femininity who had stunned him caught a fistful of his shirt, hauled him upright, and slammed him up against the wall. She pinned him there with a forearm bar across the throat.

"How come," he managed to choke out, "all the good-looking women I meet this trip wind up not liking me?"

She pressed harder. His vision started to red out.

"I am Senior Lieutenant Lu Kok Tak," she said. "I want to kill you, but my captain reserves that right for himself. You cost him his captain, his eye, and his brother."

"I didn't mean . . . to do those things," Kirk gasped. "But . . . you can tell him that . . . he's really starting to get me ticked."

She raised a hand to strike him. "No, Lieutenant," Wayne said sharply. "You are not to hurt him."

Lu Kok Tak gave her a look as if she'd like to take a

crack at *her*. But she stood back and let Kirk go. He slid down and landed on his tailbone with impact that sent sparks shooting up his spine to fountain up behind his eyes like sparklers.

He looked at Wayne. "Adding treason to your long lists of accomplishments?"

"You're the one who's playing the traitor, Jim," she said. "You've ignored your orders. You've refused to do your duty. It's fallen to these people to try to set things right."

"Klingons aren't usually the first people I'd look to for setting things right," Kirk said. "But if your definition of that includes murdering three-quarters of a million people, I guess then it's right up their alley."

"I did that," she said. "My conscience is clear. It needed doing. They were no more than cancer cells."

It seemed to Kirk that there had to be something to say to that. But his knees gave way beneath him, and he just barely stopped himself from hitting the deck with his face.

"We'll have plenty of time to discuss this later," Wayne said. "Right now we have to go."

"Shall we leave a guard?" the Klingon woman asked. She obviously did not like the taste asking Wayne for orders left in her mouth.

"No, Lieutenant Lu. Too obvious. Besides, just look at him." She laughed. "He's helpless."

The lieutenant nodded curt agreement. Wayne went out, followed by Lu Kok Tak and her two male Klingon escorts. None of them troubled to cover Kirk.

The door closed. A moment later Kirk saw a red glow and smelled hot metal. They were welding him in.

He should have leapt to his feet and done something

heroic and decisive then. Instead he huddled in a miserable heap and let them do it.

Moriah Wayne turned away from the Klingon who was kneeling to weld the door with his phaser. "When you finish sealing him in here, take your men and rejoin the others, Lieutenant Lu. If there's trouble on the bridge I'll call you."

Lieutenant Lu Kok Tak stared at that pale throat and longed to crush it. To endure the usual Earther pronunciation of her name was bad enough. *Lu* was grossly overfamiliar—the child name her grandmother called her by before she was even blooded as a hunter in the cold hills of Klingon.

The lieutenant knew nothing of the commissioner's antecedents, which was as much as she cared to. Merely by looking at her—her carriage, the way she moved—Lu Kok Tak knew that Wayne possessed muscle mass greater than the norm for Earther women, both denser and heavier. She had also clearly received some rudiments of instruction in what passed for hand-to-hand combat among the *tera'ngan*. Lu Kok Tak could have cared less. She considered herself, unarmed, the equal of a male Earther warrior —if not his better. One of their pallid flabby women was beneath her contempt.

But the lieutenant must let her live, for now. Not for this arrogant Earther's sake, but out of obedience to Kain.

"It shall be as you wish," she said huskily, and thought about dishes best served cold.

Moriah Wayne tried to effect the same swagger when she stepped onto the bridge that Kirk always had. It was her bridge now, and she needed to let these thick-skulled military types know it in a hurry.

She walked to the command chair and sat down. The bridge crew began to glance at her, uneasily and without friendliness.

"Mr. Sulu," she said, "lock main phaser banks on the nearest Discordian city."

He ignored her. "Mr. Sulu," she said sharply, "didn't you hear me?"

"I heard you," he said, looking straight ahead.

"Why aren't you obeying my orders?"

"With all due respect, you're not entitled to give orders. Ma'am."

"I am assuming command, Mr. Sulu. Now do what I say."

"No."

"Mr. Chekov," she said, "relieve Sulu of his position. Security, escort Mr. Sulu to the brig."

"Nyet," Chekov said. "Get someone else to do your dirty work, lady Cossack."

She twisted in her seat to look at the two security men who stood flanking the door. "Security," she said, "what's the holdup? We have a mutiny here."

"Security," Sulu said crisply, "please remove Commissioner Wayne from the bridge."

The two men in red shirts started forward. Wayne thumbed a button on a unit she held concealed in the palm of her right hand.

The turbolift doors opened. Klingons burst upon the bridge. The security men wheeled. One clawed for his phaser and was shot down himself before he got the weapon clear. The other launched himself at the man who had stunned his partner and grappled with him, trying to wrest the weapon from his grip.

Lieutenant Lu Kok Tak stepped from the lift, saw the two struggling, and fired her phaser at them. Both fell.

Sulu had taken advantage of the distraction to enter a quick code sequence into the helm. Then he jumped up, reaching for his own phaser. The Klingon lieutenant caught the motion from the corner of her eye. She spun toward him, dropping to one knee. His beam whined over her head and splashed against the turbolift door. Hers dead-centered his chest. He dropped.

"Hikaru!" Uhura cried, jumping to her feet. There were half a dozen Klingons still standing. They covered the entire bridge with their phasers. Uhura stayed where she was.

The Klingon lieutenant reached back and pulled the manual override next to the turbolift. This disabled the elevator and made it impossible for hostile parties to reach the bridge. She smiled. The Earthers did some things right.

A Klingon ran to the helm and stabbed at buttons with his finger. Then he turned and snarled syllables at Lu Kok Tak.

Her lips writhed back from her teeth. "The *yIntag* has locked the board!" she exclaimed. "The controls will not respond."

After the absolute blackness of descent the vent seemed to glow like an irregular red sun. Arkazha reached out and flicked off the interior lights, leaving the submersible illuminated only by the fitful dance of instrument displays and the vent's sullen glare.

"Now, Spock," she said, "open your mind."

"Why should I comply with your wishes, Doctor?"

"Because it costs you nothing. Because if you do not, a very great wrong will be done. Because if you do not, your ship and your captain might be in danger."

She leaned close. "And because if you do not, you will spend the rest of your life wondering why I brought you here."

He stared at her in the darkness. Then he nodded. Placing his hands on his thighs, he closed his eyes and shut himself completely off from her, the tiny instrument-crowded compartment, the awful impending sensation of billions of tons of water pressing down from overhead.

Then, having walled away distraction, he willed his mind to open to what might come.

And then he began to scream.

Chapter Twenty-one

KIRK'S BODY was a bag of wet sand. He got it upright again mainly by some form of levitation he didn't know he'd mastered. Those Klingon phasers must have more of a kick to them than he'd ever realized.

But he was coming out of it, slowly. He even had a plan now. All he needed was the energy to put it into action.

Which at the moment was like saying that if he had a long enough lever and a proper fulcrum, he could move Discord.

The only part of his body that had any energy at the moment was his chest muscle where the Klingon had shot him. *That* kept twitching, as if it were a wild animal struggling to escape the rest of him and live free roaming the passageways of the *Enterprise*.

He took stock of his situation, which in circumstances like this was always a mistake and depressing but something he felt compelled to do. So Kain had been up to some skulduggery all along; that was not exactly a surprise. The big question was what. He still didn't have an answer to that one.

And Moriah . . . He squeezed shut his eyes, which made yellow sparks dance behind them. *Moriah, Moriah.* He had found much in her to admire . . . in the beginning, at least. She had her principles, her convictions. He respected her obduracy because it was not much different from his own.

He had even loved her, or at least made love to her. That episode seemed distant and unreal now, as if it had happened in a dream, or to someone else. *And maybe that's because I don't want to accept that I made love to . . . something . . . that could do what she did.*

He jacked his eyes upward, toward the overhead. There was the outline of an access panel. His road to freedom. If he could just convince his still-numb limbs to get him there.

"Levitation," he croaked. "That's the secret."

A waver in air, a spill of gold. A new Klingon stood on the bridge next to the helm. He was of medium height, with black hair hanging lank from his cranial ridge. In the breast pocket of his tunic he wore a sheath of serpent-worm skin, to protect the fabric from wear by his light stylus and other small instruments.

There was that about him which said he was a computer technician.

Watching from the main viewscreen, which in turn showed him sitting in his hide-covered chair in his underground command post, Kain nodded in satisfaction. "You may relax now, Moriah," he said. *"Q'reygh* will figure out how to unlock the fire-control console long before the other *tera'ngan* have discovered anything is wrong."

The technician nodded and smiled at Wayne. He was so impressed with her that he kept nodding and smiling at her until Lu Kok Tak reached out from behind and rapped him smartly on the ridge with her fingertips. He whined a peevish complaint. Then he knelt before the helm, unfastened the front panel, and got down to work.

With a grunt and a heave, Kirk pulled himself up through the hole in the overhead. His spasm of effort knocked over the spare linen bundles he'd piled up to stand on. Fortunately they didn't make much noise.

For a moment he lay there sucking air through a gaping mouth like a beached raft dodger, with his feet dangling into the compartment. *I've got to lose some weight. I won't even make Bones nag me about it this time.*

By centimeters he wriggled the rest of him up into the Jeffries tube. Then he lay there and devoted some time to the existential pleasures of breathing. His head began to clear. He began to feel less as if his entire body were one big funny bone barked against a table edge.

He called into his mind the blueprints he and Scotty had devoted so many hours to on the journey out from Starbase 23. He had a rough idea of how to get to the bridge already. But he needed reinforcements in a hurry, and Security was not much use to him right now. That competent witch *luHoHta'* would have been sure to seal the bridge. And there were only so many burly security types he could jam in the access ducts and air vents with him.

No, he told himself. *I don't need them anyway. This is still* my *ship.*

"Helpless," he croaked. "*I'll* show you who's helpless."

Painfully but determinedly, he began to crawl.

Spock raised his head and snapped his eyes open like shutters. Arkazha tensed, not knowing what to expect.

He lunged forward for the controls. She wrapped thick-skinned arms around him. He struggled.

She held him. The very surprise of the fact calmed him slightly, returned him to a semblance of himself.

"Must—go," he said, as if he had to wrestle each word to get it out. *"They*—told me—there was—danger. Must—see."

She hesitated a moment, then let him go. He lurched to the front of the tiny craft, bent almost double in the cramped space, then folded himself into a space meant for a being half his size. He looked ludicrous with his knees up around his pointed ears, but Arkazha felt no humor. She had too good an idea what he was going through.

He set the craft onto a heading and turned on the autopilot. Then he flung himself from the pilot's seat to huddle against the bulkhead with his arms wrapped tightly around his knees.

"I first felt them in my dreams, as I slept in Deep-Sea Five," she said, settling herself beside him. "I thought I was going mad. Then I went into Hellsgate, and my head filled with the voices. I have no gift for telepathy, though, so I could never make more of them than a terrible pressure in the head."

Spock didn't answer. His eyes were squeezed shut.

His lips moved, though no sound came out. She bent an ear hole near his lips and thought she heard the ghost of a whisper: *"I—am Spock. I am a Vulcan. I am alive. I am Spock."*

She touched his forehead. It was as cold as the viewport, through which no amount of insulation could keep the lightless depths from sucking heat.

Whether he heard her or not, she couldn't tell. Maybe she wasn't talking to him, truly. Maybe she spoke for her own benefit.

"One thing I knew—they mean no harm. They cause pain by the strangeness of their thoughts. You are strong—you will endure."

She took his head in her arms and cradled it against her rubbery breast. In that way they fled through the depths, him reciting the mantra that would perhaps return his selfhood to him, her crooning an ancient Russian lullaby in a cracked and quavery voice.

Wayne sat in her chair of command with Lu Kok Tak on one side of her and a giant Klingon brute on the other, the picture of absolute authority. She felt wonderful. At last things were to be set right on Okeanos, and it was all her doing—with plenty of help from the magnificent Captain Kain and his crew. These Klingons could be a fairly coarse lot, she had to admit. But she could clearly see the innate nobility in them.

Kain, on the other hand, was bearing the delay with far less grace. He was slumping, frowning, and drumming fingers on the arm of his chair when the lumpy tech sat upright with a cry of *"pItl!* It's done!"

Kain bobbed his head. "Excellent. Lieutenant?"

Lu Kok Tak jumped for the helmsman's station.

She'd been itching to fire a ship's main phasers her whole life.

"The city Storm is right below," Wayne said. "Lock phasers onto a main governmental building."

"Commissioner," Uhura said scornfully, "the Discordians don't *have* large governmental buildings."

"Oh. Well, then, find a suitably large and impressive building, centrally located."

Lu Kok Tak was already doing that. She had a magnified overhead view of Storm up on the big screen, relegating her captain to a smaller side display. The picture scrolled this way and that as she spun the trackball mounted on the console, looking for targets. The tip of her tongue protruded from her mouth in concentration.

"Lieutenant Uhura," Wayne said, "open a channel with Storm." She smiled. "I think it's only fair to warn them what's in store."

"They won't answer," Uhura said.

"Try anyway." She pointed her thumb at the Klingon who stood beside her—*her!*—command chair. "Or I'll have *him* shake you by the scruff of your neck."

The big Klingon growled. Uhura turned toward her panel.

"Here's something," Lu Kok Tak said. She had found a circular building, which by its appearance might be either a freshwater storage tank or a sports arena. Either way, it was a reasonably imposing target.

"Commissioner, I'm getting no response," Uhura said.

"Then broadcast an all-frequencies warning! Get the people out now."

The bridge crew, including Sulu, who was reluctantly returning to consciousness, stared at her, wondering why she was suddenly so filled with compassion for the gene-altered human settlers.

"Maybe she's killed her limit," muttered Sulu. It earned him a gouge in the ribs with a truncheon from one of the two Klingons who stood flanking him.

Lu Kok Tak had succeeded in locking on to her target. With a triumphant cry she slammed the heel of her hand down on the firing switch.

Onscreen, beams of light suddenly lanced the large round structure. Metal glowed cherry red. Metal vapor swirled up like steam.

"What are you doing?" screamed Wayne. "I didn't give the order to fire!"

The Klingon lieutenant gave her a lethal look and then a Can-I-kill-her-now? look to her real commander onscreen. Kain gave her back a minute shake of his head. She shrugged and depressed the switch again.

"Forgive her, Moriah," said Kain. "She is young—her natural exuberance has the better of her."

Wayne frowned and fidgeted in her seat. She was disappointed; she had expected better discipline than this from the Klingons. But she supposed no race was perfect.

A third blast from the phaser banks. The structure exploded in a ball of rapidly expanding gas. Then all that was left was a circle wound, blue water ringed by white-glowing metal.

Wayne found herself leaning forward eagerly in the command chair. She made herself settle back. "We'll wait a few minutes," she said, "give them time to assimilate it. Then we'll destroy another building."

233

"I'm looking," Lu Kok Tak reported.

"See that your impatience doesn't overwhelm you again," Wayne said. The Klingon ignored her.

Minutes passed. Behind Kain Klingons were visible moving purposefully about. Wayne didn't know what they were doing—nor did she care. She was paramount here, this was her moment. She would *show* those arrogant mutant bastards what power was!

"Commissioner," Chekov said, "the city is breaking up."

She glared at him. A command to beat him unconscious quivered on the tip of her tongue. Then she thought about what he'd actually said.

"What on earth are you talking about, young man?"

He pointed to an auxiliary screen. A view of all of Storm filled it. As she looked at it, the fringes seemed to melt away before her eyes.

"What's going on?" she demanded.

Lu Kok Tak uttered what Wayne thought was a curse. "I do not know. But look!" On the big screen an entire block of buildings pulled away from each other. A skyway fell into the water with a splash. A long oval building submerged, trailing broken catwalks like seaweed.

"It's unbelievable," she whispered. "What are they *doing?*"

"If you'd actually paid attention to the Discordians," Uhura said, "you'd know. Every house, every business, almost every building on Discord is a *ship.* You can't threaten these people this way, Commissioner. They just pull up stakes and leave."

"Well—shoot them, Lieutenant! Don't let them get away!"

Lu Kok Tak locked phasers onto a large oval

building. It promptly vanished beneath the waves, leaving nothing but a boil of bubbles.

"I'm trying," the lieutenant said, gritting her teeth.

Gurg was a Klingon rating whose MOS was being big and ugly, a task for which nature had generously equipped him. He stood right up next to the command chair, phaser in hand, intimidating these Denebian slime-devils-who-walked-like-men with scowls from brows that didn't so much beetle as battleship. He was a man who loved his work, and he was an artist at it.

His eyes were fixed ahead. With the science station unmanned, the whole bridge complement was in his forward field of vision—an Earther design feature a good *thlIngan* could appreciate, at least one who thought a bit more profoundly about such things than Gurg. Gurg was more the direct experiential type.

Of course, no one else was paying any attention to what was going on behind them either. As a consequence Gurg was the only one who *wasn't* surprised when a phaser beam flashed from the Jeffries-tube access panel next to the inactive turbolift. Gurg was too busy being unconscious then.

Kirk had chosen to drop him first because he was the only hostile on the bridge with a weapon actually in hand. His next target was the lieutenant, who was already spinning to draw her own sidearm. She was fast as a leopard. She was smart, too. As she came around she took a step to the right and went to one knee, to spoil her enemy's targeting solution.

James Kirk was no slouch in the reflex compartment either. But he was still fuzzy from being stunned himself; in his haste to get off the first shot he overcompensated slightly. His blast struck the biceps of her weapon arm. The phaser dropped from her fingers.

She was a blur of motion, flying forward at him. Before he could squeeze another shot her boot scythed around and kicked the phaser spinning from his hand.

While this was happening, the *Enterprise*'s bridge crew was not exactly idle. Perhaps inside—irrationally—they had been expecting something like this. Their captain had a habit of coming through for them, usually in the face of the wildest odds.

Lieutenant Uhura stood up abruptly. The Klingon standing watch over her communications station gaped at her impertinence. She kneed him in the groin. As he bent double, she seized his head by the hair and dragged his face down to meet her other knee coming up. Then she let him go. He staggered backward, trying to clutch himself in two places at once. He backed into the technician, who was standing there looking befuddled.

Ferocious Klingon instinct took over. Still clutching himself with one hand, the guard half turned and began striking savagely at what he took for his new antagonist with the other. The tech wailed and fell on his rump.

Sulu pivoted and plucked the truncheon from the inattentive fingers of the Klingon on his left. Snapping his hips back the other way, he drove its heavy brass head into the solar plexus of the Klingon to his right. Turning back again, he stopped an overhand right to the head by whacking the Klingon hard on the inside of the attacking forearm. Then he slammed the truncheon upside the Klingon's head. The Klingon went down.

Senior Lieutenant Lu Kok Tak had Kirk trapped in the cramped Jeffries tube. She was firing knees into him, trying to crush his groin. He had his hips turned to the side, absorbing the blows on the great muscle of his thigh. It felt as if a giant aborigine of Taurus II was pounding him with a stone-headed club.

He managed to get a boot up and give her a desperate shove to the midriff. She reeled back three steps and caught herself. Before she could start forward again Kirk was on her, fists up, left side advanced.

She kicked at his groin. He got his hip in the way. Screaming with fury, she struck at his face. She could only use her left hand; her right still dangled like a sock still wet from the laundry. He deflected the blows with raised forearms.

She cocked her hand to strike for his eyes, fingers clawed. He snapped his left arm straight. The jab caught her right on her fine, narrow-bridged nose and broke it.

Lu Kok Tak straightened, eyes wide, blood pouring down her upper lip. The slimy Earther had actually *hurt* her.

About then the slimy Earther caught her with an overhand right to the jaw. Bone crunched. She fell in a graceless sprawl.

Kirk looked around, trying not to shake his right hand. It felt as if someone had exploded a bomb among his metacarpals. He was just in time to see Sulu batter down the Klingon he had poked in the belly with his own stick, and suddenly the bridge was clear of functional enemies.

"Touché!" Sulu cried.

"Aren't you getting your martial arts confused, Mr. Sulu?" Kirk asked. "I'm sure real *escrimadores* don't yell 'touché' when they hit somebody."

Sulu showed teeth in a feral grin. "I don't know

237

what they say, Captain. The videos don't cover that—"

"Captain," Uhura cried, "the turbolift—"

Kirk wheeled in time to see the turbolift door close. The manual override switch had been thrown the other way.

He moved swiftly to his command chair and hit the intercom button with his good hand. "This is the captain speaking. Red alert. I repeat—red alert. All hands to battle stations. This is not a drill. I need all available Security to the bridge immediately. We need many sets of passive restraints."

He paused and glanced around the bridge. "All hands be on the lookout for Commissioner Moriah Wayne. She may be armed and must be considered dangerous."

He glanced around the bridge. Anger smoldered in his belly, a feeling of violation.

"And as for you, Captain Kain—" Kirk turned to the side screen.

Only to see the Klingon shimmer out in a haze of transporter-beam glitter.

Chapter Twenty-two

KIRK LOOKED AT his bridge crew. They were all standing over the vanquished Klingons, lost somewhere between daze and triumph.

"Don't we all have jobs to do?" Kirk asked. "We're at war here, people. Attend your stations. Make it march."

Everybody dove for his or her station at once. Kirk ignored the brief resulting confusion, seating himself in his chair as if nothing had happened. He kept his right hand well away from everything.

"Mr. Sulu," he said, "shields up. I want a lock on that battlecruiser immediately. If she energizes her weapons you have permission to blast her without warning."

"Yes, *sir!*"

"Lieutenant Uhura, find me the channel Ms. dinAthos called on earlier. I want to talk to her at once."

"Aye, sir."

The turbolift door opened and Security came tumbling onto the bridge, bristling with phasers and belligerence. "Officers," Kirk said without turning, "the fight is over—here, at least. All that remains is the cleanup phase of the operation."

Security began to shackle the unconscious Klingons and carry them out. A sturdy man with curly blond hair and a blond woman, surprisingly petite for a Security officer, helped a bloody-faced Senior Lieutenant Lu Kok Tak to her feet. Her hands were bound behind her. She swayed, and glared at Kirk.

"It was luck that let you beat me," she spat. "Luck alone!"

He started to toss off a flip line about it really being all those years trying to beat Finnegan back at Starfleet Academy. Then he checked himself.

"It wasn't luck," he said in a quiet voice. "Don't kid yourself. This is *my* ship, Lieutenant. You never had a chance."

He waved his right hand in the air. It made him feel as if somebody were hacking at its bones with a white-hot saw. "Normally, I'd feel compelled to apologize for hitting a lady. Somehow I get the feeling you wouldn't appreciate the gesture."

She spat Klingon gutturals at him and tried to writhe free. "Reichert, van Pelt," Kirk said, "take care with that one. She's a handful."

The diminutive van Pelt gripped the Klingon's left arm just above the elbow and squeezed. Lu Kok Tak stiffened.

"We know *just* how to handle her, Captain," van Pelt said sweetly. The two hustled the lieutenant out.

"Sensors report only a skeleton crew on board the battlecruiser, sir," Sulu said.

"Where did the dewils *go?*" Chekov asked.

"I don't know, Mr. Chekov," Kirk said. "But I have a feeling we'd better find out soon."

"I have Ai—Ms. dinAthos, Captain," Uhura reported.

Kirk took a deep breath. "Put her on."

Aileea's face filled the screen. "I've heard of your attack on Storm, Captain." She shook her head. Tears flew from her cheeks like drops of rain. "I don't know how I could have been so wrong about you!"

"Ms. dinAthos, your plant was sabotaged by Deputy Commissioner Wayne, who, acting on her own and in flagrant violation of Federation law, beamed a Klingon explosive device next to the fusion bottle in Harmony. She then apparently beamed a party of Klingons aboard the *Enterprise.* They took temporary command of the bridge and opened fire on the city of Storm. They have now been subdued, the *Enterprise* is back under our control, and—damn. Just a moment."

He hit the intercom button. "Engine room."

"Scott here, sir. What's going on up there?"

"Pandemonium, Mr. Scott. Send four armed men to secure the transporter room at once, please."

"I'll go m'self—"

"You'll do no such thing, Mr. Scott. I need you right where you are. We may be needing full warp power at any minute."

"I'll have the drives all warmed up," Scott said cheerfully, "and purrin' like a happy kitten."

"Excellent. Kirk out. Ms. dinAthos, I apologize for putting you on hold, as it were."

She blinked moistly at him. Then her eyes narrowed to jade slits. "If this is some kind of trick—"

Kirk nodded and gave her a big, happy smile. "You've caught me, Colonel dinAthos. All these Klingons you see being carried out of here have kindly agreed to pretend to have been bloody, battered, and stunned to help me fool you into thinking we were innocent. But you, clever woman that you are—you saw right through me."

"I wish I could believe you—Jim," she said. "But —well, we've been talking to your people. We heard what you did to the people of Gamma Trianguli VI, how you destroyed Vaal, their protector, so that they would be forced to struggle to survive, to learn suffering, sickness, and death—all for their own good. What can *we* expect of you?"

"I am getting awfully tired of having that goddamned tyrannosaur head with the horn on top thrown in my face. So I got a little pompous in the heat of victory, made a silly speech. The thing was trying to eat my *ship,* damn it!

"I'm tired of fooling with you people, too. I am delivering an ultimatum, and I want it spread across the land. I want my people back, and I want them now. Otherwise I'm going to start blasting every scrap of weaponry that Mr. Sulu's sensors can find. *Starting* with those Koman ship-killer missiles you just installed back at the old homestead. Do I make myself clear?"

"Captain," Uhura said abruptly, "there's a call—"

"Please don't interrupt, Lieutenant. I'm in the middle of some good old-fashioned, overbearing gunboat diplomacy here."

"But, sir—it's Mr. Spock!"

"Put him on."

Spock's face appeared in place of Aileea's, looking haggard. Or maybe it was the light. A jumble of readouts and instrumentation framed him.

"Captain," he said, "I have just spoken to the true aboriginal inhabitants of this planet."

242

"The Susuru?" Kirk asked.

"No, Captain. I have been observing for some time that the Susuru seem curiously maladapted for life on this, their putative homeworld. They seem to have evolved as savanna browsers. The question that springs to mind is, how did that happen, on a planet where the vast preponderance of the surface is covered by water and what little dry land exists is mountainous?"

Kirk made a go-ahead motion with his hand. He regretted it promptly. "And the answer is?"

"They did not. They arrived here shortly after the human settlers did."

"Now *who* told you this?"

The image changed into . . . what? "I see what looks like a red hole cut in a black piece of paper, Mr. Spock. Do you care to enlighten me as to what on earth it is?"

"Nothing on earth, Captain, but at the bottom of the Hellsgate Rift. It is a volcanic vent. The intelligent indigenes of Discord are colonies of microorganisms that have grown up in the Venus-like conditions surrounding these deep-sea vents."

"And you . . . *talked* to them."

"I communicated with the vent-forms through telepathy, a form of mind meld. I found the experience . . . quite harrowing."

"I can see how you might. Such intelligences would be even more alien than the Horta—"

"Much as I would like to, I have no leisure to reminisce at the present time, owing to another matter of which they informed me."

"Which is?"

"This."

It lay as if wedged at the bottom of the trench, a

shadowed, vaguely triangular mass, ominous for no reason he could put his finger on. He leaned forward and squinted, as if that would do any good.

"I can't quite make out—"

"Captain!" Chekov sang out. "It's a Klingon battlecruiser!"

"No, it's not," Sulu said. "It's bigger. *Much* bigger."

It was, Kirk said. Instead of the attenuated turtle-with-wings shape of the classic Klingon *may'Duj,* this ship was a gigantic blocky arrowhead, its nose and wingtips truncated at blunt angles. It gave an impression of terrible strength.

"She's *huge,*" Uhura breathed.

Sulu was staring at his board as if in horror. "Captain, I can't find her! She must mass a quarter-million tonnes, and she doesn't so much as twitch a needle."

"Consider, Mr. Sulu—she lies at the bottom of an enormous mass of water—water with an extraordinarily high metallic content. She is surrounded by ten-thousand-meter metal walls, not to mention a powerfully fluxing magnetic field. She is not invisible —merely hidden with great skill."

The intercom chirped. "Captain, this is Satterfield from Engineering. We've secured the transporter room. We found Zellich and Tenney drugged and taped up behind the transporter control station. There's no sign of the commissioner."

"Well done, Mr. Satterfield. Call sickbay to collect Tenney and Zellich. Stay down there with your party, and stay alert for anyone beaming aboard."

"Aye-aye, sir."

McCoy came onto the bridge. "It never rains but it pours," Kirk said.

"You can say that again. Jim, what's been going on?

There I was in my office, minding my own business, reading *The Farmer's Almanac,* and suddenly there are bells ringing and lights flashing and people running all over the place, and my sickbay starts filling up with moaning Klingons."

He stopped to glare at Kirk's hand. "What in the devil's name happened to that? You haven't been hitting people with your bare fists again, have you?"

"You know I've always been a fool for a pretty face, Bones."

McCoy started to make a snappy rejoinder. Then he saw the screen and his jaw fell slack. "What in the name of heaven is *that?*"

"Nothing in the name of *heaven*, Bones. It's the latest mark of Klingon battlecruiser. Though maybe they'd be better off calling this one a dreadnought, come to think of it."

Columns of bubbles began to rise around the dark bulk. Veils of silt swirled around it.

Sulu's eyes bugged out. "Whatever you want to call her, Captain, she's coming up!"

Chapter Twenty-three

SOUND CARRIED WELL through the water at the bottom of Hellsgate Rift. Spock and Arkazha clearly heard the rumble and clatter as the great warship began to rise.

Spock raised his head. "We are close by the vessel," he said. "Clearly, there is only one possible course of action."

"You are absolutely right, my friend," Mona Arkazha said. He turned his head to see her pointing his phaser at him.

"Mona, why?" he asked. She shot him. He slumped.

Ignoring the outcry from the communicator screen, she tucked the phaser carefully into its holster and did the same with his personal communicator and tricorder.

"I know you are not unconscious," she said, lifting him under the arms as if he were no heavier than a child, "merely immobilized. You are far more durable than a normal human."

246

She propped him like a doll against the after bulkhead. He stared at her with eyes that had no choice.

"Understand that what I do is not a sacrifice," she said. "What I do, I do for myself. You and your friends are welcome to share in the fruits—if any."

She turned her face to the video pickup. "Captain Kirk, one to beam aboard. I trust you can lock on your friend's communicator?"

"Mr. Sulu's trying," Kirk said. "The storm has broken up over your head, but the same factors that hid the Klingon from us are making it tough to lock him in."

"We've got him!" Sulu sang out.

Kirk nodded. "Are you sure you don't want us to beam you up, too, Doctor? The big boy is taking it slow now, so he doesn't lay himself open on a jagged metal outcrop, but in half a minute or so things are going to get mighty uncomfortable down there."

She smiled. "I'll be fine, Captain."

She turned, bent, and kissed Spock on the forehead. Then she climbed into the pilot seat and took the controls.

"Anytime you are ready, Captain."

Her instruments began to fluctuate madly. The lights dimmed, and she heard the strange song of the transporter behind her.

"Farewell, my friend," she whispered, bleeding power to the impellers. A great roaring rose around as the vast warship engaged its impulse drives. The slow irresistible surge of displaced water shoved the little craft back, dangerously close to the deadly canyon walls.

She played jets and vanes expertly to keep clear of

sharp metal buttresses that seemed to reach for her. The roaring grew louder as she oriented the submersible. The canyon filled with a hideous blue-white glare.

She applied full forward power and sent herself hurtling toward Leviathan.

Dr. McCoy was standing by the transporter platform to catch Spock when he appeared and toppled bonelessly forward. Nurse Chapel stood by with a gurney. She helped McCoy maneuver the immobilized Vulcan aboard.

Qeyn HoD wa'DIch settled himself into his captain's chair. The thrill of impending battle sang in his veins, the rush all true Klingons found more addicting than any drug. Moriah Wayne stood at his side. He paid her no attention.

"Get me Kirk!" he shouted. "I want to watch his face as he dies!" And he threw back his head and laughed.

He felt a tremor run through his ship. He frowned. If they had kissed a wall, his helmsman would kiss his *kligat*. He had not waited and worked and forborne so long to have his wild ride ended before it fair began.

"What was that?" he snarled.

"Captain," his instrument officer reported, "a small undersea craft seems to have rammed us near the outboard starboard impulse drive nozzle. There was no damage."

"So one of your Discordian friends decided to make a final heroic gesture." He reached up. Moriah's pale hand slipped into his black gauntleted one. "It was futile, as all such ultimately are."

Wayne snuggled happily against his powerful biceps. "Not all of them," she said.

He laughed again.

"Captain Kirk," said the handsome mustachioed face on the screen. "We meet again. Prepare to die."

"Bold words, Kain. Can you back them up? Or are they as hollow as your professions of peaceful intent?"

"My intent has always been peaceful, Captain. I see you looking skeptical. Well, hear this: I shall not know peace until you are dead. I am about to kill you. Then I shall be a peacemaker indeed."

He swept his arm around. "Behold my ship," he said, "five years in the building, at a yard so secret the Federation had no inkling of its existence—until eight of our months ago. Then we caught one of your robot probes skulking about. We had to assume the facility was compromised."

He smiled. "Our discovery of this world was a gift of Destiny, Kirk. It enabled us to bring her here and conceal her at the bottom of the sea, where you would never find her with all your sensors and spycraft, while the finishing touches were applied."

"Since you seem inclined to talk, Kain, just what *is* that monster?"

Kain laughed. "She is a prototype battleship, Captain. I helped design her myself. When we have destroyed you, she and I, she will have proven herself worthy to spawn a long line of warcraft."

He fingered his long jaw. *"Monster,* you called her—and you spoke truly. I have the discretion of naming this vessel. I have held off doing so, since it is most propitious to name a ship on the very brink of battle, that she may be christened in enemy blood. I am a generous man. So I shall honor the superstitions of your friends and allies.

"I name her *bIQ'a' veqlarg'a'*, Great Demon of the Ocean. Or, to be succinct—*Leviathan.*"

"The Devil in the Sea."

"Coming to kill you. *Phasers fire!*"

Five thousand meters of water still lay above *Leviathan*. No matter; the water molecules in the path of her phaser beams simply ceased to exist. The weapons bored twin holes through the water and leapt toward space.

Enterprise's shields coruscated. "Phaser banks charged, ready, and locked on, Captain," Sulu said.

"One-quarter impulse power, Mr. Chekov. Hold her in this orbit. Mr. Sulu, hold your fire."

"But, Captain—" Sulu looked back over his shoulder.

"I said, hold your fire, mister! Let him waste his charge boiling water. I want our banks to be full when he breaks the surface."

"The power of those weapons is unbelievable!" Chekov breathed.

"I'm not sure our shields will hold long enough, sir," Sulu said.

"Sure they will, Mr. Sulu. All you need is a little faith. Engine room!"

"Scott here, sir."

"I need more power to the shields, Mr. Scott."

"We're already running at red line, sir. If I give ye much more, the dilithium crystals may blow out altogether. And then it's good-bye, warp drive."

"It's good-bye, warp drive, if he punches through our shields, too. Not to mention everything else. Give me more power, Mr. Scott!"

"You've got it, Captain."

"He's approaching the surface, sir!" Sulu sang. "Five hundred meters and counting."

"He's coming fast, sir," Chekov said.

"On my mark, mister—wait for it!"

"Our shields, sir!" Sulu exclaimed.

"Here he comes!" cried Chekov.

"All phasers fire, Mr. Sulu!"

Red beams stabbed downward from the *Enterprise* to drench *Leviathan* in deadly glare. "Captain, our shields are going," Sulu said.

"Hold her steady as she goes, mister. Keep firing."

The shields went down. One Klingon beam missed the *Enterprise* altogether. The other bit into the strut that connected the central engineering hull to the starboard warp engine pod. Kirk grimaced in physical pain as he heard the shriek of metal sublimating away into space, transmitted through the fabric of the hull.

"Steady!" he commanded. Sulu turned a strained pale face to him.

The Klingon beams winked out.

"Their batteries are exhausted, Captain!" Chekov exulted.

"Keep hammering them, Sulu!"

Freed of the crushing weight of water *Leviathan* accelerated quickly to hypersonic speed, splitting Discord's sky with a scream. But she could not move fast enough to escape the searing caress of *Enterprise*'s main battery. Her shields flared, flickered, and fell.

Enterprise's beams touched the bare metal of *Leviathan*'s hull. Her armor was thick and tough, but it simply vanished in puffs of superheated gas at the touch of those energy lances. The twin beams stabbed deep into the giant warship's guts.

"Captain, sensors show his phaser bank accumulators approaching full charge," Sulu reported. "Our shields are starting to come back, but they won't stand up long to what he's mounting."

"Full power to impulse engines. Get us around the planet, Mr. Chekov."

Again *Leviathan's* phasers reached for them. The shields immediately began to flicker. Energies leaking through made Kirk's hair stand on end.

"Mr. Scott, forget about the shields. We need more impulse power now!"

The chief engineer didn't even bother to protest. "You're the captain," he said, and gave the orders to his people.

And then they were around the world's edge, and her blue limb cut off the enemy's beam.

The bridge crew cheered. "Belay that noise!" Kirk snapped. "We haven't won anything but time."

He stared at the image on the main screen—Discord belying her name, looking utterly serene. Unreal to think that death lurked behind its placid face, that a killer used that face as a blind. Unreal unless you thought about what the planet was *really* like, as opposed to what it looked like from way up here.

"First things first. Mr. Chekov, shape us a new orbit around the planet—use your imagination. It won't do to come around the world on the same trajectory he's seen us in. He's liable to greet us with a spread of disruptor bolts."

The turbolift hissed open. "Jim," he heard McCoy say, "I tried to stop him."

"Really, Dr. McCoy, your concern is misplaced. You would be better advised to tend the captain's hand."

Kirk spun. "Spock! Are you all right?"

"Naturally, Captain. My indisposition was no more than momentary." He walked to the science station and bent over the panel as if he'd just stepped away for a drink of water.

Kirk had actually forgotten his broken hand until Spock mentioned it. Then it began to throb like Discord thunder. He let McCoy call Nurse Chapel back up from sickbay to dress his hand while he listened to damage reports.

To his relief he found that no one had been killed or injured. There was substantial damage to the strut, but not enough to seriously compromise its structural integrity. Or so the damage-control detail hoped.

"What about shields?" Kirk asked.

"Virtually nonexistent, Captain."

"Mr. Scott, get me my shields back."

"There's only so much I can do, Captain. We've got one dilithium crystal cracked already. I've got a team replacing it—"

"No time. *Shields,* Scotty."

He punched off and looked around the bridge. "The question is, how badly did we hurt him?"

"We hurt him, Captain," Sulu said. "I saw enough to know that much."

"But the next time he hits us," Chekov said, "he's liable to finish us."

Kain smelled smoke on *Leviathan*'s bridge and frowned. He had heard screams when the *Enterprise*'s beams struck home. It took a lot to make a Klingon scream.

Screams and smoke—not good. Damage reports showed he had taken heavy losses in lives and metal. But *Leviathan* had both in profusion.

"It's strange," Moriah Wayne said. "I'm really surprised, but I wasn't afraid."

"If you were a Klingon," he said, not hiding his contempt, "lack of fear would be a given, not a virtue."

He found himself oddly pleased at the way her face crumpled, as to a blow. Then he gave his attention to more important matters.

"Vang," he called.

"Captain," his tactical officer replied from the weapons console.

"What is your assessment?"

Vang paused. He hesitated to offer opinions to a man with Kain's reputation, either as a tactician or as a man possessed of a dangerously unpredictable temper. One time at which Kain's temper was absolutely predictable, though, was when his orders were not obeyed instantly and fully.

"*Enterprise* is wounded," he said cautiously, "but remains a dangerous foe."

"*Fagh!*" spat Kain, dropping his hand to the *kligat* hilt. Vang recoiled. "You're as vague as an Earther. Tell me something I can *use,* damn you!"

"We can wait, using impulse power to remain stationary relative to the planet surface, and let him come to us. We outgun *Enterprise,* Captain. We can put that advantage to good use—"

He let his words trail off as Kain leaned forward, a dangerous shine in his eye.

"You are advising us to sit passively and *wait?* What are we, Susuru, that we fear to seize the initiative? Is this the best you have to offer, Tactical Officer? Perhaps you would prefer to watch the final battle from outside the ship—without the encumbrance of a suit."

254

Wayne gasped and clutched his arm. Vang turned ashen.

"When—when the time comes to close, we should rush upon them as rapidly as we can," he said. He rushed the words from himself, fearful of saying them, but more fearful of holding back. And then what he dreaded most to say: "Response times for Federation crews are . . . consistently quicker than our own. We can negate that advantage if we can dictate the instant at which the engagement begins, and then get close enough that our greater firepower can quickly overwhelm our foe."

Kain smiled. "I begin to believe you can *think*, Vang. Well done."

He leaned back and patted the commissioner's hand. "Be patient, my dear. Soon you will have the pleasure of watching James Kirk die."

Chapter Twenty-four

"WHERE IS HE?" muttered Sulu.

"If only we could see through the planet."

"And if wishes were horses," McCoy said, "then beggars would ride."

"Oh, but we can, Doctor," Spock said. The glow of his board cast satanic highlights over his face.

McCoy blinked. "We can? Can what?"

"We can see through the planet."

"Why, that's absurd."

"Fortunately it is not. I am detecting a clear neutrino track." He pressed a button. A dot appeared, seemingly making its way slowly across the ocean of Discord. "The trail of *Leviathan*. As even you may be aware, Doctor, most neutrinos lack both mass and charge, and can pass through the core of a planet unimpeded."

"How is it possible that *Leviathan's* emitting, Spock?" Kirk asked. "She must be equipped with neutrino baffles just as we are."

"Was, Captain. Computer, bring up the images of *Leviathan* captured during our firing pass."

"Affirmative." In slow motion *Leviathan* boiled out of the sea and hurtled into the air. Energy beams flared like linear suns.

"Generate and display a graphic of structural damage detected prior to contact with our phaser beams."

The image lost substance, became a schematic, and rotated level, then side on. A red spot appeared at the stern.

"Impact damage highlighted," the computer said. It was being good today. Probably because Wayne wasn't present to take offense.

"Now highlight the neutrino baffle on the outboard starboard impulse drive."

A blinking yellow circle appeared around the dot.

"Mona Arkazha did not die altogether in vain, it would appear," Spock said softly.

"I'll say she didn't! Plot an intercept course, Mr. Chekov. Mr. Sulu, arm all forward photon torpedo tubes. Mr. Scott, how're repairs coming on those shields?"

"We've got enough to hold him off a wee bit, sir," came the reply, "if he shines nothing on us hotter than a flashlight."

"We'll try not to give him the chance to do more than that," Kirk said.

"Just how do you propose to do that, Jim?" McCoy demanded. "Appeal to his better nature?"

Kirk bit the tip of his thumb. "No," he said after a moment's consideration. "Cheat. Mr. Sulu, what's the status of that battlecruiser?"

"Shields are up, sir."

"How many aboard?"

"Before their shields were raised, sensor readings

257

indicated twelve individuals, all Klingon," Spock said. "Two on the bridge, four in engineering, and six manning phaser and disruptor batteries. Inasmuch as the shields rendered their transporter beams inoperative at the same instant they blocked our scanners, it is logical to presume the number has not changed."

"How long till we come in line of sight of *Leviathan?*"

"Twelve hundred twenty-one point seven seconds, Captain."

"Excellent. Lieutenant Uhura, broadcast a message to the *Dagger*. They have three minutes to lower their shields and stand by to be boarded. Security, I want six men with phasers and body armor in the transporter room in two minutes." A moment's hesitation. "Make sure they're volunteers. This could get hot. Mr. Chekov."

"Aye, Captain?"

"Take over weapons control. Plot a photon torpedo launch. When *Leviathan* appears around Discord, I want them there and waiting for her. Mr. Spock will continue to monitor her neutrino track; if she changes course, inform me at once and recalculate launch time and trajectories accordingly. Understood?"

"Aye, sir!"

"Captain," Uhura said, "the Klingons are responding . . . are you *sure* you want to hear this?"

"The standard abuse?" She nodded. "I'll take your word for it, Lieutenant."

He rose. "Mr. Spock, you have the con. Unless the *Dagger* surrenders in—one hundred fifty-one seconds—I want you to open fire on her with all phaser banks, and continue firing until her shields go down. Then cease fire. Understood?"

"Captain—" He stiffened. "Understood, sir."

"What about me, sir?" Sulu asked.

"Mr. Sulu," Kirk said, "you're a would-be swash-buckler. Care to try buckling on a swash for real?"

"Would I, sir!"

"Then follow me."

He turned to go. McCoy blocked his path.

"Jim," the doctor said, "have you lost your mind?"

"Probably. Now please excuse me—we all have an appointment with *Leviathan,* and we don't want to be late."

Kirk held his arms out to the side as Sulu fastened the clamshell polymer armor vest around his chest. It was crowded in the transporter room: the six security volunteers, Reichert and van Pelt among them, gathered by the platform in a knot of tense readiness they were all trying not to show; Dr. McCoy and Nurse Chapel standing by with emergency medical equipment; Mr. Scott himself at the transporter controls.

"Bridge to captain," Spock's voice said from the bulkhead speaker. "We have taken the Klingon vessel under fire."

"Well done, Spock. Keep pouring it to them until they agree to lower their shields—or until we batter them down."

He turned to Scott. "Remember, Mr. Scott—the very instant her shields drop, beam me and Ensign van Pelt onto the bridge. Then beam Sulu and his party into her engine room. Then stand by to beam aboard prisoners and any casualties."

"I'm ready, Captain," he said, refraining from pointing out it was the third time Kirk had issued the identical set of orders.

"What about the Klingons at the weapons stations, Captain?" Sulu asked.

"They're split into two groups of three. We can isolate them in place, and I can't spare the men or the time to secure them. The art of the cutting-out expedition is the art of the possible."

"Jim, this isn't your *job,*" McCoy said pleadingly. "Starship captains are supposed to *command.* They're not supposed to go haring off on boarding parties with cutlasses in their teeth."

Kirk laughed. "I'm leaving out the cutlasses this time, Bones. Come on, Doctor. All the years we've been together, you should know by now I *always* beam across. I'm too old to change now."

"Jim, adolescence has to end sometime. Even yours."

"Whatever phase of life I'm in," Kirk said, "my main concern right now is seeing that it lasts longer than the next sixteen and a half minutes."

"Captain, her shields are weakening," Chekov reported over the intercom.

He glanced at van Pelt. The two stepped onto the transporter stage and drew their phasers. The security woman's looked huge in her dainty fist.

"Kirk here. I'm standing by."

"Her shields are down—"

Before Chekov finished the *Enterprise* had gone away. In its place the Klingon bridge took form, cramped and dark.

And crowded; a third Klingon, a portly lieutenant with a fringe beard, stood talking to the slight Captain-Third who sat in the command chair. A warrant sat at the helm.

Three faces turned toward Kirk and van Pelt, their beards surrounding toothy *O*s of surprise. Three red flashes lit the cavelike bridge.

Kirk gazed down at the three slumped Klingons and

let out a slow breath. He felt a strange sense of anticlimax.

"Nice shooting, Captain," van Pelt said, moving forward to make sure their victims were actually stunned and not shamming.

"You're no slouch yourself," Kirk replied, aware that she had fired twice to his once. Well, *she* was the professional security person; he was just a starship captain, as Bones kept pointing out.

His communicator chirped. He unhooked it, whipped it open. "Kirk here."

"Captain, this is Sulu. Engine room secured, sir."

Feeling acid in his gut, Kirk asked, "Anybody hurt?"

"Herring's down, sir. He doesn't look good."

"Have Mr. Scott beam him back at once. Keep me apprised of your situation. Kirk out. *Enterprise,* give me a time check."

"Nine hundred twelve point seven seconds until contact, Captain," Spock replied.

"Let me know if *Leviathan* changes course. Kirk out." He snapped the communicator shut and tried not to think of one of his people injured. It could be worse, he knew, but just now that answer reeked of self-justification.

He sat in the captain's chair. Van Pelt stood up from wrapping restraints around three hairy sets of Klingon wrists and stepped away from the captives, who were beginning to stir and make seismic noises deep in their bellies. She took out her own communicator and hit the transmit button twice. The Klingons glowed and disappeared in *Enterprise*'s transporter beams.

"What about the weapons crews, sir?" she asked.

As if in response, a blast of Klingon vocables came from the intercom. Kirk grimaced. "Captain," Spock reported, "the Klingons remaining on board the *Dagger* have activated anti-intrusion screens. We can neither beam boarders into those positions, nor beam their occupants out."

"All right," Kirk said, "my move." He snapped up a cover beneath his right palm and depressed a rocker switch. A klaxon sounded.

"All compartments are now sealed by vacuumproof blast doors," he said, "with mutiny locks activated. We should be thankful for Klingon paranoia, Ensign. Nobody can move from his station now—weapons stores and even service access panels are locked out."

And that, he reflected, *is one reason I was able to take* my *ship back single-handed.* Like the ancient Japanese, the Klingon made an ideal of total obedience; and like the ancient Japanese, they were kidding themselves. Assassination and revolt were routine means of advancement. If a superior was not capable of protecting himself against the ambitions of his underlings, he was clearly unfit to hold his position. The warrior who supplanted him, with or without confederates, was deemed his rightful successor.

Repugnant as the system was to Federation morality, it worked in its way. But it produced certain inefficiencies. One of them was that unrestricted access to any part of a vessel did not exist in the Klingon service, no matter how severely that complicated damage control or even routine maintenance. It therefore had not occurred to Lieutenant Lu Kok Tak that Kirk might be able to find a way out of his cell—or onto the bridge.

Naturally, it hadn't occurred to Commissioner Wayne either. *You underestimated me, Moriah,* he thought with a twinge. *Again.*

He pressed the intercom switch. "Attention, all Klingon crew," he said. Klingon officers all spoke English—advanced education was an important mark of caste distinction among Klingons. If the ratings didn't understand, their officers could translate. "This is Captain James Kirk, USS *Enterprise*. I am now in command of this vessel. I am ordering you to put down your weapons and surrender."

"Never!" a voice shouted back from the speaker, ragged with rage. "It is Lieutenant Vokh who speaks, and I cast defiance in your pale face. We shall die at our stations. And we shall take you with us, *tera'ngan*."

"If that's the way you want it," Kirk murmured.

"I know you can fire the weapons from up here, Captain," van Pelt said, "but what about sabotage?"

"Good question, Ms. van Pelt. The answer is, they'll have to cut their way in, which'll take them a while."

"And we don't know how long a while, sir."

He shrugged. "No. So we'll just hope it's long enough."

He studied the controls. They were labeled in Klingon script, of which he had only minimal command. It didn't matter. He wasn't as obsessive about Klingon naval architecture as Scotty was, but he had a good grasp of the layout of a battlecruiser's bridge. Just as the Klingon boarding party had known how to operate the *Enterprise*.

He checked the weapons systems. Phaser banks were full and ready to fire. The two forward photon torpedo tubes were loaded. Once they were gone the tubes were useless, but as long as he did not exceed performance norms—or take damage—Kirk could fly and fight the Klingon vessel. At least until the Klingons in the various weapons stations figured out a way to cause mischief.

It took them just over ten minutes. The clock display on the Klingon tactical display showed one hundred eleven seconds when a purple light began to blink on the arm of the captain's chair.

"What does that mean, Captain?" van Pelt asked.

"I don't know," Kirk said, "but I suspect nothing good."

A roar of triumph burst from the intercom: *"Qapla'!* We have breached the photon torpedo locker. We will now manually detonate the torpedo and take you with us to oblivion, Kirk!"

"Are you sure you want to play it this way, Vokh? It'll take you a couple of minutes yet to get the cover off the weapon's manual override panel. By that time, your ship is liable to be a plasma cloud anyway."

A pause. "Do not make sport of me, Earther."

"Nothing could be further from my mind, Lieutenant." He opened his communicator. "Kirk to *Enterprise.* Mr. Scott, begin beaming the boarding party aboard, commencing with Mr. Sulu's group."

Seconds passed like eons. Kirk watched the main screen, on which hung the image of Discord. He was on the night side now. The planet was a black disk.

At thirty seconds to contact van Pelt shimmered out.

"Lieutenant Vokh," Kirk said over the intercom, "this is your last chance to drop your intrusion screens and be beamed to safety."

"Prepare for death, Earther."

"I have, Lieutenant."

He pressed a button. The *Dagger*'s shields snapped

on. He was cut off from rescue now—alone with the Klingons and their bomb, waiting for *Leviathan* to rise with the sun in a handful of heartbeats.

"Captain," Spock's voice said, "are you sure the course you are following is wise?"

"No, Mr. Spock. It's just the one that gives us—or at least the *Enterprise*—the greatest chance of survival."

And Eris struck the limb of the world alight.

Chapter Twenty-five

"PHOTON TORPEDOES AWAY, CAPTAIN," Chekov's voice reported.

"Very good, Mr. Chekov. Reload and prepare to engage on my command."

"Qeyn HoD wa'DIch," Vang exclaimed, "sensors detect a vessel about to come into line of sight!"

"He's early to our appointment," Kain said, tapping gauntleted fingertips on the arm of his chair. "All weapons lock on."

The helmsman goggled at his panel. "IFF transmissions received. She's *taj,* sir! Her shields are up."

"Why has she changed orbit?"

"Perhaps she's managed to engage the Earthers, Captain," Vang said.

"If that's so, I'm surprised she hasn't been blown out of space—*Enterprise* could take her at one swallow. Lock phasers on to her, and keep an eye out for *Enterprise.* I smell a trap."

Vang actually turned a startled glance back at his captain, then obeyed. A moment later he yelled, "She's locked on to us!"

"Open fire."

The *Dagger*'s screens lit up like Federation Day fireworks. Beyond the glare splash of *Leviathan*'s phasers against them Kirk could see the monster herself, black and huge.

"Captain," Spock said from the *Enterprise*, following the hijacked battlecruiser at a range of ten thousand kilometers. "Jim. The *Dagger*'s screens can withstand the force of *Leviathan*'s main batteries for no more than twenty point two seconds."

"Don't I know it, Mr. Spock," he replied, watching the shield-strength indicator bar drop steadily toward zero. "Mr. Scott."

"Standing by, Captain."

Kirk's own phasers were blasting away at full power. The display showed *Leviathan*'s screens straining to stand off the little cruiser's comparatively puny weapons. *Enterprise*'s first pass had wounded the monster. *But did we hurt him enough?*

The indicator hit bottom. The fireworks on the big screen went out.

"Now, Mr. Scott."

Kirk saw the whole front of the bridge begin to glow red before his eyes as *Leviathan*'s mighty phasers reached for him. "Any time now, Mr. Scott," he said.

"And now, Earther," Vokh's voice bellowed from the intercom, "we all die!"

James Kirk felt a familiar twisting sensation. He winked out of the captain's chair a millisecond before an intolerably bright phaser blast tore through the

267

bridge and reduced it to dissociated subatomic particles.

"Be my guest, Lieutenant," Kirk said as he materialized on *Enterprise*'s transporter stage.

"Qapla'!" Vang exclaimed as *Dagger* blew up. "Success!"

Moriah Wayne clutched Kain's right shoulder. He scowled. "You fool," he said, "we've just destroyed one of our own ships! Can't you see it was just a diversion?"

"Sensors indicate a vessel approximately ten thousand kilometers aft of the wreckage of *taj,* sir," the helmsman reported.

"Our shields still hold," Kain said, leaning forward with a predator's smile. "You've bought yourself a few seconds more to breathe, Kirk, no more. All weapons lock on."

And Vang shrieked, *"Photon torpedoes incoming!"*

Kirk appeared beside his own command chair in time to see the remnants of the nebula that was all that was left of *Dagger* fading from the screen. To its left shone the three miniature suns that were *Enterprise*'s photon torpedoes, about to strike *Leviathan*.

"Captain," reported Sulu, back at his own station, *"Leviathan* has locked on to us."

"All weapons fire, Mr. Sulu."

His earlier mention to Sulu of the nautical adventure novels he had grown up loving reminded Kirk of the blasphemous prayer of the fighting sailor of rag wagon days.

"For what we are about to receive," he intoned, "dear Lord, make us thankful."

Shields crumpled like wet tissue paper. A beam lanced the living-quarters saucer through and through. What it touched flared and vanished, bulkheads scarcely less readily than human beings. It cut upward, out, grazing the bridge and sending the atmosphere shrieking forth in a gale.

It was common bridge discipline to keep loose objects off the bridge, against just such an eventuality. When it came, it was astounded how much stuff had managed to find its way there anyway: papers, lightweight computers, light pens, Kirk's favorite coffee mug—and Sulu.

With a yell he sailed toward the hole that yawned into blackness. Chekov just managed to catch him by the legs, hug his boots to his chest, and cling.

And the photon torpedo spread hit.

One missed entirely. The second spent itself overloading *Leviathan's* shields, leaving her hull unprotected.

The third missed the bridge by mere meters and ate its way along the centerline of the ship, destroying the central warp drive tube and the inboard impellers to either side. The torpedo and the secondary explosions in its wake killed a quarter of *Leviathan's* crew in less than half a second.

The final hit struck into the starboard wing of the blunt arrowhead that was *Leviathan*. It found the locker for the starboard photon torpedo tubes and set off a chain reaction that simply ripped that side of the ship away.

Leviathan hurtled toward *Enterprise*. All systems were failing fast. The three hits had snuffed over four hundred lives, and secondary explosions continued to rip at the mighty warship's guts. She was dead already.

But like the prehistoric monster her name and bulk suggested, it took *Leviathan* a while to die. And as she died, she struck back with demonic fury.

Leviathan and *Enterprise* passed each other on nearly reciprocal orbits a mere five hundred kilometers apart. In contemporary terms that was broadside to broadside.

Leviathan's shields were gone, but her phaser batteries were almost intact. Their awesome power burned through *Enterprise*'s remaining screens in seconds. As the great ships passed, they clawed each other's sides like beasts.

Enterprise struck *Leviathan*'s bridge a glancing blow. The heat of its passage sent random hyperspeed jets of vaporized metal spurting away from it; one of these caught Vang in the chest and threw him back, burning. The upper part of him, arm still outflung in a final macabre gesture, was sucked out the hole in a black cloud of his own blood.

The same gas jet that killed the tactical officer severed Kain's left leg just below the knee. Ignoring the gush of blood, Kain seized Moriah Wayne around the waist and, thrusting with all his strength with his good leg and the raw end of his stump, won through the afterhatch a heartbeat before the armored emergency panel slammed shut.

Depleted by being fired at *Dagger,* the charges in *Leviathan*'s phaser banks went first. *Enterprise*'s armament was weaker, but it rang hell through the compartments and passageways of the doomed ship before it too winked out. Bleeding clouds of debris and condensed air, the combatants hurtled away from each other, around the world named Discord.

Eris, watching, laughed radiation. She was a cruel goddess.

As part of her upgrade at Starbase 23 *Enterprise* had received a new system for rapid sealing of breaches, as long as they weren't too severe. When the computer detected a loss of integrity a field sprang into being, surrounding the bridge with an airtight bubble of force. The occupants could continue to breathe—as long as power kept being supplied.

Miraculously, none of the bridge crew was hurt. The rest of the ship was not so lucky. Kirk paid only enough attention to damage reports to form an accurate assessment of his ship's fighting capacity.

"Scotty," he said, "get us some shields back."

Down in Engineering, Scott's face was bright with sunburn from the backscatter of the beam that had ravaged his section. There were tear tracks in the grime on his cheeks.

"Our main reactors are gone, Captain," he said. "So're twenty of my bonny wee men and women. Evidently y'think I'm a miracle worker."

Twenty dead in Engineering alone. Kirk briefly closed his eyes. *Don't think about it. If you reckon the butcher's bill now, you'll never have strength to do what remains to be done.*

"Evidently I do," he said hoarsely. "Don't make me out a fool, Mr. Scott."

Leviathan circled Discord like a moon whose face was gouged with glowing wounds. On one-quarter impulse the *Enterprise* shaped orbit to intercept.

"This is *Enterprise* calling the Klingon vessel *Leviathan*. *Enterprise* calling *Leviathan*."

"I am here, Kirk." A laugh. Snow flurried across the

main viewing screen, and then there was Kain, a bloody gash on his cheek and his patch ripped away to reveal the pucker of pink scar tissue where his left eye had been, huddled in the emergency bridge with a handful of his officers. There was a crude pressure bandage affixed to the stump of his leg. It was already black with blood.

Commissioner Wayne stood behind him, the green gown she had been wearing torn in an almost artful way, her hair in theatrical disarray. She looked entirely beautiful—and entirely mad.

"I am not so easy to kill as you expected, eh?"

"I didn't expect this to be easy," Kirk said in a full voice. "And it hasn't been. But I don't want to kill you, Kain. I'm calling on you to surrender. If you do, you and your crew will be treated honorably."

The Klingon thrust himself up from his chair and balanced on his surviving leg to shout, "Do you think you can escape me so easily, Kirk?"

Kirk ignored the outburst. "I also call upon you to surrender the person of Deputy Commissioner Wayne." He moistened his lips. "She will be returned to the Federation to stand trial on charges of treason and genocide."

Wayne put back her head and laughed. It was a jarring, wild sound.

"It's you who's fighting the Federation, Kirk!" she shrilled. "It's you who's the outlaw rebel. We serve the cause of peace and justice—"

Kain wheeled. The *kligat* flew from his hand, a glittering wheel. It struck Moriah Wayne in the pit of her stomach. Blood erupted. She doubled over and collapsed into a mewing knot of pain.

"I grew tired of her yapping," Kain said, "and she

had served her purpose. She was only a means to an end, Kirk—only a means to strike at you."

Kirk's eyes narrowed. Almost he gave the order to open fire. It was like opening his flesh with a knife to speak instead.

"Give it up, Kain. What point is there in continuing this—this carnage?"

"Honor. *Revenge.*"

"Words."

Kain pointed to his raw socket. "You cost me an eye. Is that mere words? You cost me my bond-brother as well. How, oh, how do you explain that away?"

"Kras was your bond-brother?"

"He was."

"I'm—sorry. I didn't know."

Kain stared at him in white-faced fury. "Almost twenty years of my life I devote to stalking you, to planning the perfection of my revenge—for *this?* So you can say you're *sorry?"*

He raised his hands above his head. "Phasers—"

"—*fire!"* James Kirk yelled.

Beams of destructive energy struck both ways. *Enterprise*'s shields, kept in place by little more than Lieutenant Commander Scott's raw will, held for a handful of milliseconds.

It was all they needed to. Captain of the First Rank Kain, his crew, and *Leviathan* all became a giant ball of plasma that glowed like a sun and quickly dissipated into nothing.

Chapter Twenty-six

"IT STRETCHES the limits of credibility," Spock said, "given the immensity of space, that two sets of political refugees of utterly different species, coming from entirely different directions, should happen upon the very same previously uninhabited planet within a few short years of each other."

The *Enterprise* circled Discord, not whole, but patched up enough to make it back to Starbase 23 for repair. Some injuries would take longer to heal—the seared and broken crewfolk in McCoy's overloaded sickbay and the holes in the entity that was *Enterprise* that the dead had left behind.

Alongside the starship orbited the transport fleet and its escort, *Enterprise*'s sister ship USS *Potemkin*. A steady stream of lighters passed back and forth between planet and fleet, storing up provisions for the long journey to come.

"Come now, Mr. Spock," Kirk said. "Surely stranger things have happened. Like—"

He held his hands up from his lap, apart, as if holding open a book. Everyone else on the bridge turned to stare at him. Silence stretched long and loud.

"Well, ah," Kirk said, "anyone else who thinks of one, feel free to jump right in."

"Well, it happened this once, anyway," McCoy said, "and the odds be damned. Maybe this will make you rethink your belief in the omnipotence of that precious logic of yours, Spock."

"A single anomalous event is as likely to make me forswear logic, Doctor," said Spock, "as the apparent success of a voodoo doctor in making a seriously ill patient rise up from his deathbed is to make you trade your medical tricorder for a rattle and beads. Although"—and for a moment Kirk could have sworn he was almost at risk of smiling—"now that I think if it . . ."

"Don't say it!" McCoy said. "Don't even say it."

"Captain," Uhura said, swiveling from her console, "now that it's all over, I can't help feeling sorry for Commissioner Wayne."

"A tragic case," Spock said.

An investigation had been launched back in the Federation. Commissioner for Interspecies Affairs Hightower had been a close friend of the late Councillor Cornelius Wayne. He had taken the councillor's brilliant but unstable daughter under his wing. He had also, it seemed, expended a great deal of effort covering for her.

Or maybe he was covering something darker, something deeper. New evidence about the councillor himself was coming to light, tales of violent outbursts which his enormous influence had kept hidden for years. Staff from the Wayne household on Jotunheim confirmed that the councillor had brutalized Moriah mentally and physically. Perhaps he had done more than that.

However much Hightower had known about Cornelius Wayne's maltreatment of his daughter, his efforts on behalf of his friend and his protégé had bought the commissioner nothing but trouble. Moriah's defection had turned the spotlight of scandal full-bore on the Commission for Interspecies Affairs. A great many irregularities were being illuminated.

Two traditional foes of Starfleet—Wayne senior and Hightower—were in the process of being utterly discredited. Kirk got no satisfaction from the fact. The whole thing made him feel sad and sordid. He would be happy to put Discord and its memories behind him.

A call for Kirk came from the surface. He accepted. Aileea dinAthos smiled from the screen.

"How're the repairs coming, Jim?"

"Good enough for government work," he said, "though I doubt you feel that's a very high standard. How about down there?"

"We'll endure the loss of Harmony—we've learned a lot about enduring, over the years. Storm is coming back together, but it's taking on a whole new character and will probably wind up having a new name . . . the market decides that, too, in a way."

"How do you feel?"

"Relieved and happy and scared and sad, and somehow kind of empty," she said. "It's hard to think about the war being over after all these years."

"You'll miss the excitement, won't you?"

A shy smile and a nod. "I'm afraid so. That's one reason Vares tend to look down on what I've done for a living most of my life—it gets to be hard to do without. No matter how much we think we hate it, when we're away, we start feeling a craving for it."

Kirk looked thoughtful. How he'd feel when he no longer got to command a starship . . . was something that didn't bear thinking about. "Sufficient unto the day is the evil thereof," as Bones would say.

"The funny thing is," she said, "I still can't hate the Susuru. I won't make excuses for them . . . but it's easy to see why they were always afraid of us."

The Susuru were afraid of *everybody*. For excellent reasons.

Kirk never saw Swift nor any of his Five of Fives again. He didn't inquire too closely into what had happened to them. The Klingon captives taken aboard the *Enterprise* had been contemptuously straightforward about their intention of enslaving the Susuru and looting their planet, just as soon as they'd served their function of baiting the Empire's worst enemy to his destruction.

Swift's successor as Lead Walker was a much younger Susuru named Wise, which Kirk hoped wasn't overly optimistic. Whether he lived up to the name or not, Wise was much more forthcoming with information than his predecessor.

The Susuru had begun as a peaceful, mainly agrarian people. Over what seemed to Kirk an enormous period of time they had developed a technical civilization, including limited spaceflight.

Then had come invasion by a race of beings with only one discernible agenda: to exterminate all other intelligent life in the universe.

Three times had the Susuru started life anew on an uninhabited planet. Three times their tormentors had found them and destroyed all but a few who managed to win free. The final time, somehow, the Susuru had developed warp drive—or acquired it from somewhere; the Lead Walker either didn't know or didn't care to say.

They had spent years traveling through space, hoping to put enough light-years between themselves and their enemies that they would never be found. Then the warp drive broke down. In two hundred years of sublight travel, the first marginally habitable world they had been able to reach was Discord. They didn't like it there—but they didn't have any choice.

They were horrified, half a local year after their arrival, to find they were sharing the planet with a race of backwards-built, hairless bipeds. Naturally, the Susuru tried to destroy them. Alien beings were a menace. If they could, they would destroy the Susuru.

The problem was, the Susuru weren't very good at war. And the Discordians wouldn't fight fair, and come onto the land in bunches so they could be conveniently eradicated. They made the Susuru come after them in boats.

The veldt-roving Susuru *hated* the sea.

They didn't like the Klingons, either, when the Empire stumbled across them. But they were easy marks for experienced operators like the Klingons. Their leaders were hungry to consolidate power over their own people and rabid at the prospect of being able to purge the planet of the hated intruders. Even if the intruders happened to have arrived first.

And the Klingons promised to do it all with a minimum of muss and fuss, no down payment, easy monthly terms. The Susuru were not the first race to bite on that one. Kirk sadly doubted they would be the last.

* * *

"The strangest thing," Aileea said, "the hardest thing for me to get used to, in a way, is that, just because the Susuru were willing to fight for Discord, it never meant they *liked* it here. They just hated us worse than they did the planet."

"And now the Federation is seeing to resettling them," Kirk said. "They'll still have to learn to put up with neighbors. But at least they'll be living on a comfortable planet."

Discord's true natives, the colony-forms that inhabited the Venus-like microenvironments of the volcanic vents at the bottom of Hellsgate, had no objection to the Susuru and the Vares continuing to inhabit their world. Quite the opposite: They were able telepathically to perceive everything that occurred on Discord, above and below the sea, and they found the colonists of both species entertaining.

But the Susuru had had enough of the world they called Island and had taken the Federation up on its offer of a ride out.

"I wonder if they'll adjust," Aileea said.

"Do you care?"

She shook her head. "No."

And he laughed a little and shook his head, because he found her answer mildly appalling and incomprehensible. And yet he knew she was a warm person, willing to risk her life for a friend and extend the hospitality of her childhood home to a near stranger, one whose possible goals might include the disruption of almost everything she held dear.

She's a complex one, that's for sure.

"You're staying a few days yet, aren't you?" she asked.

"A few days only," he said. "We're going back with the first transports."

"Well, I know Hikaru wants to spend a little more time with Gita before you go. And Jason and Uhura wanted to visit the ranch. Why don't we make an expedition of it, do some diving, teach you some more about our local wildlife."

A smile stretched itself slowly across his face. "You know," he said, "I think that might be just what the doctor ordered."

"Speaking of doctors," Aileea said, "why don't you ask that marvelous Dr. McCoy along? He's been working himself to death, and there's nothing more he can do for your wounded now. My aunt Maritza's a surgeon in Serendip. Maybe she could teach him a thing or two."

And maybe I'm not so eager to put Discord behind me after all, Jim Kirk thought.

STAR TREK®
THE GREAT STARSHIP RACE
by Diane Carey

When a friendly, alien people called the Rey make contact with the Federation, they are thrilled to learn the galaxy has a large number of intelligent races. To bring the myriad cultures to their world, the Rey host a celebration - inviting spacefaring peoples to send representative ships to compete against one another and the Great Starship Race is on.

As the Federation's flagship, the *U.S.S. Enterprise* under the command of Captain James T. Kirk, is sent to compete. But the event takes a dark turn when a Romulan warship arrives and demands to join the race. Soon, Kirk and the Romulan commander are engaged in a deadly game of cat and mouse and, for Kirk and his crew, the race becomes a struggle for survival. Faced with treachery at every turn, Kirk must protect his ship from relentless attack and prevent the annihilation of an entire world.

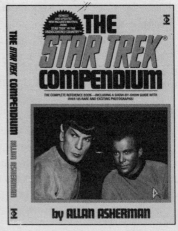

For a complete list of Star Trek publications, please send a large stamped SAE to Titan Books Mail Order, 19 Valentine Place, London, SE1 8QH. Please quote reference ST61.